MEL HOGAN, a renowned song writer and musician, has worked with various artistes and has an enviable list of credits to his name.

Mel immigrated to Australia with his family in the mid-sixties, and after he left school he put himself through college and achieved an honours degree in classical music.

While on a recent record-promotion visit to Australia, Mel met with an unfortunate accident, resulting in an 'inconvenient' broken knee. With his promotional plans in turmoil and his leg in a flexible splint, it was damage-limitation time.

A few nights later, while drifting in and out of restless sleep, Mel began dreaming of an adventure set in the future. By the next morning the adventure was implanted firmly in Mel's memory.

Two years later, the adventure has been written!

Children of the 23rd Century
The Secret of the Lost Planet

CHILDREN OF THE
23RD CENTURY
BOOK I

THE SECRET OF THE LOST PLANET

Mel Hogan

ATHENA PRESS
LONDON

ISBN 10-digit: 1 84748 042 X
ISBN 13-digit: 978 1 84748 042 2

First Published 2007 by
ATHENA PRESS
Queen's House, 2 Holly Road
Twickenham TW1 4EG
United Kingdom

Printed for Athena Press

To Tasman, Elliot and Ann

Chapter One

Outside Aurora's study window, the very first changes in colour of a mid-May sunset began to burn red and yellow through the haze of pollution reaching to the horizon, although the sky directly above was still a deep blue. Her home was high enough in the hills overlooking North Nevulae, over the worst of the pollution, for their air to be clean enough without having to filter it.

Elegantly perched like a flamingo behind her ornate antique birch-wood desk, Aurora was poised with pencil in hand, ready to enter her most private and personal thoughts into her old tattered, leather-bound, coffee-stained journal, which she affectionately referred to as her Bible.

It was time for Aurora to reflect on the significant memorable and some not-so-memorable events of the final passing year at the institute.

Whoa! What a great day to celebrate the end of a very manic and exhausting year, she began to write. *I've put my heart and soul into my studies in preparation for this crucial final semester. I certainly haven't had time for any late night socialising, that's for sure. Not that I am complaining, though; it suits me at this stage of my life. This year has been my hardest and most gruelling year to date. I feel as though I have fought an epic emotional battle, actually.*

Father often complains that it's not natural to always have my nose buried in science journals and encyclopaedias while continually scanning the World-Wide Web, searching for any new revelations. Sometimes I become so preoccupied I lose all track of time. He insists that a healthy, sixteen-year-old, beautiful and intelligent young lady should hit the town occasionally, and that I should go out more regularly with my best friend Crystal. (I snuck the intelligent part in.)

Papa has a comprehensive index of old-and-new-age books about our planet and its environment, a passion that both he and I share. I suppose a few of my friends reckon I am quite fanatically focused on conservation and the protection of our environment. They are entitled to their opinion. I love this wonderful land of ours, but we need to preserve vital life-giving resources or it is all going to fall into a screaming heap around us.

Aurora paused for a brief moment to gaze at the spectacular collage of atmospheric sunrays electrifying the afternoon sky-scape, a fantastic visual display seldom seen these days, while busily chewing on the end of her pencil, completely mesmerised by the array of wonderful bright sparkling colours.

I have been so very critical of certain people this year, even to the point of arrogance at times, which is so far out of character, especially when it is to do with that rat-face Blackie. Like, what planet is she on anyway?

Poor old Nigel Dougal-James; I've given him a bit of a battering as well, but he just will not take the hint, for goodness' sake. Both Nigel's and Blackie's parents are big-time property developers and seem to have little or no regard for our environment. It riles and consumes me when some unscrupulous individual or giant corporation does something that could endanger the survival of our species!

Crystal constantly reminds me that you cannot choose your parents. Thank goodness I have been blessed with my father. Sometimes I wish I could be an average, normal young girl, like my best friend, Crystal.

(Hey! she thought. *Where did that bitchy comment come from? It's entirely unfair. I hope she doesn't ever find my journal and read it! I think she would certainly take offence at that off-the-wall remark!)*

Crystal is an accredited honours graduate, like myself, and the best friend and confidante a girl could ever wish to have; only difference is I have a few more doctorate letters after my name. That sounds a bit snobby but it's certainly not meant that way. Hard to believe that we are both still only sixteen years old! I think we deserve a little self-praise and adulation; a self-administered pat on the back wouldn't go astray either if I say so myself!

Diverting slightly, I have to go to the silly annual Leaders' Ball tonight with Crystal, accompanied by two pimply-faced rascal boys who do not deserve a mention this early in the day. I would rather tuck myself under my warm sweet-smelling duvet and read a good novel. There I go again! What am I like? Preferring hot cocoa and slippers to a night on the town!

Papa always tells me that I am just like my late mother; she was a homebody and a wonderful human being. I wish I could have known her; I reckon we would have been the best of friends, real soul mates. I really miss her. Papa always says that she is nearby or upstairs, looking out for both of us. I often hear him saying good night to her. I do love my dad.

Just then, the intercom light on her desktop communicator began flashing. She touched the Answer icon on the screen and the doleful face of Riley, her father's elderly butler, came into view. 'Miss Lane has arrived,' he announced, in one of his more doleful voices. For some reason, Riley seemed to find it difficult to refer to Crystal by her first name.

The Leaders' Ball was being held at the swanky Grosvener Private Club north of Queen's South Side, one of the few elite areas left on the planet.

Decisive as always, Aurora closed her journal, bolted up from her desk chair and strode out of her study. She made it to the cosy lounge area, which Riley insisted on calling 'Miss Aurora's parlour' between her bedroom and the corridor separating her suite from her father's, just as Riley, carrying Crystal's zip-bagged ball gown by the hook of its hanger, was showing her friend in. 'Just put her gown in my wardrobe, please, Riley,' she ordered politely.

Crystal held up her make-up case. 'I decided not to embarrass the poor man by making him carry this, too,' she not-quite-giggled in her soft, flat Kiwi accent. She was tall and striking, her Maori-Irish ancestry making itself clear in her proud, dark, freckled face. She had grown up by the sea, but her family had been forced to abandon their home due to rising sea levels and had lived in a high mountain valley since she had been nine.

The immediate topics, however, after Riley had withdrawn and the ball gowns had been brought out, were the Future Leaders' Ball and related matters.

'To tell you the truth, girl,' Aurora grumbled, as she zipped her friend into her stylish grown-up gown, 'I really wish my dad wasn't so keen for me to go to this silly ball. I'm really not in the mood.'

'Really? I'd never have known,' Crystal said sarcastically. 'Oh, c'mon, stop whingeing about going to the ball and get into your frock. It could be a real hoot, for goodness' sake.'

Aurora was wearing an even more grown-up low-back, clingy, neck-to-floor dress in a sort of metallic-champagne-coloured fabric that moved with her. Crystal was in awe.

'You look fab and dangerous, you foxy lady. Oh! I do like that on you, babe,' Crystal said laughing. 'It's so sleek and it hides all the bumps and bulges.'

'What bumps and bulges? Speak for yourself, you horrible girl!'

'Touchy! Did I stumble onto a hair trigger here? Venom!' Crystal purred.

Aurora sniggered. 'I'm going to ignore that comment. Don't you just love this fabulous new fabric, just developed by Monty Engel's?' she announced, in a phoney-sounding fashion-commentator voice. 'Stays cosy on the muscles, but it sure lets you dance.' She moved her hips in the current dance style. 'I sure hope Nigel doesn't try to grope me if they play any slow music.'

The rascally Nigel Dougal-James, her date for the ball, was a matter of convenience: good family, good student at the Capital Region Institute of Medical Studies, bland-looking, boring and entirely too free with his hands.

'Nah,' Crystal assured her. 'Haven't you heard? The band's going to be Batteries Not Included.'

'Great, I like them. With BNI, it's always everyone in a big ruck in the middle of the floor, shakin' sandbags at full tilt. Too bad, Nige,' she said laughing.

They laughed about this and about Crystal's date, Booker Parmentier, and about where the after-parties were going to be and who was going – and with whom – while they did each other's hair and make-up.

'I wish they weren't having it at that stuck-up hoity-toity Grosvener Private Club this year.'

'Yeah, I know. It's a great place for people with three first names, like Nigel Dougal-James.'

'And with three last names, like that obnoxious Drexel Pigott-Baines…'

'Who don't give a toss about anybody but themselves?'

'Or about anything except money and status.'

Crystal giggled. 'Don't forget their lack of interest for anything happening above their waists.'

'And we're right back to…'

The girls spoke in unison, saying 'Nigel Dougal-James' together, laughing.

'Of course,' Aurora said, pulling herself into a haughty attitude, 'we intellectual women are above all that.'

'That's one thing that bothers me about you, Aurora.'

'What's that?'

'Why you haven't manipulated one of your dad's security men to find out who that Greek god was who we saw through the hole in the shower-room wall at the Interacademy Sports Festival last year.'

'What? The one from the UFA?'

'Well, why haven't you?'

Aurora became queen-like again, 'Simple, I am not interested, that's why,' she said, secretly hiding the fact that she had found out ages ago who he was and that she had on occasions gone out of her way to watch him on military parade. This had caused a great deal of inward confusion. Aurora had spent hours staring at the ceiling, wondering what all the fuss was about. *Boys; who needs them?* was her final conclusion before she turned the lights out.

Crystal chuckled, 'And not only that; you're too embarrassed to admit otherwise!'

Clive, the Gazers' family chauffeur, drove them to pick up their dates in Admiral Gazers' state-of-the-art limo, a Roller Glider. Lopez, a highly-trained security agent assigned to the Gazers' household, rode next to Clive up front. Admiral Gazers' prominent position meant that Aurora rarely went anywhere without an agent by her side just to make sure she was safe. Clive was a great hulk of a man, 195 centimetres tall and a weighty 110 kilos at least. He had a South African accent. Lopez was of an indefinite age and with an indefinite accent, when he said anything at all. He was medium-sized, dark and wearing, as always, an expensive-looking, dark pinstriped suit.

The first stop was to pick up Booker from his student hostel near the university. Booker was an intense-looking young man, a year older than the girls.

'Hi, Cris; hi, Rora,' he muttered shyly, as he climbed into the back of the Roller. His rented evening clothes fit him badly.

'Hey, Books,' Crystal said, taking his hand. 'It's good to see you.'

He blushed and shook his head. 'It always seems so bizarre to me that you act like you like me.'

'Oh, get over it, Booker,' Aurora almost hooted. 'Everyone I know likes you. Well, almost.'

He looked down at his not-quite-shined shoes, then at Crystal's hand holding his, and said, 'I don't know if that's true or not, Rora, but that's not what I meant.'

Laughing, Crystal leaned over and kissed him high on the cheekbone. His eyes rolled briefly up into his head. 'Sorry,' Crystal said, giggling, 'but you were looking so cute with those big brown puppy-dog eyes that the devil made me do it.'

Booker closed his eyes and breathed deeply, saying nothing.

In less than ten minutes, they were back up in the leafy hills of the exclusive suburb of Grosvener, where they stopped off at the Dougal-James stately home, not far from the club, to pick up Nigel. Unlike Booker, Nigel was turned out flawlessly, from his every-strand-in-place dark-blond hair through his custom-tailored evening clothes, which he owned, to his manicured fingernails and shiny dancing shoes.

As he settled into his seat, he said, 'Aurora! More lovely than ever!' and tried to put his arm around her shoulders, but she deftly slipped his smooth move and left him clutching air. He turned and took Crystal's hand and bent over it in the continental manner, intoning, 'Ah, sex kitten, stunning as always. Hey, Books! How's it hangin'?'

All three of them were polite enough not to roll their eyes, realising that, although Nigel was irritating – something all three of them were too polite to tell him – he was essentially harmless. 'Get your seatbelt hooked up, Nige,' was what Aurora finally said.

The Grosvener Private Club had been built by wealthy people during a period of ostentation and looked something like a scaled-down version of a late-twentieth-century airport terminal, with high ceilings and enormous tinted-glass walls looking out over the golf course.

Arriving at the grand entrance, Aurora was surprised to be greeted with an out-of-character 'hello, darling' from her old nemesis Blackie.

Suspiciously, Aurora exchanged careful-with-the-frocks-and-make-up hugs with her. Crystal and the others shoved their way past, hoping that Blackie would not spot them; fortunately for all concerned, Bailey Spragg, the self-appointed Campus fun machine, caught her eye first.

Whisper had it that he was the ultimate party animal; a recent survey conducted throughout most of the girls' dorms during the mischievous midnight mayhem, when adolescent hormones, along with the pillows, were flying all over the place, voted him the cadet most girls would like to go on a date with besides, of course, the acclaimed 'Greek God' Ethan Knight. Aurora did not share that same view; she thought Bailey was a cocky, arrogant upstart pig.

The boy's conversation soon drifted, as usual, to martial arts. The girls always found the topic quite boring. It wasn't as if Aurora didn't have an interest in martial arts; after all, one of her passions was ancient hand-to-hand combat techniques. She was the regional inter-academy judo champion in her weight class and was also inter-regionally competitive in karate and taekwondo, as well as being a certified self-defence instructor. She just didn't want to talk about it twenty-four hours a day and was getting quite irritated.

'Come on, guys, change the channel; I'm dying here! Can someone please show some initiative? I need some stimulation now.'

The 250 or so ball-goers had clustered into a couple of dozen groups of three or four couples each. Aurora spotted first the other young scientists present, several of whom drifted by to say hello to Crystal and her. Crystal had fun pointing out a couple of clusters of either negligently or flamboyantly dressed young leaders from the Academy of the Arts: a group of highly-regarded painter and sculptors, a couple of groups of movie-makers and actors – the largest of these groups clustering around Edison Bates, whose student film, *The World of the Lost*, had become an international sensation and had made him an instant celebrity – a group of serious musicians and a group of dancers. 'Just leave it to Edison,' she said, laughing, 'to wear an opera cape lined with cherry-red satin!'

The girls' dates had paused in their conversation as Aurora had vented her frustration. They looked at each other when she'd finished.

Finally, Nigel said, 'Oh, lighten up and have some fun, girl.'

'Yeah; come on, Aurora, it will get better I promise. At least give it a chance. Keep it cool, babe,' Crystal suggested.

The club's PA system, which had been playing some bland syntho-pop at a discreet volume, started to fade the music out, and the few groups of people who had been dancing to it began drifting over to where a reception line had formed.

Taking Booker's arm, Crystal said, 'C'mon, friends: time to be polite; what say we go and mingle?'

No one seemed that eager to move.

'Well, come on!'

'All right, I'm right behind you, for goodness' sake.' Aurora glared, wide-eyed like a startled rabbit.

Most of the ball-goers had shaken hands with the line-up of club officials and other notables in the reception line. With formalities finally over, the band started to kick some welcome life into the action-starved occasion. Soon, nearly all the young people were going wild out on the polished real-parquet floor dancing as a demented mob. Arms, legs and elbows, were flying everywhere, some deliberately aimed at Blackie and company.

Miraculously, Aurora seemed to be enjoying herself and tiny little beads of perspiration started to appear on her brow, indicating to everyone, including her dance partner, Nigel, that she was getting into the mood of things at last. The other members of her entourage were swimming in sweat and really boogieing to the beat.

Having arranged for Clive to collect them at 12.30 Lexus time, Aurora had an attack of guilt, admitting that she may have been a little out of order with her stuck-up attitude earlier.

'See, told you it would get better, luvvie,' Crystal scoffed.

'OK, Crystal, I concede you were right! Now, let's not make a meal of it all right?'

'You can make it up to me later.'

Twelve thirty had soon arrived. Aurora seemed a little reluctant to leave; normally, she would make any excuse to put a little distance between herself and Nigel's roaming hands, but tonight was quite different. She was soaking up the atmosphere and rolling with the thump of the beat. Nigel was ever so confused;

he hadn't experienced Aurora being so nice and accommodating to him before and he was making the most of it while it lasted.

Spotting Clive enter the ballroom, Aurora gestured to show that she was aware of his arrival. Clive took up his post just near the west wing side exit, where the Roller Glider was parked in stationary mode. Being familiar with all the exit points, Clive favoured the west wing because most of the patrons always elected to leave by the grand entrance, so there was far less likelihood of congestion.

Crystal had earlier accepted an invitation to an after-party Edison Bates was throwing on the set of his new short movie, and, although tired and a bit grumpy, Aurora couldn't tell her friend no. She signalled to Clive, who left his post by the exit to get the Roller primed and ready to go.

About fifteen seconds after Clive went out to get the limo, about twenty-five scruffy young men, with five or six similar young women, burst into the ballroom. Although uniformly dirty, they all wore elaborate hairdos dyed in multiple bright colours, their faces were all tattooed with a spiral pattern of small blue daggers with red tips and their shabby clothing was all coloured red and blue in a mix-and-match hotchpotch. They were also all brandishing machetes and a variety of clearly home-made weapons. One of them, clearly the alpha male of the group, waved a semi-automatic handgun about and fired a round into the ceiling.

The band immediately stopped playing and ducked for cover as the thug with the gun shouted, 'OK, everybody, let's make this quick! Give your cash and any jewellery to my brothers and sisters as they go by and then we're outta here!'

The gang moved menacingly through the ball-goers for less than a minute, grabbing handbags, watches, wallets and necklaces, threatening the more reluctant young leaders with their weapons.

When one particularly large and toothlessly ugly gangster reached Bailey, however, he received an unwelcome surprise, as Bailey easily disarmed him, knocked him to the floor and stomped on his head. Immediately, about five additional thugs surrounded Bailey, but their leader raised his gun and aimed it in that direction, shouting, 'Get outta my line of fire or I will put a round in yer belly!'

Then Lopez, who had been watching the approaches to the club from the front, burst in through the double doors and put a cluster of bullets into the armed leader's chest from a distance of about thirty metres.

Some of the gangsters immediately took off toward the kitchen doors with their booty, but the ones surrounding Bailey grabbed Crystal to use as a human shield on their way out, putting a sharp blade at her throat and shouting, 'Let us go and the lady won't get hurt!'

Bailey and Lopez froze for a moment, working out what to do next, but Aurora, already on the edge, reacted reflexively to Crystal's abduction. She landed a kick to the head of the thug who had grabbed her friend, grabbed the wrist of his weapon hand and twisted it until the knife fell to the floor, and then delivered another kick to his kneecap, sending him to the floor as well, screaming with pain. The other four foolishly turned their attention from their hostages to Aurora, giving Bailey the opening he'd been looking for. He seemed to fly through the air to smash his foot into the face of one as Aurora slashed the bridge of another's nose with the side of her left hand, following up with a stiff jab to the same place with the four knuckles of her right while Bailey used the momentum of another one charging at him to send the fellow flying a couple of metres to land awkwardly and painfully on the floor. Bailey and Aurora hit the fourth aggressor simultaneously with a high-low: the heel of Bailey's right hand into his larynx and the side of Aurora's foot into his kneecap.

Lopez, who had come charging into the room, shooting the legs out from under some of the fleeing gangsters, took charge of restoring order as a squad of ten police troopers arrived at the front of the club in two police hover-modules and came running in through the front doors. Still, at least a dozen and a half of the raiders managed to escape with their loot.

As the police troopers made a big show of arresting the injured and wounded gangsters, Aurora spotted Nigel and Blackie, with a couple of her girlfriends, gingerly tiptoeing away from the safe confines of their convenient hiding place, which was well away from the danger. Aurora seemed to hypnotise Blackie, forcing her to gaze straight into her eyes. Aurora shot a stinging glare back at her: a look so cutting that even Blackie found its jagged edge hard to dismiss. As for Nigel, 'the brave', he just hung his head in shame.

Chapter Two

Ethan Knight, a sixteen-year-old officer cadet at the Universal Flying Academy, was graduating as Top Gun Flight Captain. His parents and his dog, Jack, made the long journey from their old, vine-covered little home in Kingstonia, a leafy suburb about sixty-five kilometres from the urban sprawl of Nevulae, to be with their son on his special day.

A consummate scholar, Ethan had excelled in everything he had ever attempted. Possessing a 183-centimetre athletic frame; smooth olive skin; jet-black, naturally wavy hair; high cheekbones and large, deep-set, dark-blue eyes, he was, according to his female fellow cadets, a real hunk of eye-candy.

His best pal at the Academy was Ralph Logic Baxter, whose strong point was his superior intellect. Unlike Ethan, however, he'd been overlooked when they'd been passing out the good looks. His frizzy, fire-red hair flew out of control in every direction. He was barely 155 centimetres tall, but his courage made up for what he lacked in height, and, just like his pal Ethan, he was always ready to face challenges enthusiastically and head-on. Acne spots and huge craters covered his round face, playing havoc with his dating prospects by rearing their ugly heads at the most inopportune moments. This, combined with his freckles and thick, heavy eyebrows that grew together over his pug nose, made life seem brutally unfair to him.

Ralph was well-known at the Academy as Ethan's eternal shadow. It seemed to their fellow students that they were always by each other's side, and they were, indeed, like brothers. Hanging around with his best pal suited Ralph just fine, as Ethan was usually surrounded by plenty of girls. This, however, could sometimes prove frustrating. Ethan studied and trained hard and had many interests that seemed to consume him, but the pursuit of the opposite sex wasn't yet one of them, as he refused to allow himself to be overcome by his natural adolescent hormones.

Ralph, however, was more than ready to take over that tediously unpleasant job for him.

'Well,' Ralph had said once, with a crooked grin, as he'd prepared to walk Agnes, a female cadet with short, straight, shiny blonde hair and pale grey eyes – and who was almost a head taller than Ralph – to class, 'it is a hard task. I will try to serve my pal as well as I can.'

Ralph was also graduating, and he had achieved the status of Dux of the entire school, a distinction only earned by one other pupil in the UFA's illustrious history.

The Headmaster, Dr Jonas Mickleson, called Ethan's name. It was time for him to proceed to the stage, dressed in a scholar's cap and gown bearing UFA's distinctive silver blue and green lightning-bolt symbol, to receive his diploma.

Ethan's family sat at the front of the auditorium. Feelings of pride and deep, unexplainable emotion filled his parents when he appeared on stage to a hero's welcome of thunderous applause. *That's my boy*, his mother, Bella, thought silently. His father, Connor, managed to whistle from a slightly dry throat. Lapping up all the attention, Ethan acknowledged his parents with a slightly red face and a huge grin. Jack joined in the fun by turning somersaults, getting all tangled up with Connor in his lead.

Waiting nervously in the wings, Ralph wondered if his parents had been able to make the journey from their home in Corona, not far from Kingstonia. He sadly thought that it was highly unlikely, however, as he had received word a couple of weeks earlier that his father, Jacob, had been injured at work while testing minerals he'd found inside a meteor that had crashed to Earth the previous day.

Jacob worked as a scientist at Nevulae Technological Institute. The authorities there had been playing down his injuries in their e-mails to Ralph, giving him the impression that his father had received a slight crack on the head and was undergoing tests in hospital as a precautionary measure. The truth was that a highly volatile combination of gases had ignited, leaving him lying unconscious and bleeding on the ground. Ralph's mother, Inger, had been keeping a twenty-four-hour-a-day vigil at her husband's bedside, hoping that he would be well enough to make it to his son's graduation, but it hadn't been looking good.

Dr Mickleson announced in his deep, mellifluous voice over the PA system that it was time for Lieutenant Baxter to step up onto the stage and receive his diploma. Dr Mickleson had a tremendous voice and enjoyed having occasions to use it. Ralph deliberately hung back, waiting, hoping to allow his parents more time to arrive.

'Where are they?' His nervousness showed in his voice.

'Come on, Ralph. Could this be the very first time you've been late for anything, let alone your own celebration?' Dr Mickelson allowed a little chuckle into his voice, which raised a slight chuckle from the well-wishers in the auditorium. Ralph's parents were still nowhere to be seen. 'Come on, please.'

Ralph really wanted to share his proud and special moment with his parents.

Pull yourself together, Ralph said to himself, silently. *Time to get up on that stage and receive my award.* He took a deep breath. *I've held things up long enough.* He turned and launched himself for the door and swept through into the auditorium – not just entering, but making an entrance – and the audience met him with a reaction similar in enthusiasm to the one they had given his pal Ethan moments earlier.

Dr Mickelson stepped back up to the microphone and let his voice boom out. 'Can I have your attention, please?' He then tapped the microphone to make sure it was turned on and that everyone could hear him clearly. 'In the Academy's entire history, no other cadet has ever achieved higher grades than this young man standing before you, Lieutenant Baxter, and some very distinguished individuals have attended the Academy over the years. Thirty-three years ago, however, a young officer cadet did actually manage to equal Lieutenant Baxter's achievement. That person went on to become one of the world's most loved and respected leaders. He insisted on being here today to present Lieutenant Baxter with this well-earned diploma.'

A scarlet flush rising up his pale neck to his freckled cheeks, Ralph turned to Ethan in the hope of some answers. 'Who's that?'

Ethan raised his eyebrows and shrugged his shoulders, silently mouthing the words, *Beats me*!

His voice at its most sonorous possible colouration, Dr

Mickleson intoned, 'Please be upstanding and welcome on stage World Minister and Commander of the Universal Defence Fleet, the Right Honourable Admiral Harlius Fonce Gazers.'

The admiral stood on stage for over five minutes before the cheering and clapping died down enough for him to say a few words. Standing 193 centimetres tall, Admiral Gazers was a tower of a man, lean but strong, good-looking in a rugged, well-worn sort of way, with a genuine sparkle in his bright blue eyes. Nudging fifty, he was fitter than most men half his age.

Finally, Admiral Gazers spoke slowly and effectively into the microphone, remembering how his own illustrious career had begun at the academy. 'It's very humbling,' he reflected, in his deep, strong voice, 'for me to have the opportunity to stand on the exact same stage where I stood as a young, green-necked officer cadet over thirty years ago, on a day during which I became a recipient of the same award I am about to present to Lieutenant Ralph Baxter today. We should all be very proud of this young man's enormously outstanding achievement, and I am honoured to be able to share in this very special moment in history: two men, three decades apart, living the same rare experience.'

Ralph naturally enjoyed hearing the admiral singing his praises, but he still felt a deep sadness, as he wished that his mum and dad could hear all this, knowing what warm, satisfying pride and fulfilment they would be feeling.

Unfortunately, Ralph was unaware that his mother had arrived just in time to hear every kind word. She had known for years that her son would reach great heights academically, but this was something beyond what she had, deep in her heart, expected; he had gone to a totally different level. She wished that her husband could be with her to share in this fantastically special occasion and to make her son's day absolutely perfect. He had looked pathetically sad, lying in that big hospital bed, when she had left that morning. It had seemed to consume him.

Ralph's preoccupation with trying to spot his parents far outweighed his awareness of the admiral's presence; it even clouded his immediate memory of his own achievements. His mind played dirty tricks of distraction on him. He stopped listening to what the admiral was saying, as visions of images, past and present, floated in and out of his head instead. He wondered if his father's injuries were far more serious than the authorities had told him they were. He even wondered if his father had died.

Admiral Gazers handed Ralph the diploma symbolising his accomplishment. Ralph, preoccupied, seemed barely to know what it was. He looked down at it with what seemed like an uncomprehending look on his face. The admiral stepped back and gestured for Ralph to step up to the microphone.

Over the PA, Dr Mickleson's voice intoned, 'And now Ralph Baxter, Dux of the Universal Flying Academy, will say a few words for us.'

Ralph, however, just stood in place, his eyes scanning the crowd.

What's up with Ralph? Ethan wondered silently. His friend's distress was obvious, and he understood intuitively that Ralph needed him. He only processed this understanding in his own mind for a moment before he made a firm decision and walked back out onto the stage to see what he could do.

Ethan saluted the admiral smartly, said, 'Sorry for my untimely interruption,' and then dragged a protesting Ralph a few steps over to one side.

'What the hell is going on, bud?' he whispered urgently. 'Man, don't you realise that the world's most famous person is on stage, immortalising your place in academic history? You need to snap out of it and concentrate, Ralph, and fast.'

Ralph didn't answer. Faced with no other choice, Ethan brought him back down to Earth with a sharp dig in the ribs with his elbow, raising a yelp and a 'Hey, man!'

'Well, something got your attention!' Ethan winked at him. 'I needed to do something. You were going to pieces up here.' He looked out at the crowd, which was shifting and muttering impatiently, and said, 'Hey, isn't that your mother walking over here?'

'Where?' Ralph looked to where Ethan was pointing. Sure enough, he saw his mother walking quickly towards them, obviously anxious to make sure her son was all right after seeing him go to pieces on the stage.

Ralph dropped his bottom lip and mouthed, *I'm OK, Mum. Where's Dad?*

Inger gave her son a brave smile and a wave, called out that she'd talk with him after the ceremony and turned away discreetly before he could see her wiping tears from her eyes.

'For your information, pal,' Ralph informed Ethan, 'the admiral's just the second most famous person in the world. Dad's on the top of my list. Judging by the way Mum's acting, though, I don't think he's coming today.'

Ralph walked back to the centre of the stage and looked at the microphone as if it were going to bite him. He then stepped up to it and said, 'Thank you, Admiral Gazers, distinguished faculty and my fellow cadets,' before his eye caught a glimpse of something going on near one of the auditorium's side doors. He stepped back from the microphone and turned his head to his friend. 'Ethan, what's going on over there?'

'Looks to me like an Egyptian mummy jumping up and down and waving a pair of crutches in the air, trying to attract our attention, Ralph. Now, that's a common, everyday occurrence, isn't it?'

'That's Dad for sure! He's made it! Great!'

Ethan looked at him sideways. 'How can you tell with all those bandages?'

'I know my dad. I knew he'd make it.' He looked over at his friend with a shy little smile. 'What shall I do? Keep the admiral and everyone waiting a little longer? What's another five minutes or so? I've already kept them waiting longer than I should have – or shall I just jump off the stage and make a run for it?'

'Take a deep breath and think about it,' Ethan advised, then he said, 'Oh hell, Ralph, go for it,' realising that his best friend's father was more important to him than any accolade at that moment.

Realising Ralph had seen him, Jacob forgot about his injuries for a moment, thinking this was just what the doctor ordered. *Such a sweet pill to swallow*, he thought to himself. *Bucking the odds to be here with my son on his graduation day is just the tonic. Yes, indeed, this is the best start for me on my road to recovery*.

Ralph jumped off the stage, landing gracefully despite his short, awkward-looking frame, and made a beeline towards his father.

Dr Mickelson tried to stop him, making a grab for his arm, but was far too slow, and Admiral Gazers halted him, anyway, saying, 'Let him go, Jonas. Can't you see that the boy needs his father right now? And I'm sure his father needs him. It sticks out a mile that it's far more important for them to be together at this time. We can wait.'

Dr Mickelson felt the powerful emotions going through everyone. He took a deep breath and answered, 'I'm with you on that one, sir,' as he wiped perspiration from his thick, black-rimmed glasses with his silver-green-blue striped tie.

Inger had joined her husband after running from one end of the auditorium to the other, sobbing all the way. Her face showed the intense pleasure and relief she felt, and also her wild amazement that he had made it to Ralph's graduation ceremony, goodness knew how.

Ralph came running up and flung himself at his father, wrapping his arms around him and nearly knocking him off his feet.

Jacob laughed warmly and said, 'Steady on, son,' then hugged Ralph back as best he could. It was clear that even this gesture of fatherly love caused him some discomfort and pain.

Swelling with pride, this connection to what is best about the human species forcing a surge of emotion into his heart and then throughout all of him, Admiral Gazers began to clap softly, encouraging the whole audience to follow suit and to rise to their feet, cheering.

Ethan, who had felt sorrow for his pal a few moments earlier, now felt extremely proud of him.

'Please explain, Jacob,' Inger demanded, her voice trembling with a mixture of feelings; she then made a visible effort to compose herself before continuing. 'Didn't I leave you half-dying in hospital this morning, barely able to talk, let alone walk? And now you turn up, as right as ninepence – apart from the bandages and crutches, that is. I mean, what is this: a medical miracle?'

'Quite simple, darling. Earth, wind, and fire couldn't have kept me away from the biggest day in my son's life. I did have to do lots of sweet-talking to be let out, though. Those doctors and nurses should get jobs as prison-camp guards. I had to promise on my oath to be back in hospital straight after the ceremony. I did, however, manage to commandeer an air ambulance and controller.'

'Thanks, Dad. It means a lot to me, but are you feeling OK?' Ralph's voice showed his concern. 'Do you need to sit down?' He started looking around for a conveniently-sited seat.

'Hey, Son, don't you worry about me. I'm as tough as old boots. It'd take more than a little old everyday explosion to keep me pinned down. Now, give your father a hug.'

Ralph glowed with his father's public display of affection and planted a huge smacker on the side of his cheek. He didn't mind showing how relieved he was to see his father again and to know that he was all right. The colour returned to Ralph's cheeks and he seemed back to his old self.

'Go back up there, son,' Jacob told him, 'and finish accepting your diploma. It's what I came here to see.'

Back on the stage, Ralph again thanked the admiral, this time for being so patient and understanding, and then turned to talk to everyone present.

'I didn't try to win this award,' he told them. 'I just tried to take advantage of the opportunities the Universal Flying Academy made available for me to learn, and to think, and to dream. I just love to do these things, y'see? The more I learn the better I feel. The better my mind is trained to think, the more I like it. Without a dream, there's no point in all the rest. The academic ranking is just a side effect showing how much the Academy helped me to learn and how well the Academy trained me to think. Thank you. And thank you again.'

The applause was loud and sustained.

Afterward, Ralph rushed from the stage again to be with his parents. A few minutes later, Ethan joined them, almost bursting to tell Ralph some fantastic news that he had just received. He didn't want to interrupt the family reunion, however, so he paced up and down, the seconds seeming like hours to him, waiting for an opportunity to butt in. 'C'mon, come on, Ralph,' he mumbled under his breath.

Nearly exploding, Ethan eventually couldn't contain himself any longer and blurted out, 'Excuse me, Mr and Mrs B, but I need to talk to Ralph right now.' Not giving him the opportunity to object, he grabbed Ralph's arm and forcibly marched him over to a quiet corner of the auditorium's lobby, leaving Jacob and Inger open-mouthed.

'What's so freaking urgent, pal?' asked a clearly irritated and slightly disgruntled Ralph.

'I'm leaving on my first mission thirty days from now. Admiral Gazers just gave me my orders.'

Ethan was almost quivering with excitement, but Ralph, so animated a moment before, fell almost deathly silent. Ethan, still pumped up, asked him, 'What's up?' He grabbed Ralph by the shoulders and squeezed them in a friendly way. 'I thought you'd be pleased for me.'

''Course I am. I'm over the moon.' His pain and disappointment were clearer than even his sarcasm. 'But what about me? I'm coming, too, aren't I?'

'I'm sure you'll receive your orders soon.' Not expecting Ralph's dejected reaction, Ethan tried to play down his extreme excitement. 'Maybe we'll be together, Ralph, and maybe we won't. That's the military. Maybe other things are destined for you, and they'll be great things, for sure.' Trying to comfort his friend, he suddenly sounded older and wiser than his sixteen years.

'How long will you be gone, and where are you heading?' Ralph asked, like a little boy lost.

'It's a voyage of exploration and I'll be away for six months. We'll be looking for inhabitable planets. I'm going to save the world.'

'You will need a science officer, then, won't you? I can help in that department.' Ralph was quick off the mark.

'Fleet Command has already picked the crew. I don't have any influence over that decision, Ralph.'

'Surely there's something you can do, buddy,' he pleaded to Ethan's soft, caramel-like centre, a tactic which had always worked well in the past. Not wanting to let it go, and giving Ethan a really hard dose of pressure, Ralph reminded him, 'Brothers should stick together, you know; wherever one goes, then the other should follow.' He began to think that his cleverness had nearly won Ethan over.

'It is not that easy, Ralph. We're in the military now. We can't make our own decisions.' Ethan looked firmly yet pleadingly into

Ralph's eyes as he continued. 'We have to follow orders, no matter how we feel.'

Ralph thought he still had half a chance, and pursued Ethan like a terrier. 'You can swing it. Promise me you'll at least try, please?'

'What's keeping the boys?' asked Bella. 'They've been talking for ages!'

Connor was in the dark as well, so they slowly made their way over to have a nosy.

'Ethan's received orders to go on a mission,' Ralph told them, 'and he hasn't heard anything about me going along on the mission, too, and I can't say I'm happy about my best and only pal just skiving off on a mission without me. Being the wonderful son you've raised so well, though, Ethan's promised to try to get me assigned to the mission as part of the scientific crew.'

'For goodness' sake, Ralph! I haven't promised you anything of the sort. I said that I would see about trying if I could. Leave it at that, please!'

After all the excitement and emotion of the day, Jacob was feeling definitely washed out and decided to put wisdom ahead of emotion. He apologised to everyone that he had to leave so early, and said, 'And, really, really: congratulations, boys. All the best to you both for a great first mission and safe return home. We are all blessed to have two such great potential leaders in our midst. The world is a better place with you boys in it. We can sleep soundly in our beds tonight, knowing you two are around.' He smiled. 'Now, I had better get to mine, otherwise the prison-camp guards will have the dogs out and then give me heaps of static when I do get back. Interrogation! Walk me out to the air ambulance, babe. I think it's time to leave.'

Ralph's parents turned and moved off towards the waiting air ambulance, Inger helping Jacob stay on his feet. A white-uniformed pilot-paramedic leapt from the side of the vehicle after lowering and extending the gurney to help Jacob lie comfortably down.

Ralph immediately turned and pounced on Ethan. 'You haven't forgotten about that promise to try to get me on your mission, have you?'

'Blimey, Ralph! We only talked about it two minutes ago. I'll try, OK? So back off a little.'

Ethan's little display of irritation was only an act. He thought, deep down, that it would be great to have his best pal with him on his first mission. He silently agreed with Ralph that his computer and scientific skills, but most of all his friendship, would certainly prove to be a great asset during the coming months.

After seeing Jacob into the air ambulance, Inger turned to go and rejoin her son. She was just outside the auditorium and heard what the boys were saying. She was not deliberately eavesdropping, but the boys had been talking just loudly enough for her to hear as she approached them. She thought to herself that, if Ralph were allowed on the mission, he could not be in better hands; she trusted Ethan implicitly. She was a strong believer in destiny; if her son was meant to go, then so be it.

Ralph spotted his mother coming back into the reception area. 'Hey, Mum,' he called out. 'Were you just around the corner there?'

'Not for long, son, but I heard enough. Do you want me to have a word with Admiral Gazers for you?'

'I didn't realise you knew the admiral,' exclaimed Ralph, surprised. Both boys looked confused.

'Harlius Fonce and I have been friends for years: since well before you were born. It would have been great to meet up with him today. It's such a shame to miss him after all this time.'

'Oh, it's Harlius Fonce, is it? So you know him quite well then, do you, Mum?'

'Never you mind. Let us just say "well enough" and leave it at that. Stop trying to read anything more into it. We were just really good friends, that's all.'

'I think it's really up to Ethan to try and persuade the admiral,' Ralph decided. 'He's our Commanding Officer. I'd hope that being that should carry a fair bit of weight. His briefing is scheduled for 09.00 hours at the Grand Assembly headquarters tomorrow morning.'

Chapter Three

While handing Ethan his orders at the graduation ceremony, Admiral Gazers had also told him that he would have to appear at the Grand Assembly meeting the following morning, in connection with the mission, and had invited Ethan and his family to his private home for an informal briefing and a little supper, adding that he thought it would be a good idea for them to have a talk in order to provide Ethan with some preparation before he was thrown to the wolves.

'There's no reason to pretend otherwise,' Admiral Gazers had told him. 'So much power in one room is daunting for the best of us.' He'd then offered to have Clive, his personal chauffeur, pick them up at 6.45 p.m. Ethan hadn't been able to say no.

Standing outside the auditorium, the Knight family discussed this news after Ethan had relayed it to his parents. Connor, wanting the family to spend as much time together as possible before Ethan left to prepare for his six-month mission, said, 'Well, I, for one, am thoroughly grateful that Admiral Gazers has invited the entire family.'

Ethan, however, was eager to take off and have fun after leaving the admiral's. He took a deep breath and told his parents, 'Later on, Ralph and I really do deserve to spend some quality time together, celebrating our graduation. So, Mum, Dad, after the meeting, I'll just leave you two to retrace old footsteps and memories.'

Ralph and his mother were staying at the Paradise Apollo Inn, a nice little boutique hotel only five minutes from the large and luxurious Planet Plaza, where the Knights were staying.

I'll give Ethan five minutes before he knocks my door down, wanting to hit the town tonight, Ralph speculated, after checking in. *He's so predictable when it comes to having a good time.*

Looking out of his first-floor hotel window, he saw his pal down below, just as he'd expected.

Ethan shouted up at the window, with a huge grin, 'Hey, Ralph, want to hit the town tonight and celebrate?'

Ralph called back down, 'Are you coming up, or what?'

'No need. Ask your mum; I'll wait down here. I can't be bothered climbing all those stairs. I've got places to go, people to see, things to do.'

Ralph gave Ethan the thumbs-up from the hotel window.

'Great, then, mate!' Ethan yelled up enthusiastically. 'I have my meeting with the admiral at seven, so I'll see you at ten, then. OK, Ralph? Don't be late, and watch out; we're in for a bumpy ride.'

Ethan dashed off to prepare for his meeting with the admiral. Halfway down the road, he realised that he'd forgotten to tell Ralph where they were going to meet, so he stopped, raced back and shouted, 'I'll be at the Golden Gate Centre on the North Side. There's a great Cyber Lounge there that's in right now.'

Ralph was still at the window, waiting for this crucial information. He'd known his friend would do just as he'd done. He shouted back, 'Right.'

Admiral Gazers had arranged with Ethan to have Clive pick them up at 6.45 p.m. but, being well aware of Admiral Gazers' reputation as a stickler for promptness, the Knight family left their suite at 6.40 to take the lift down to the ground floor of the hotel's atrium lobby.

As they walked into the scenic glass lift, Jack slipped in behind the rest of the family, trying not to be noticed. Spotting him, Ethan half-shouted, 'Where are you going, you naughty boy? You can't come.'

Jack tried the tactic of rolling onto his back and exposing his tempting, soft, pink belly, clearly intending this to change his mind, as it had many times before. This time it failed to achieve its objective, as Ethan pointed to the hotel-room door and commanded, 'Go back inside!'

Jumping up as if accepting defeat, Jack ran from the lift, darting about all over the place Ethan and his parents were momentarily preoccupied with the fantastic view through the lift's glass sides thirty-three floors up, allowing the dog some extra time of freedom. Pushing his luck, Jack tried to induce Ethan into forgetting about refusing to chase him all over the place.

Ethan, of course, had no intention of chasing him and shouted to Jack, 'I'm going to sort that naughty dog out, now!'

Sensing he was in deep trouble at the change of tone, Jack slid along the marble floor tiles on his belly, wanting anyone to scratch and forgive him.

Being an old softy, Ethan conceded, 'All right, just one, then you're going back to the room, you naughty dog.'

Descending from the thirty-third floor, Ethan could see one of his all-time favourite transporters pulling up outside the hotel. 'Wow, look at that, Dad! It's a Roller Glider! They're the most luxurious limos on the planet. What a beauty! I'd love to have a go in that.'

'It's probably waiting for someone rich and famous, like a rock star,' Connor told him. Listening to rock music was Connor's favourite pastime.

Bella, though, realised immediately that the vehicle was waiting for them. 'That's for us,' she said. 'Hold on to your hats, folks; we're going in style.'

Clive, looking remarkably large and dignified, was waiting to greet them outside the lift. He welcomed the family on behalf of Admiral Gazers, led them out of the hotel's main entrance and opened the rear hatches to the Roller Glider with his remote, inviting Mrs Bella and Mr Connor (as he addressed them) to climb aboard and offering them assistance in doing so. He then turned to Ethan and said, 'You can join me in front, if you like.'

'Really? Insane, man! Thanks, Clive! I've never been up close to a Roller Glider, let alone been allowed to sit in one.' Looking at everything closely every centimetre of the way, Ethan climbed into the front passenger seat. 'Closest I've got to one of these before now is a picture in a motoring magazine. My pal Ralph used to come 'round to my place and we would daydream in my bedroom about flash transporters, and I told him one day I would own one of these.'

'Well, I hope your dream comes true, young man,' Clive told him as he fastened his seatbelt. 'I'm sure it will if you want it enough.'

The fifteen-minute journey didn't seem to take long enough. Ethan examined the control-and-communications console and fired questions at Clive about each of its screens, keyboards, potentiometers, laser-optical cursor controls, switches, buttons and rheostats, one after another, sometimes forgetting to breathe.

'Whoa, man.' Clive smiled calmly. 'We've got plenty of time. Take a breath or you'll pass out, and we can't have that.'

'Point taken.' Ethan gulped.

'OK then, my man.' Clive's face broke briefly into a grin before returning to its usual calm-and-watchful expression.

Ethan blushed a bit, but then asked, 'Just how did you do that, Clive – shift the focus on that screen?'

It seemed to all three Knights that the ride had been all too short when Clive announced, 'Just around this next corner and we have arrived, folks. Dead on the dot of seven o'clock.' He guided the Roller Glider into a custom-made entryway, deflated the tyres and brought it to a smooth halt. He pressed the keys on the console that secured the vehicle and released the seat belts.

Clive pressed a button and the doors hissed open. He was instantly out of the limo and standing by the open door to the back seat where Bella was sitting.

'When I first became a chauffeur,' he told them, 'my first limo still had those manually-operated doors, and I would automatically move smartly to open the doors for my passengers. Old habits die hard.' He offered Bella his arm in assistance.

Connor moved with exquisite slowness in climbing out of the Roller Glider, milking a few more moments to drool over it. 'I might never get the chance to see one of these things again,' he explained.

Ethan, also moving slowly, said, 'We're thinking the same thoughts, Dad.'

Clive looked at Ethan, who had moved over into the driver's seat and was testing the controls, imagining that he was driving it. He looked back over at Bella and Connor and said, 'I'm going to have to prise that young man's bum out of there with a special tool I have just for that purpose.'

Not wishing to push his luck any further, Ethan hopped out voluntarily. 'Thanks, Clive. That's a stonking car. Thanks heaps.'

'My pleasure, young man. Now that everyone's on their feet, shall we?' He inclined his large head in the direction of the door leading away from the limo port.

He led them down a short corridor with a silver-coloured wall on one side and floor-to-ceiling windows looking out over a large and colourful walled garden on the other. They came to a huge pair of doors made out of solid oak, with giant, lifelike brass lion-head door handles.

'They must be worth a fortune!' Ethan whispered. 'Probably cost as much as our entire house in Kingstonia!'

Clive pressed a remote button that made a chime ring on the other side of the doors. 'I'll be leaving you here. I have to take the Roller Glider to its hangar-port to check its systems – something I do after every excursion. It's another old habit.' The doors started to open. 'Riley will look after you now. He'll take you through to Admiral Gazers.'

Riley, old and dignified, appeared in the doorway, wearing a crisp, starched old-fashioned dark suit.

'Ah, Riley, there you are at last!' Clive greeted him with a touch of sarcasm in his voice. 'This is the Knight family.' He gestured to each as he said their names in turn.

Riley turned to the Knights and said, 'Please follow me inside, if you will.'

Stepping through the giant doors into the reception hall of Admiral Gazers' fabulous home a whole new world unfolded in front of Ethan's eyes. They were all standing in a veritable palace, stunned into silence.

Antiques from all ages and cultures were everywhere in the spacious reception hall. The furniture was French Renaissance, hundreds of years old and in perfect condition; the high ceilings were covered with murals painted with such skill, colours, and perspective that they took the family's breath away – something Ethan had only seen in old books about the now-destroyed Sistine Chapel. Famous, priceless paintings from four centuries of artists adorned the walls.

Art had been one of Ethan's favourite subjects while he'd attended Kingstonia Preparatory School before going to Universal Flight Academy. The paintings were much more impressive in real life than they had been in his school art books.

Riley allowed the family to appreciate the beauty for a couple of moments, and then bowed slightly in the direction of an archway leading to a corridor. 'Follow me, please.'

'Where are we following you to?' Ethan asked.

'It will be best if you feel completely relaxed and refreshed when you meet Admiral Gazers. This home has a section designed as a relaxation zone. This way, please.'

'Feel free to use any of the facilities,' Riley informed them as he led them down a wide hallway, the walls of which were also covered with great art between occasional mysterious doors. 'The relaxation zone,' he continued, as they walked, 'is fully equipped with a championship space-ball table, a skittle bowling lane, a state-of-the-art sound system with over 20,000 recordings in all genres on its hard drive, and, of course, a natural mineral spa and luxury changing room, amongst other amenities. I am sure, Mr Knight, you will be interested in the fully-stocked bar, containing an extensive selection of only the finest beverages.'

'No need to be so formal, Riley. We know each other now, so just call me Connor.'

'I'm happy with that, if you insist, Mr Knight.' Riley was clearly not accustomed to informality. 'Now I must inform the admiral of your arrival. Shall we say twenty minutes of rest and relaxation? Will that be enough?'

'Oh, plenty,' the family confirmed in unison.

'Sounds more like an order than a question to me,' Ethan observed.

'I'll be off, then.' Riley bowed ever-so-slightly, turned and walked out of the room.

Ethan immediately started to explore the relaxation zone, as curious as a young puppy. He looked in cupboards, picked objects up to examine them and fiddled with the controls to the music system and the giant-screen interactive digital games. Bella constantly reminded him to be careful not to drop or otherwise damage anything; everything seemed enormously expensive and she feared that the possible consequences of an 'Oops!' might include enforcement of a you-break-it-you-buy-it rule.

'Please, Ethan,' she begged. 'It would take you for the rest of your lifetime and more to earn enough to replace even the smallest of these things.'

Ethan heard his mother, but he was too curious and confident in his own ability to avoid disaster to stop what he was doing.

'Whoa, this house is unbelievable. There are so many nooks and crannies to explore that I don't know where to look first.'

Bella shrugged hopelessly and went to lie down in a soft-massage machine. *After all*, she told herself, *we're supposed to be here to relax*. She noticed the machine's music and scent control panels and chose Irish harp music and jasmine.

Ethan swept his surroundings with observant eyes. Then his curiosity led him to explore some of the doorways leading off the relaxation zone and the hallway leading to it. Wanting to take a better look at a curious door between two mid-twentieth-century surrealist paintings about halfway down the hall, he put his hands in his pockets and casually made his way down towards it, thinking that, if he were sprung, he'd make out that he was lost. He practised looking innocent, strolling oh-so-casually with his hands in his pockets, whistling naïvely, unaware that this sort of obvious behaviour usually had the opposite effect.

Nearly reaching the door he wanted to explore, Ethan was startled by hearing a young female voice behind him asking, in a sharp tone, 'Where do you think you're going, young man?'

Too frightened to turn around, he answered, 'I'm lost, ma'am, and looking for the relaxation zone.'

'You've just come from there, haven't you, Ethan? Aren't you really snooping?'

'No, honestly, I'm not. And how do you know my name?'

'Well, turn around and I'll tell you.'

Ethan still didn't turn around. He could be hard-headed sometimes.

'Are you going to turn around, or do I call for help? I can scream really loudly, you know.'

'No. No need to do that.' Ethan turned slowly, wishing to put a face to the voice. What a face! He had unwittingly bumped into the most beautiful girl he'd ever seen, and could only manage a high-pitched, awkward-sounding voice. 'Everything in this house is so beautiful, and – may I be so bold? – that's including you. What's your name?'

'You can dispense with the cheesy clichés, Ethan! I happen to be the admiral's daughter, Aurora, and your attempted flattery leaves a lot to be desired.'

'I agree it's a pretty awful, feeble attempt,' he admitted, 'but I mean it, and I hope you can make allowances for my inexperience and lack of polish and smoothness.'

'Well, I won't hold it against you this time, but it's about time you got back to the relaxation zone and your parents, isn't it? Your meeting with my father is in five minutes. Yes, I know who you are. Who else would be walking around my house, having a good old nose?'

'Will I see you later, Aurora?' Ethan's voice made it clear that seeing her later was what he really wanted to do.

'If you're lucky. Now, you should get back. You do not want to keep my father waiting. Do you know where to go?'

'Yes, I do. Thank you, Aurora. It's just down the hall on the right.'

'Then you were snooping. I knew it.' Aurora smiled like the cat that had the cream.

Electing not to continue digging a hole for himself, Ethan took his leave of the situation and quickly returned to the relaxation zone.

At that precise moment, Riley arrived to escort them to the meeting, asking, 'Did you all enjoy the facilities afforded you?'

'I certainly did.' Connor spoke for himself allowing a little hiccup to escape.

'I perceive that you found it, then, Mr Knight,' Riley intoned, with a thoroughly suppressed smile.

'Found what? And call me Connor.'

Riley touched his nose in a diplomatic way of saying: *I know it's our little secret.* 'How about you, Master Ethan? Get up to any mischief? Meet anyone you like?'

How did he find out? Ethan wondered, thinking Aurora must have told him. Not wanting to incriminate himself, he just grinned and said nothing, feeling glad that Aurora may have mentioned something and hoping he had left as good an impression on her as she had on him.

'Are we all ready, then?' Riley asked. 'We need to make a slight detour via the telecommunications room on the way. It will only take a moment.'

He led them all towards the same doorway at which Ethan had nearly arrived before having been pleasantly sprung by

Aurora. Riley asked them to wait outside for a moment and then went through the door, accidentally leaving it slightly ajar. Ethan's natural instincts got the better of him, and he took a sneaky peek.

'Have a look in there.'

'I wouldn't do that if I were you,' advised Bella. 'You'll get into trouble; trust me.'

Ignoring her good, sound advice, Ethan looked in at a beehive of activity going on inside the room. People were everywhere, some engaged at sophisticated work stations and others moving amongst them. Ethan found it so intriguing that he gestured for his father to take a look.

Connor at first was a little apprehensive, but succumbed to his inquisitive nature. Riley, noticing that he'd left the door slightly open, promptly walked over and slammed it shut, looking them both in the eye as he did so. He discreetly didn't mention the incident when he came back out, and Connor and Ethan weren't about to mention it either.

Riley, having obviously achieved whatever his objectives in the telecommunications room had been, politely asked, 'Will you all now kindly accompany me to where Admiral Gazers is waiting to receive you? It is only down the hall. You would have found it earlier, Ethan, if you had been able to keep looking.'

I am saying nothing, thought Ethan.

Riley ushered them into what was obviously a conference room. Everything seemed to be of dark wood and well-cared-for dark leather, all of which seemed to glow in the indirect lighting. Ethan noticed several discreetly-placed control panels. The room's central feature was a huge, round table not dissimilar to the one used by King Arthur and his knights. Ethan turned to his father and whispered, with a grin, 'I hope we can hear what the admiral's got to say.'

Chapter Four

The admiral rose from a deep leather chair at the far end of the room and strode forward with his arms extended in front of him in greeting. 'Welcome,' he told them, in his deep, soft voice. 'Welcome to my home. Please sit down.' He gestured towards some comfortable-looking chairs, upholstered in real leather dyed a dark green. His eyes sparkled and well-worn smile lines crinkled at their corners. 'I trust you all enjoyed the ambience and facilities of the relaxation zone. Did you appreciate the malt, Connor?'

'Good drop, that,' Connor replied, smiling. 'Allow me to express my gratitude for that pleasure. Thank you very much. I'm sad to say that I did leave you some, though,' he chuckled.

'I'm glad you liked it, and I do agree it is a mighty good drop. But shall we get down to business? I will be directing most of the evening's conversation at young Ethan, lad; you come and sit over at this part of the table, opposite me. What is important is that you need a clear understanding of what to expect tomorrow morning at the Grand Assembly.'

Ethan was all ears.

'At tomorrow's meeting, I will be introducing you to the largest gathering of world leaders ever assembled in history. I have just been informed that our Supreme Ruler, Ziekiel Landon, will also be attending. Something big is in the wind.' He smiled mysteriously.

'The leaders you will meet tomorrow are either top professionals in their own fields or much-loved and respected representatives of nations. Or both. Each of them is highly trained or highly educated. As a minister myself, I always find it difficult to be in the company of so many people who deserve and expect such large amounts of respect. It will pay you not to forget this.' He paused, waiting, but Ethan said nothing.

The admiral smiled with approval and continued, 'However, I can tell you that the board of ministers have been following your career closely and are fully aware of your achievements to date, and of your clearly-assessed potential. That is why, upon your graduation, I presented you with orders for the mission upon which you are about to embark. I cannot discuss the details of that mission right now for security reasons, but all will unfold tomorrow at the meeting. I can reveal, however, that, if your mission is successful, you will be hailed as a national hero for all eternity.'

Ethan was much more than speechless. His parents, far across the table, were also struck dumb. Aware that their son was about to embark on an adventure of a lifetime, they were both deeply concerned for his safety.

Connor stood up and caught the admiral's attention. 'Please excuse my interruption, sir, but I feel this is important, and I'm sure I'm speaking for my wife about this as well as for myself.'

'Go on, Connor,' the admiral said graciously.

'Ethan is barely a man. Really, he has just graduated, and – he's our only son. Both his mother and I are deeply concerned at the level of responsibility that you're placing on his shoulders. After all, for one so young—'

'I appreciate your concerns, Connor,' Admiral Gazers interrupted, his voice showing both sympathy and authority. 'I have an ambitious young offspring as well, but please do not underestimate your son's ability.' His facial expression was kind but firm. 'Ethan's shoulders are broader than anyone who has ever graduated from Universal Flying Academy, including my own. He can carry the weight, and youth is his biggest asset. Not only are his reflexes at their peak developmental point for rapidity, but he has not been subjected to the bad habits that come with age, which will help in the clarity of his judgements and prevent his ability to make strong decisions from being clouded. This combination of youth and ability will enable him to become a great leader.'

Stunned by Admiral Gazers' words, Connor sat back down again and squeezed Bella's hand. She squeezed him back, not saying a word, but she could feel his anxiety, along with his mountain of pride. Still not convinced, Bella wished to turn back the clock a little so that she could have more time with her son.

Straightening his back, as he always did in moments of pride and adulation, Ethan felt as if he'd added another few centimetres to his already-tall frame and tried to reassure his parents that he was ready to leave the nest and serve his world.

'Now,' the admiral went on, briskly, 'there's someone who you need to meet.' He pressed his left hand down flat on a cleverly-disguised panel set into the table's top. A door opened across the room and in walked a short, wiry man wearing a nondescript brown suit. He strode athletically, despite seeming to Ethan to be old, his nearly-bald head being fringed with curly white hair.

'This is Willis,' the admiral introduced him when he stopped, clearly ready for anything, a metre or so from them. Ethan noticed that he was not getting Willis's title or first name. 'Willis,' the admiral continued, 'this is Captain Ethan Knight.'

Ethan stood up and extended his hand. 'Willis. Good to meet you.'

Willis shook Ethan's hand firmly and said, 'Captain Knight.' He spoke evenly, in a voice without any distinguishing characteristic other than its blandness. 'You will need to be acquainted with World Assembly protocol. I will now brief you on the process of getting into the Great Hall for tomorrow's meeting.'

Willis reached into the pocket of his suit's jacket and extracted a fifteen-centimetre-long, shiny-metallic, pin-like object with a largish, rounded head. 'This titanium pin and recorder,' he explained calmly, 'is calibrated to match the readings it takes of the unique pattern on the iris of any individual's eye. It can store 2,000 patterns and digitally transmit any pattern required over any one of, um, several securely encrypted bands to security installations, wherever we might locate them.'

He held the pin up in front of Ethan's right eye and placed his forefinger into a depression on its bulb-like handle. A small, pale green light indicated that the pin was scanning Willis's fingerprint; it then changed to white, indicating a match. Instantly, another pale green light scanned back and forth and then up and down over Ethan's eye, then disappeared. Willis replaced the pin in his pocket.

'There you go,' he said; 'that's part one of your security clearance. Just don't change your eyes before tomorrow morning.' He smiled fleetingly.

'I'll try not to.' Ethan smiled back. He didn't know whether to like Willis or not. There didn't seem to be much about him to like, but there didn't seem to be much to dislike, either. 'You said "part one". How many parts are there?'

Willis's quick smile came and went again. 'Only two. The second one involves logging your cranial functions; in short matching your brain waves, as everyone's are different. First, I'm going to give you a series of fifteen numbers to memorise in order. I'm told you've displayed a rapid memory at the Academy.'

'Well…' Ethan drawled, sounding unsure; 'of course, I'm flattered, but fifteen numbers… How big are these numbers?'

'They vary from one to three digits; nothing complicated.'

'No, of course not,' Ethan assured him, but he thought, *Fifteen numbers! Blimey, does everybody have to do this?*

Willis touched a Rotary International pin in his lapel, and the door through which he'd entered slid open. A man came in, carrying what looked like a shiny motorcycle helmet with various lights and controls on it. The man carrying it was medium-sized, dark and wearing an expensive-looking pinstriped suit. Willis said, 'Thank you, Lopez,' and took the helmet.

Lopez stepped back to stand near the wall. Willis didn't introduce him; instead he turned to Ethan and started to explain, patiently, 'This is a cranial-logger headset: not the same as the one at the entrance to the Great Hall building, but it can transmit what it reads digitally via any one of several securely encrypted bands to the appropriate security installation.' He placed the headset over Ethan's head and showed him how to adjust it for comfort and fit.

'Now, Captain Knight,' he continued, 'I hope they trained you well in relaxation techniques at the Academy, because you have to be very careful to relax. The process is so complex and the sensors are so delicate that any distraction is extremely likely to cause it to halt operations. Should that happen, an amber light will appear on the control panel – in the case of this unit, near the top of the translucent visor – immediately leaving the individual being logged back at the beginning. Wait for the control light to turn white and then try again. What you don't want is for the control light to turn red, because then you get arrested. You want it to turn green. Is the headset fitting comfortably?'

Ethan nodded. 'Yes, sir.'

'Your numbers are now appearing below the control-panel lights on your visor. Memorise them now, but stay cool.'

Ethan looked at the list of numbers with despair, thinking, *Not only do I have to memorise fifteen numbers to get into that joint, but I've got to remember them without sweating. What if my brain can't produce any wave atoms? What if I have dry ducts, in between concentrating on what's happening at the meeting? Welcome to the real world, Ethan. I'm not sure I can handle such a big ask.* Still, he focused his mind on the numbers, and, as he memorised more and more of them, the ones he had memorised faded from his vision and the light on the control panel changed from white to a very pale green to an increasingly bright and vivid shade of green. Within a few minutes, the numbers had all disappeared and the light was a brilliant green.

Willis then touched a control on the side of the headset and it loosened up automatically. He removed it from Ethan's head.

'So, then,' Admiral Gazers said, smiling, 'now we have you inside the building. About what happens next, I'm afraid I have little that I can tell you, other than to be prepared for the unex-pected. Be prepared to be tested. Don't let the World Ministers intimidate you, but it is extremely important that you show respect, listen carefully to everything you are told and only speak when invited to do so.'

The admiral stood up. 'Well,' he said, his eyes crinkling with his smile, 'thank you – all three of you – for taking time at such short notice to come here and have this meeting with me. I would not have felt right taking young Ethan to that meeting tomorrow without these things being understood. Now, how about a little light refreshment to close the evening?'

As they entered the supper room Ethan got a very pleasant surprise: as he followed Riley through the door, the first and only thing that caught his eye was Aurora. She honoured him with an amused smile, and then she turned her eyes towards his parents, who had followed him in, and said, 'Welcome to our little supper, Mr and Mrs Knight – or may I call you Bella and Connor?' She returned her smile to Ethan. She seemed to be suppressing an urge to laugh.

'Ethan and I have already met.'

Ethan was dumbstruck and couldn't make a sound for fear it could be the wrong one.

Admiral Gazers took Connor by the elbow and led him to a side table bearing a new bottle of sixteen-year-old single malt and two crystal glasses. 'I don't think a drop before we eat would be out of order; will you join me in one, my good man?'

Connor wouldn't dream of declining such an invitation.

As he poured, Admiral Gazers said, 'So, tell me, Connor: how is your business coping with the current economic situation?'

Connor was a food scientist, who had branched out from operating his own research facility to also owning three soybean warehouses with processing plants and four enormous commercial chicken-rearing barns. He told the admiral that costs and demand were both rising.

Riley, meanwhile, had served Bella with a glass of old sherry and Ethan and Aurora with orange juice. Ethan felt intensely uncomfortable to be standing there with his mum facing him on his right and Aurora facing him on his left. Whenever he looked at Aurora, he started to flush slightly, embarrassing him somewhat in front of his mother.

Aurora noticed all this and found it charmingly funny. 'I understand you're going to the Cyber Lounge in Golden Gate Centre after supper,' she said, smiling.

How did she know that? Ethan wondered to himself, but he said aloud, 'Yes, that's right. I'm meeting my friend Ralph there. Do you know it?'

'Oh, yes; I used to go there quite regularly with my best friend Crystal, but lately I have had my head down studying intensely, so I haven't had the time. It's OK.'

Riley and a slender, middle-aged man with a slender beard, wearing a dark suit like Riley's, came into the room, bearing trays. The two hosts showed the three guests to their chairs at the table.

Somewhere in the general conversation, Ethan got enough nerve up to ask Aurora, 'Are you studying tonight after supper?'

'Oh, yes; I have to write up the notes of an experiment I was working on today.'

'Then,' – he tried not to gulp too obviously or stumble over his own tongue – 'do you think that you'll be going over to the Cyber Lounge later?'

'I don't know. It depends on whether any of my friends stop by and offer to go with me and if Clive is on duty. Anyway, if I do, it won't be until late.'

'What is it that you study, Aurora?' Ethan was amazed to hear the words come out of his mouth as if he were just plain Ethan asking just plain somebody else a normal question, rather than the usual 'Ethan whose body chemistry was running riot doubling his heart-rate' daring to approach the young woman who was causing that reaction in him.

'Physics and geology, mostly.' She shrugged. 'Call it geophysics.'

'What she hasn't mentioned,' Admiral Gazers put in, obviously proud, 'is the time she spends three times a week with a group of poor children whose parents have abandoned them. They live in an old, abandoned underground tube just outside central Nevulae and survive the best they can without joining any of the criminal gangs that pretty much run things down there. Aurora brings them food and teaches them some basic things, like reading and maths and science and self-defence.'

'Dad!' Now it was Aurora's turn to turn red.

'Wow!' Ethan was impressed. 'I think that's really great! Isn't it dangerous, though?'

'Clive stays with me,' Aurora explained, 'and, usually, Lopez, and we meet in a small building I've rented – basically, little more than an old garage – almost next door to the big courthouse downtown. We call it Glebe Hall. There are always heaps of troopers around. Really, those children face worse every day. And I know there are just a few dozen of them, while there's millions who need help, but I have to do what I can do. Dad, the World Ministers just have to do something to stop all this ugliness.'

'Yes, Aurora,' Admiral Gazers said, more to all four of them than just to her, 'you're right. I can't say much more right now, but the World Assembly is coming closer to being able to do something soon, and I think Captain Ethan Knight just may play a big role as events unfold.' He popped some pasta into his mouth.

Ethan, completely entranced by Aurora and what she'd been saying, could only think to say, 'I'll just do what I can do.'

'I'm certain you'll come out a champion,' Aurora said, with a secret little smile, 'just as you were in sport for the UFA.'

'You know about that, too?' Ethan sounded amazed and a bit bewildered. 'How?'

'I've taken part in a few Interacademy Sports Festivals myself, too. Judo. You just didn't notice me there.' Her secret smile still confused him.

'Yes, I'm sorry,' he confessed. 'I didn't watch the judo.'

Her unexplained tinkle of laughter bewildered him still more, but he could have listened to it all night.

In what seemed to Ethan to be hardly any time at all, Admiral Gazers said, 'It's time you were going if Clive is to get you to your friend on time, Ethan. I know how it is with young friends. Our peers are always important to us.'

Riley and Marcel entered the room and everyone stood.

'Oh,' Aurora said, as if just remembering something. 'Father, weren't you going to invite Ethan back to have dinner with us on Saturday?'

'Oh, yes! That's right. You will come back for dinner on Saturday, won't you, Ethan? I realise I may have put you on the spot, though. You don't have to answer right away.' He laughed. 'You must have made quite an impression on my daughter.'

Aurora looked with just a touch of anguish at her father, then looked away.

'Yes, sir – I hope so! I mean, I would love to,' Ethan spluttered, blushing again, trying unsuccessfully not to sound too eager. 'This Saturday, you say? I can make that. Thank you.' He was extremely excited, but tried not to let it show. He thought, *Yes, yes!*

'Then it's settled. Clive will collect you at 7 p.m. Saturday. Is that OK?' asked the admiral as he walked, chuckling, in a direction other than the one in which Riley was leading the Knights.

As he escorted them through the corridors to the Roller Glider's port, Riley gave Ethan a wink and said, in his deep, formal, almost sombre voice, 'See you on Saturday night – and look your best, won't you?'

Chapter Five

Once outside the Gazers' residence, Ethan quickly jumped into the front seat of the Roller to pre-empt his dad or even Clive from changing the seating arrangements of the drive to the Gazers' house. He sat glued, eyes forward, not saying a word, hoping that Clive would hurry up, get in and drive.

As soon as Clive got in behind the controls, he started peppering him with questions. 'Clive, are you familiar with the Golden Gate Centre? How long does it take to get there? What's the Cyber Lounge like?'

Before starting the Roller Glider, Clive answered, 'I can show you what it's like, if you wish, my boy,' as he flicked a switch to reveal a video life screen ascending out of the dash control panel. Punching in a sequence of numbers, he allowed Ethan to see a complete virtual real-time tour of the Cyber Lounge. He showed him how to change images with a little joystick on the side of the screen and told him, 'You can take it from here.'

'I can't believe it. This car has everything!' Ethan's grin split his face in half as he panned around the Cyber Lounge with his finger on the joystick. 'Do you ever take the admiral's daughter there?'

'Ah, you've met Aurora, then?'

'I certainly have.' Ethan sighed. 'I think she's great.'

'Aurora and her friend Crystal used to meet up with girl-friends from university at the Cyber Lounge every week, but until recently, as you know, she has had her head down, studying very hard for her last term exams. I normally drive her there personally and take her home again. She's a very special and talented young lady. Don't be fooled into thinking she's just a beautiful face, though; she's a fully qualified geophysicist and has been training as a science officer for voyages of discovery. As young as she is, she already has over 400 hours of exploration time to her credit. That makes her number one in her field – and she's barely sixteen.'

Ethan thought, *Mmmm!*

'I have the pleasure of Miss Aurora's company more than anyone else,' Clive continued, as he guided the Roller away from the Gazers' neighbourhood and through the hillsides towards the Golden Gate Centre, 'except her father, of course. He always makes enough time for his daughter.'

'I've been invited to dinner with Aurora and Admiral Gazers this Saturday night, and I can't wait,' said a slightly embarrassed Ethan, picking a little thread from the armrest of the seat. 'I've done nothing but think about her since I met her before our meeting with the admiral.'

Not letting on that he already knew about the Saturday dinner, Clive told him that he was one privileged, lucky young man, as most of the young officers and dignitaries' sons throughout the Grand Assembly were vying for her attention.

'Pays to snoop around, don't it, eh?' Clive chuckled.

'Isn't anything sacred?' Ethan muttered to himself.

'Not when it comes to Miss Aurora,' Clive told him absolutely. 'Only her well-being is sacred. She's more precious than anything to the admiral, and to us all.'

Ethan's parents were all ears, but they did not say a word in case Ethan got a little embarrassed; they just looked at each other and smiled.

'How much longer do you think it'll take us to get there, Clive?' Ethan looked at the precision flyer's chronometer on his wrist. 'I'm meeting my pal Ralph there at 10 p.m. The meeting with Admiral Gazers took longer than expected, and I definitely don't want to be late.'

'I think we can manage it.' Clive smiled, already aware of Ethan's meeting time with Ralph. 'Now, the traffic is at its worst between here and there at this time of the night, but leave it to old Clive. We'll make it there by 22.00 hours; just watch us.'

He wasn't wrong about the traffic. By the time they got to the North Side's central business district, everything was at a standstill and the clock was ticking.

It wasn't long before Ethan exploded, 'This is hopeless! I think it'll be quicker for me to get out and walk! What do you think, Clive?'

Clive was getting a touch frustrated as well, although he was careful not to show it. He did, however, decide to do something about the situation, as his pride was on the line and he didn't want Ethan to be late. 'Watch this, folks,' he told them. 'I'm not really supposed to use this facility except in an emergency, but I think we can agree that this qualifies, don't you?' He smiled.

Bella and Ethan agreed in unison.

'OK, then; here we go. Ethan, you see that orange oval on that screen there? The one that says "Turbo Lift" on it?'

'Yes, sir.'

'It's heat-sensitive to fingertips. Just press your forefinger to it lightly.'

Ethan leaned forward, reached over to the screen and pressed the orange oval with an experienced touch. He was familiar with this sort of control from his Flying Academy training. The Roller Glider immediately rose up until it was hovering more than four metres above the road, rather than the fifty centimetres of the other modules. They were suddenly sitting higher than any other vehicle in front of them, whether land-car or hover-module. Clive activated the controls and the Roller moved forward, driving clear over the top of the vehicles in their way.

Looking down at the vehicles below, Ethan and his mother stared in disbelief, and the drivers of the cars on the ground were looking up with the same reaction.

With a smile, Clive told them, 'We can only hover at about this height while going forward. I hope we don't come across a huge tanker or transporter. That could prove most interesting, don't you think?'

'There're no tunnels on this route, are there, Clive?' Ethan half-muttered.

'Now, that would be interesting, wouldn't it?' answered Clive, tongue-in-cheek. 'I guess we'd just have to go over them, road or no road, eh?'

'I think so,' Ethan almost stammered in awe. 'Fantastic machine, this. Is there nothing it can't do?' he marvelled '

Clive brought the Roller to the entrance of the Golden Gate, set it gently back down on its tyres dead on ten o'clock, and told them, 'Now you know that, when I make a promise, I'll do whatever it takes to keep it. You should never have doubted for a moment that we wouldn't make it on time. Remember that.' He smiled at them confidently, but Ethan wondered if he noticed a touch of relief on Clive's face, and was that a faint film of perspiration on his upper lip?

Ralph had only just arrived at the Golden Gate Centre moments earlier, and he had watched the Roller Glider's smooth landing and its pinpoint easing to a halt. Not realising that Ethan and his mum and dad were inside, he pushed his nose up against the window to get a closer look, thinking there was no one in the back. It was not every day that he could get this close to such a great car. Ethan, seeing Ralph do this, did the same from the inside. Ralph, seeing a squashed, disjointed face peering back at him, jumped back in fright.

Ethan let the power window down with a barely audible hiss and began to laugh. He pointed to Ralph and, in between merry gasps of breath, said, 'Got you there, you minger!'

Ralph stepped back, still startled by the realisation that it was his pal in there, and called out, 'What the flippin' 'eck are you doing in that fantastic machine?'

'You shouldn't be sticking your big spotty nose in places it shouldn't be, then, should you, Ralph? If it'd been the wrong person, you might've got yourself arrested – or even beaten up!'

Ralph, who'd focused in on the words 'spotty nose', quickly examined his face for craters, thinking, *Not tonight, please!*

Ethan was still hooting with laughter, tears rolling down his face.

'Ethan!' Bella said, sharply. 'Don't you be so mean to your friend.'

Still laughing, Ethan leaned out the window of the Roller Glider. Ralph returned to the glamour machine and gave it a quick once-over before telling his friend, 'It's heaving here tonight, mate.' He gestured vaguely behind him at the Cyber Lounge. 'I think we could have some real, serious fun. Watch me and you might just learn something, me boy!' Ralph had more front than a mega-mall; what he lacked in good looks he made up for in agreeable rubbish.

Chapter Six

It had been graduation day for many of Nevulae's institutions of learning and training, and the Cyber Lounge was the party destination of several groups of young graduates. The place was buzzing with excitement: hundreds of young people dancing to loud music and talking animatedly, some playing cyber-football and other cyber-games on giant screens placed here and there, others playing laser billiards and other lounge games, and the party was spilling out onto the pavement in front. Ralph had never seen so many pretty girls all in one place. Whispering and giggling, two of them were pointing to the Roller Glider, where Ralph was standing, talking to Ethan. They were probably wondering if there could be someone rich and famous inside. Ralph believed that they would appreciate his introducing himself, so, straightening his collar and tie and ineffectually licking down his hair, he walked over to do just that.

Ethan looked away from Ralph's escapade with the two girls and gave the control console of the Roller Glider one last, loving look. He spotted a toggle switch he hadn't noticed before, and, on an impulse, he reached for it to see what it did before he said goodbye.

Noticing too late what he was up to, Clive reached to stop him and called out, 'Don't pull that one!' too late.

Clive's seat quickly reclined, forcing him flat onto his back in the supine position. Trying to quell his frustration and irritation, Clive politely asked Ethan to toggle the knob back into its original position. Ethan, not really having noted what its original position had been, gave it his best shot, causing Clive's seat to come flying up until he was sitting bolt upright, with his face pushed hard up against the windscreen.

'Thank you, my boy, that'll do nicely,' Clive managed to grunt, talking through his nose, as he reached over and readjusted his seat.

Ralph returned to the Roller Glider and reached through Ethan's open window to tap him on the shoulder and whisper, 'Let me in, mate.'

Ethan turned around, glad to have an excuse to look away from Clive without being rude or too embarrassed. He looked at Ralph and almost started laughing again. 'Why are you whispering?'

'Just let me in. I'll tell you inside,' said Ralph hurriedly, as he kept looking back at the small crowd of girls still standing outside the Cyber Lounge, giving them a brief smile and short wave.

Sensing Ralph's urgency but being in a mood to have a bit of fun with him, Ethan turned to look through the front windscreen and said, 'I'm not going to let you in, Ralph, until you tell me exactly what you're up to.'

'Let the poor boy get in the front with you, Ethan,' Clive ordered him, clearly in no mood for this particular type of fun.

Bella joined in, demanding, 'Open the door and let Ralph in, for goodness' sake – and don't be so mean. Can't you see the boy is suffering out there?'

Feeling outgunned and definitely outnumbered, Ethan opened the door for Ralph, who immediately gave him a full-on pinch on the flesh-hanging part of his underarm – a real, bruising nip – as he climbed in. Ethan yelped with pain.

'Thanks, mate,' Ralph told him as he settled in. The front seat automatically adjusted itself from one wide, comfortable, contoured seat to two narrower, still-comfortable contoured seats. *How does it do that?* Ralph and Ethan both wondered silently. Ralph began to look around.

'What was that for?' Ethan, still rubbing his throbbing arm, glared at his friend.

'Well,' Ralph looked him straight in the eye and said, in a reasonable tone of voice, 'There's me out there, doing what a man has to do – which is lining up some interesting conversation for us tonight – and you leave me standing out in the cold. I'm not a brass monkey, y'know.'

Ethan looked out of the window in the general direction to-wards which Ralph was gesturing and received a long, lingering smile from one of the girls standing on the pavement: a stylish-looking young woman with a chic black outfit and straight black hair. Hitting the switch to close the window, he turned to look at Ralph with exasperation and resignation. 'What have you been saying to those girls, and what lies have you spun?'

The girls were still standing and waiting outside the Cyber Lounge, going nowhere until something started happening. Clive paid close attention to all this.

'Spit it out, Ralph,' Ethan badgered him. 'What's going on, then?'

'It's only a bit of harmless fun. I just happened to mention that…' Suddenly, Ralph found it hard to come out with it, and went into a defensive posture as Ethan went for a back-of-the-arm pinch.

'Come on, Ralph, you can't stop there!' Clive talked to Ralph with a familiar tone, as if they had known each other for years. Although he had never met Ralph until just then, he clearly liked him. 'I'm intrigued now. There's obviously something going on.'

His eyes on Ethan's hands, Ralph pleaded, 'Promise you won't inflict any pain on me and you'll go along with the plan I've set up?'

'It depends on what you've got me into, Ralph.'

'It's not that bad! Come on, people, lighten up. OK, I'll tell you.' Then, in a rush of earnest-sounding words, he did tell them. 'Well, you see, it's like this: I mentioned to the girls that I'm meeting my best friend, Prince Knight of Kingstonia, here at the Cyber Lounge tonight, and that that's you sitting in the Roller Glider. That's all I said.'

'That's all, eh?' Ethan was certainly not amused and spoke in an unfamiliar, high, squeaky voice, trying to clear his throat. 'Prince Knight?'

Clive was grinning from ear to ear, making sure not to make a sound until it was safe to do so.

'How could you, Ralph?' Bella smirked.

'There's just one more tiny little thing,' said Ralph sheepishly. 'I promise this is everything. I told those girls that you're single and on the lookout for a girlfriend, while mentioning that, being your most trusted friend, I can introduce them to you.'

Clive laughed. 'And feathering your own nest at the same time, no doubt; clever boy, Ralph. I like your style.' He was enjoying himself, feeling far removed from his mundane routine of enduring long, uneventful days and nights on the road, mostly driving stuffy dignitaries around without so much as a by-your-leave. For him, it was a welcome change to be in the company of such innocent and exuberant young people.

'What do we do now, then?' Ethan was sulking. 'I'm not going in there with everyone thinking I'm a prince. Wild horses couldn't drag me into that place now.'

'You are such a wimp, Ethan. Anyway, I have a plan that will work, for sure, and, before you shoot me down, listen: all you have to do is smile and wave, pretending to be Prince Knight from Kingstonia, and leave all the talking to me. I'll tell the girls that, due to royal protocol, you aren't allowed to have verbal contact with them unless in the privacy of a secure location. I mean, you're still in your captain's uniform and you look great. All you have to do is act the part and leave the rest up to me. How hard can that be, eh? It'll be a breeze.'

Ethan thought, *And pigs will fly*. He was enormously less than eager to co-operate with Ralph. In addition, he worried, *What if Aurora finds out that I'm going around masquerading as Prince Ethan Knight of Kingstonia. Someone's bound to mention that a 'Prince Knight' visited the lounge during the week; it's not every day that something like that happens, if ever. Aurora's an intelligent girl and would draw the right conclusion straight away and know it's me. Who else does she know with such a name?*

Ethan was absolutely infatuated with Aurora and he did not want to stuff things up with her at this early stage. In fairness to Ralph, he conceded, he hadn't told him about her yet. If he had, maybe Ralph would have thought twice about putting his best pal in this position; then again, maybe not.

'Are we on, then?' Ralph pushed it.

'I suppose so,' Ethan said tentatively, 'but, if I feel it's not going well at any stage, I'm out of there, with or without you. Is that clear, Ralph?'

'I hear you, mate. Relax man; chill out. It's going to be a great night. Now, listen to my plan: if this is okay with you, Clive, you'll get out and go 'round the glam machine to open Ethan's door, then, loudly, but without being too obvious, ask him, "What time would Your Highness like to be picked up this evening?" Ethan will then answer by saying, "Thank you, Clive, but would you send the Star-Bird for us? I'd like to travel home tonight in that." Clive then informs Prince Knight that his father is on official business in Buenos Aires and travelling in the Star-Bird, so it's not available until tomorrow when he returns, but shall he send the Eurocopter instead?'

'Is that it?' asked Clive.

'That's all I can think of for now.'

Ethan just did not want to listen.

'OK!' Ralph rubbed his hands together. 'Isn't this exciting, imagining how it's all going to pan out? I can't wait! Try to make sure that the girls can hear what you're saying, Clive, that's crucial – and, Ethan, you tell Clive not to worry about the Eurocopter, just bring the Roller Glider at half past midnight. That will give us a couple of hours of quality time to socialise with our new-found friends, who are eagerly awaiting an introduction to His Royal Highness,' – he giggled – 'and still let you get some sleep before your meeting tomorrow.'

'I'm not comfortable doing this, Ralph. Something is bound to go wrong. It always does.'

'You're making a mountain out of a molehill, mate. It's just a bit of harmless fun.'

'Harmless?'

'Oh, come on! What's wrong with having fun? Since becoming a Captain of the Fleet – this afternoon! – you've turned all serious. No one's going to get hurt. In fact, having the opportunity to meet a real live prince will be something for these girls to talk about for years to come. It's something they can boast about to their friends: a fairytale come true, the high point of their lives.'

Still immaculately dressed in his finery from his meeting with the admiral earlier in the evening, Ethan certainly looked the part. Out of pure habit, he rubbed little bits of dust from the toes of his shoes up against his trouser legs, rejuvenating their highly-glossed shine. They were so shiny that he could still see the worried look on his face in the reflection. Ethan tried always to look immaculate, and this combined with the military influence from the Academy to embed the fine points of personal grooming firmly in his daily routine.

'I'm as ready as I'm ever going to be,' he grumbled. He was thoroughly un-enchanted by Ralph's plan and objected to it strongly, but he was psychologically unwilling to let his best friend down. He knew that Ralph always looked up to him, seeing him as a real lad – and, as his mum always said, 'boys will be boys'. He conceded silently that, if not for Aurora, he could well be up for this.

'Let's be having it, then,' he burst out with half-hearted jolliness, trying to kid himself and almost, but not quite, succeeding. 'You know what to do, then, Clive?'

'Affirmative,' Clive replied, acting like a secret agent in a low-budget movie. Ralph gave Clive a who-are-you-trying-to-kid? look. Ethan snickered.

Clive got out of the Roller Glider and proceeded to follow Ralph's script. He strode in his most dignified manner around the vehicle and stood before the opening front door to allow Prince Knight and his entourage to emerge, making sure that the waiting female admirers outside the Cyber Lounge heard him well enough when he announced them.

Ethan was becoming more convinced that the entire enterprise was a lousy idea. *I'm sure that Clive is going to tell Aurora about this*, he thought. *It's going to ruin everything.*

Ralph was standing in the wings waiting to escort Prince Knight into the lion's den, when it seemed as if all hell broke loose. Ethan emerged from the Roller Glider and girls rushed at him, screaming and struggling frantically with each other to get close to him – and not just the two girls Ralph had lined up, either; at least a dozen were having at him. People with cameras seemed to appear from nowhere and the light from their flashes and mini-floodlights brightened up the night sky.

With all the increasingly hysterical pushing and shoving going on, Clive found it difficult to control the people surrounding Ethan, and his face started to cloud with worry. Clive was a trained bodyguard as well as a chauffeur, but he had never had to manage a mob of out-of-control young women before and wasn't certain as to which of the tactics in which he had been trained would be the appropriate ones for him to use.

Bella closed her eyes, wanting it all to go away. She hoped that the boys knew what they were doing. Connor just stayed mute and smiled.

Ralph was trapped amongst the crowd, not able to get close enough to help, thinking, *This is not supposed to happen! Ethan is going to kill me twenty-five times for this!*

Dozens of party-makers spilled out from the inside of the lounge onto the pavement outside, giving Ethan a reception normally reserved for celebrity rock stars, movie stars or, well, royalty. He forgot for a moment that that was just what he was supposed to be.

Ralph managed to get close enough to grab Ethan's arm and, playing down his own concerns, whispered, 'So far, so good. We're cruising.'

'We're cruising? Are you crazy? Look at all these people! When all this is over, you're dead, and I'm not joking,' Ethan hissed.

'Don't be too rash; we're nearly through the front door.' It was an expression they'd shared when up to mischief at the Academy.

'We'll see.'

Ralph started asserting himself with the crowd, barking orders to get out of the way, shuffling Ethan through the press of well-clothed young bodies. Young men as well as girls pressed in on him, wanting to shake his hand and offering to buy him drinks. Ralph tried not to show his concern that the crowd, instead of thinning out, had started growing larger now that the word had got around that there was a famous person in the club. It was not the situation he'd expected. *It was only supposed to be a little intimate evening with two girls, that's all; and look what's happened! Everything's spiralled out of all proportion; Ethan's sure to be hating this. I am in the deep muck now, for sure*, he thought. *I hope they say something nice over my grave.*

'All right,' he shouted. 'Back off, you mingers; you aren't supposed to be this uncool! Back off!' He shoved someone who had grabbed at Ethan.

Several large bouncers appeared, all with the authority and the ability to keep people out of the club, and took up Ralph's theme, barking, 'About your business, then!' and 'A higher standard of conduct, please!' and 'Behave yourselves, now!'

The crowd, although remaining clearly curious, quickly calmed down. Clive gave Ethan and Ralph the thumbs-up sign and returned briskly to the Roller Glider.

Ethan looked after him in despair, wondering if he was going to tell Aurora about this, and felt certain that he would want to melt into the cracks in the pavement if he did. Ralph, employing the help of the bouncers, ushered Ethan into the Cyber Lounge and to a table in a niche against a wall. It was barely ten fifteen. Predictably wishing to kill Ralph slowly, Ethan looked over at his friend with cold fury in his eyes, but decided that torture would have to wait until later.

'Wow, Ethan, do you see what I see?'

'What, the gorgeous babe in black? She's been giving me the eye ever since we arrived.'

'In your dreams, pal! She's way out of our league!'

'Speak for yourself, Ralph.'

'I think she is coming over, what shall we do?'

'Why ask me? Aren't you the expert, Ralph? Don't tell me your famous computer sensors have crashed.'

A long-legged creature of beauty, fashioned in skin-tight black Lycra, managed to easily manoeuvre her way through the crowd and under the bouncers' guard, provocatively positioning herself across the lads' table. 'Hi, boys. I'm Gwendolyn Black, but all my friends just call me Blackie.'

The lads' eyes were bolting out of their sockets in sheer delight. Unfortunately for Ethan and Ralph, that brief, nervous feeling of heavenly pleasure was quickly extinguished and substituted with the dull, unpleasant ache of anguish.

From out of the confines of the crowded darkened room appeared a ghastly shadow, a deathly figure that could send shivers up a thirty-foot Great White's back bone.

'Hello, guys.' A distinct chill filled the air, causing Ethan's pulse rate to rise immediately, while Ralph just stood frozen to the floor with his mouth gaping wide open.

'So, the rumour is true: we have a dignitary within our midst.'

'Reptile— I mean Nat— Nathanial,' Ethan stammered.

'Well, hello, Prince Ethan Knight,' he sneered. 'What's the flavour?'

Ethan tried to stare Nathanial down, but got a reminder of

Lieutenant Clegg's annoying habit of never looking directly at whomever he was talking to.

He laughed humourlessly. 'Man, if it isn't just like you, Ethan, acting like you're better than other people.'

'What's your game, Clegg? Why are you acting like a jealous moron?' Blackie interjected.

Ralph desperately wanted to say something, but the words would not resound from his vocal cords.

'Yes, just get to the point, pond scum.' Ethan scowled.

'Well, Gwendolyn, I have probably just saved you from potentially the most embarrassing situation of your young, sweet, innocent life. I will accept your gratitude later.'

Blackie just rolled her eyes. 'In your dreams, snake face,' was her response to that horrible thought.

'See our Prince here? He is an impostor! I've got more royal blood than he has; in fact, even my mangy old flea-bitten dog has. Prince Ethan is a mere flight captain from the Universal Flight Academy in Nevulae, which happens to be my headquarters also. His struck-dumb geeky cohort standing beside him, with the big mouth full of dodgy fillings, is Lieutenant Ralph "Logic" Baxter, also known, amongst other things, as "the joker".'

Miraculously, those unkind words seemed to instantly bring Ralph back to the land of the living. 'Hey, look who is painting the kettle black here,' he snapped.

'Go on, Reptile. Remember, I outrank you; be very careful,' warned Ethan.

'Yes, Clegg, don't stop there. I am intrigued, to say the least, and very amused.' Blackie was all ears.

'Wait a minute!' Ralph piped up. 'There's no need for all this personal unpleasantness, Nathanial. Let's all sit down and have a melonesto or two. I will even pay; can I be any fairer than that?'

'I am sure we can work out our differences; what do you say, Nat?'

'It will take a lot more than a few free bevvies to bring me 'round, you couple of blockheads. I think I am in the driver's seat, don't you, Prince?'

'Come on, Clegg, we were only letting our hair down and having a bit of fun. There's no harm in that, is there? It's not as if we have conned people out of their life savings or mugged a little old lady for her loose change.'

Blackie found the humour in Ethan's retort, and smiled at him.

'Oh, the Prince has found his voice at last. I thought you were going to let that upstart be your negotiator all night.'

'I have no need for a negotiator to act on my behalf you weasel; I can talk for myself, thank you.' Ethan was getting really agitated. 'Yes, and enough of the insults and profanities, especially directed at my expense, all right? I might develop an inferiority complex, just like you.'

'Shut it, numbnuts. You are the main cause of many of my sleepless nights and anxieties; I was the butt of many of your practical jokes on campus. You constantly made my life a misery; it was sheer hell at times. Now it is your turn to suffer. How's it feel to be on the opposite end of the stick?'

'Well, I can't deny that I was a little naughty, and so was Ethan.'

'Thanks, pal,' Ethan growled.

'But we didn't mean you any harm. What can we do to make it up to you, Nat?'

Blackie was enjoying every minute of the to-ing and fro-ing, and constant grovelling; she was in her element. Normally it was she who was dishing out the dirt and applying the pressure, tightening the tourniquet.

'Nothing at all! You are both in a great deal of trouble,' Clegg drawled. 'Impersonating any dignitary is a disciplinary offence, let alone royalty; now, that could even be a capital offence.'

'Who's impersonated any royalty, toe rag? I sure as hell never said a word about it, and there's a bunch of witnesses to back that up. If a bunch of stupid people draw some wrong conclusions by overhearing some friends having each other on, that's their problem.'

'Save it for the Disciplinary Tribunal, but I'd leave out the bit about "toe rag" when addressing the Chief Judicial Officer.'

'What are you on about, Nathanial? Why are you threatening a ridiculous prosecution over something you can't prove and which didn't hurt anybody? I mean, what's your problem? Jealous?'

'Don't give me that infamous attitude, Captain Top-Gun Knight! I've got nothing to be jealous about. I know I'm a better pilot and space-jockey than you'll ever be.'

'Oh, yeah?'

'Damned right, and you know it!'

'Then how about this: we go back out into the Cyber Lounge now and get into the Simulex22 Dogfight game. If I shoot you down, you leave it off with your childish prosecution, and if you shoot me down – which you won't – then I'll file an application with the Academy to forfeit my Top Gun fighter status title to you.'

'OK, you're on; let's do it!'

'Woo, we've got a showdown,' shouted an excited Blackie, instigating a stampede of onlookers.

They strode to the part of the Cyber Lounge where the bigger digital games were located and were lucky enough to find an empty Simulex22. As Ethan had feared, like the rats behind the Pied Piper, everyone was now crowded around the games master. Some were taking bets on the outcome. Nearly all wagers were on Ethan, though.

Ethan and Nathanial each fed the Simulex22 a five money-unit note, strapped themselves in and switched it on. They had an audience of maybe two or three dozen, watching the contest on a big screen set over the game module.

Inside his simulated cockpit, Ethan carefully noted the controls as the simulator screens came to life all around him. The touch-screen control on the console in front of him lit up, showing two sets of icons: one with the three symbols for scissors, paper and rock, the other with four choices for battle environment: low-altitude ground and sea support, stratospheric air cover, ionospheric patrol and deep-space search-and-destroy. He touched paper and ionospheric patrol.

A moment later the screen showed him that Nathanial had touched rock, meaning Ethan got his choice, but it also showed that Nathanial had also chosen ionospheric patrol, meaning that the victory in scissors-paper-rock had made no difference.

Then the touch-screen showed the scissors-paper-rock icons again, along with icons for attack and defend. Attackers had the advantage of (usually) first target identification. Defenders had the advantage of (usually) limited vulnerability. This time, Ethan touched scissors and attack. Nathanial's choices flashed up on the screen: rock and defence. Again, no difference.

Ethan absorbed all this without emotion. Combat was the way each pilot found it.

Next, the touch-screen showed scissors-paper-rock again, along with initial attacker orientation: down from space, from around the ionosphere and up from the stratosphere. Who won this choice would make a big difference.

Ethan touched rock and, of course, down from space. Nathanial, who was certain to choose up from the stratosphere, touched rock also. Ethan would have to attack from around the ionosphere.

Finally, the screen showed icons for the three types of ionospheric patrol craft. This choice would be hidden from the opponent until the first sighting – if the first sighting was such that it could be determined.

Ethan picked the Bright-star, a craft noted more for its defensive than its offensive features, even though he was on the attack. He figured that Nathanial could never shoot him down, with all the Bright-star's defensive features, and that he himself didn't need all the latest offensive bells and whistles to get through any defence Nathanial would be likely to put up.

The simulator flashed him his co-ordinates and his screens showed him what the pilot of a Bright-star would see when at the co-ordinates. The whole set-up process, from inserting the money to receiving the co-ordinates, had taken about a minute.

Outside the Simulex22, the crowd cheered. Ralph was quietly confident that the reptile would be no match for his pal.

Ethan, figuring that Clegg would probably be started on the other side of the ionosphere or close to it, set out along the upper-atmosphere's circumference near top speed, at the limit of the Bright-star's sensors' ability to detect bogies, knowing that Clegg would win the game if Ethan failed to engage with him within ninety seconds. Clegg started manoeuvring his Thor Thunderbolt-Seven in random evasive patterns, changing direction and profile every second or so, but within eleven seconds Ethan's sensors had picked up his image.

A Thor Thunderbolt-Seven, eh? All firepower, but vulnerable from above if set at the wrong attitude, he thought in a flash, as he took the Bright-star in at an angle to the direction in which he guessed – correctly – that Nathanial was going to jig next, his attitude poised to dive under the Thunderbolt at the instant that his screens told him that Nathanial's trackers had locked onto him; then, just as Nathanial let loose with an awe-inspiring volley of smart missiles and bendable lasers, bringing a gasp from the audience, Ethan moved his controls with incredible speed, dipping the Bright-star off at an odd and continually-changing angle into a tight loop at a punishing number of Gs, its sensor-benders deflecting the course of the Thunderbolt's barrage, which missed the Bright-star by barely more than a kilometre – which, in ionospheric warfare, was no more than a whisker. He twisted this tight loop into a wide, irregularly parabolic loop at top speed, up and over the Thunderbolt, also at a punishing number of Gs, and then down at it at just the angle at which it was most vulnerable, sending one heat-seeking high-speed missile into its fuselage, causing all the Simulex22's screens to light up with the virtual explosion. The whole dogfight had taken just a few seconds.

The crowd cheered. Money changed hands.

Clegg was the first to climb out of his Simulex22 cockpit, his face red with embarrassment and anger. He looked around for Ethan, saw that he was still in his cockpit, and then turned on Ralph. Pointing his finger at the short, ginger Dux, he snarled, 'Your mate may have got lucky this time and won our bet – which I'll honour, because I'm a fellow-officer and officially a gentleman – but I didn't have any bet going with you, you little turd, so watch your back. I may just come up with some way to make trouble for you about all this.' He then stalked from the Cyber Lounge.

It was another half-minute or so before Ethan emerged from his cockpit. His face was sombre, rather than triumphant. Clearly in a state of considerable distress, he said, 'Excuse me for a moment, please,' and did a runner for the front doors.

Twenty minutes later, he emerged from the shadowy alley between two restaurants about thirty metres from the Cyber Lounge, where he had been hiding and fuming with anger at Ralph. To his surprise, he felt a sort of pity for his arch-rival Clegg, not bitterness.

Chapter Seven

Ethan saw the Roller Glider coming along the transport corridor from the direction of the Gazers' house. He broke cover and got to the front of the Cyber Lounge, where Ralph and Blackie were both waiting. He made a point of eye contact with Blackie; they both smiled at each other, and then Blackie went back inside the lounge.

Ethan was quick to be right by the Roller's passenger-side doors as they hissed open, ready to jump inside immediately, but he froze as he saw Aurora and another girl emerging from the back seat. Out of the corner of his eye, he could see Ralph approaching.

'Ethan!' Aurora exclaimed with a semi-shy smile, clearly glad to see him. 'I talked Clive into bringing Crystal and me here when he came to pick you and Ralph up. I thought I'd surprise you.'

'Well, yes… uh… yes, I'm – I'm really shocked – I mean surprised. Pleased to meet you, Crystal.'

'And me you,' she replied.

'Hey, Captain!' Ralph could have a surprisingly loud voice for such a short man sometimes. 'Aren't you going to introduce me to these two lovely young ladies?'

Ethan was feeling really guilty about his earlier subconscious flirtation with Blackie, but he somehow managed to recover enough of his dignity to answer.

'Oh, uh – Ralph, this is Aurora Gazers and her friend Crystal…'

Unfortunately for all concerned, Blackie happened to decide to take an impromptu stroll outside, spotted Ethan, looking quite loved up, talking to Aurora and put two and two together. *Time to get bitchy to protect my interest*, she schemed, even though she really had no claim. Ethan had barely said three words to her all evening; his eyes had done most of the talking.

Crystal spotted her first and, before she could get a word of warning out to Aurora, the harsh tone of Blackie's raspy voice began to invade and contaminate the otherwise serene airwaves of a very balmy night, which took everyone, including Clive, by surprise.

'Well, if it isn't the ice maiden, Aurora Gazers. Haven't seen you at the lounge for a while; been on annual holidays at the nunnery?'

Oh no, thought Ethan, who was now hyperventilating. *I'm sprung; they know each other. I knew tonight would be an horrific disaster. Ralph, you are dead!*

'Do you know this little madam, Aurora?'

'Yes, Clive, you could say we're acquainted. Hello, Gwendolyn.' Blackie hated it when Aurora called her by her full name. 'Are you here with Brillo?' He was her scruffy long-haired on-and-off Hell's Angel boyfriend.

'Matter of fact, no. I am here with that handsome officer, Ethan Knight, and his friend, Ralph, actually, and we have had a superlicious night together; haven't stopped dancing.' She winked. 'Have we, boys? Let's do lunch, luvvie, and I can tell you all about it.'

Before Ethan could respond with an unrehearsed denial, Crystal instinctively came to the boys' rescue.

'Come on, folks, let's go down to the Café Tropicana; there seems to be a really bad odour coming from somewhere around here.'

'It's all right, Crissie, my dear: no need to get uppity and leave on my account; I've had enough of this emotional melodrama, anyway.'

'If the crap – I mean "cap" – fits, Gwendolyn!'

'My chauffeur will be here any moment now. Ah, talk of the devil; here he comes in our brand new Mercedes Fantasia. Now, that's very good timing in my book.'

Ethan breathed a sigh of relief and silently promised himself that, if he was fortunate enough to get out of this crazy mess, he would never allow Ralph to entice him into a similar situation again.

Ralph whispered to his friend, 'Am I missing something here? What's going on, and what's your relationship with Aurora and Crystal?'

'I will tell you later, Ralph; now give me a break and shut it.'

As Blackie was about to depart, she called out to Aurora, 'Remember, let's do lunch. I think we both have a lot in common. See you, Ethan; thanks for a great night. Now, don't be a stranger; you will remember our little secret?'

'What does she mean by that remark, Ethan?' Aurora asked.

Clive raised his eyebrows and waited with bated breath for Ethan's response, thinking that it would have to be very good.

'Oh, it's nothing, really. She has the hots for Ralph, but he is not in the least bit interested, so she wants me to have a word in his ear for her.'

'Oh, is that all, Ethan?' Aurora was not the least bit taken in. 'I think you have it the wrong way around, don't you? It's you who she has the hots for. Tell the truth; I wasn't born yesterday.'

Whoops, Ralph thought. *Now the penny has finally dropped: these two are an item. Ethan sure kept that a big secret, and I had better bail him out here or it could all end in tears.*

'Sorry to butt in, Aurora, but Ethan is telling the truth. Blackie would not leave me alone all night in the lounge. It was unbearable; she just would not take the hint. She's a touchy-feely woman, that; not my cup of tea, that's for sure. Make sure you don't make any rash promises on my account, Ethan.'

Clive used Ralph's unconvincing explanation as a convenient window, to diplomatically lead into, 'I think we should be getting back; young Ethan here has an important meeting at the Great Hall early tomorrow morning.'

'That's OK with us, Clive; I, for one, have lost all enthusiasm for continuing this misadventure anyway. Crystal and I will ride in the front, and the boys can have the back; I think that will be adequate distance between us for the moment. Maybe they can both concoct some more unrealistic excuses on the way home, but nice try, Ralph. Ethan must be a true pal.'

Ethan took a deep breath and slumped back into his seat. He looked over at Ralph and thought, *Ex-pal, to be precise. You're a dead man walking; what a fine mess you have got me into. Aurora will probably never talk to me ever again after tonight.*

Ralph was fully aware of his miscalculations that evening, and opted to keep his lip well and truly buttoned all the way back to his hotel, just for his own safety.

Ethan was very glad to see the welcoming sight of his warm bed; it wasn't as comfortable as his bed at home, but it ran a close second. Ethan was dead on his feet and felt as though he had ridden an emotional rollercoaster for most of the night. He was completely drained.

He could not sleep a wink, and tossed and turned all night, totally convinced that, after his and Ralph's abominable behaviour, Aurora would probably never speak to him again. The thought of that mixed with the unfortunate events of the disastrous evening was an unwelcome emotional cocktail, and the last thing he needed the night before the most important event in his life. He had to have total clarity for the meeting, otherwise that could end up a major disaster as well.

This was where all of his military training and discipline would have to kick in and get him through. He would have to act on instinct and instinct alone for the early part of the meeting; hopefully; he would be able to pull himself together and see it through.

'How'd it go last night, son?' Bella asked, tongue in cheek, as she took away his hardly-eaten breakfast, convinced that something had gone terribly amiss last night, judging by the long face and loss of appetite.

'I'd rather not go there, Mum, if you don't mind.' Ethan stood up and stretched. 'Let's just say a total disaster. I just want to forget the whole experience. Oh, and I'm never going to speak to that Ralph Baxter again.'

'OK, son; you can tell me later.'

'Oh, c'mon, boy.' His father chuckled heartily. 'You can tell us all the gory details!'

'Dad, it's 07.00 hours. I haven't the time. The limo's going to be here at eight, and I'm not even ready!' He scurried into his bedroom, kicking Jack out as he tried to sneak in behind him. The last things Ethan needed just then were dog hair all over his uniform and an interrogation from his dad.

Noticing his nicely-folded and pressed uniform lying out on the dresser with his highly-polished shoes sitting on a piece of newspaper on the floor, Ethan ran out and planted a big kiss on Bella's cheek, saying, 'Thanks, Mum. You didn't have to do that.'

'You need to look your best today,' Bella told him, with some tears in her eyes. Sometimes, Ethan had no idea why his mum got all teary-eyed over what seemed to him to be non-tearful things. 'I thought you might be a little worse for wear from your night out with Ralph, but don't get used to it.'

Ethan took the lift down, so as to be ready to go when Clive arrived dead on the dot of 08.00 hours. But he didn't feel ready for possibly the most important day in his young life; all he could think of was Aurora.

Chapter Eight

As Clive guided them into the traffic, Ethan looked around himself and asked, 'Why isn't Admiral Gazers taking the Roller to the meeting?'

'Actually, Mr Cloudy Day, Aurora organised it,' answered Clive. 'The admiral is taking the Eurocopter. Aurora is certainly looking out for you, Ethan; you're a very lucky boy.'

'Especially after last night's antics; she has got such a kind heart. I thought I had ruined everything,' Ethan choked out, 'especially when that dipstick Ralph cooked up that cock-and-bull story about him and Blackie.'

'Ah, so that's why you were looking like someone had stolen your favourite blue denims off the clothes line.' Clive could see the colour gradually return to Ethan's cheeks, and the strained look of anguish disappeared and returned as a slight smile. 'Feeling better now, my boy?' he asked.

'Much, thank you, Clive; lead me to my Peers, if you will. How long will it take to get to the lions' den – I mean meeting, Clive, my man?'

'About thirty minutes. We're going via Sarantio Suspension Bridge; the Great Hall is a few kilometres on from there. It usually takes less time, but security measures have been put into place to protect the meeting, and those will take up an extra few minutes. We'll still get there in plenty of time. Everyone is on Code Red. You'll be in the company of some of the most influential people on Earth today.'

Ethan tugged at his shirt collar and loosened his tie a bit, feeling somewhat dry in the throat.

Noticing this, Clive told him, 'There's ice water in the fridge there,' and pointed to a small door on the top of a console between their seats.

'You're a life-saver, mate. Thanks heaps.'

As they approached the Sarantio Bridge, the atmosphere outside became increasingly on edge. Police and Domestic Order troopers were on every corner; armoured personnel carriers were patrolling the streets; barricades had been erected at what appeared to be strategic locations, especially at intersections. 'Detour' and 'No Entry' signs were everywhere.

'There's only one way in,' Clive told him, 'and there's only the one – same – way out.' He glanced over at Ethan, who seemed just a little pale at the sight of it all, and asked, 'Are you all right, son?'

'A little intimidated, if I can be honest, Clive, but no need to worry; I'll keep it together. I know how to do whatever it takes.'

Clive smiled his approval.

As they pulled up at the first security checkpoint, Ethan gazed in awe at the anthill of Domestic Order troopers swarming all over the bridge.

A heavily-armed trooper wearing a gas mask approached the Roller Glider, looking menacing, and ordered in a muffled, almost non-human voice, 'Please display your identification, gentlemen, if you will.'

'That's a familiar voice.' Clive smiled. 'It's Le Clerc!' The muffled voice coming from the gas mask reminded Clive of his skittle-bowling partner at the Orbit Dome a couple of seasons before.

All the trooper did was repeat, 'Please display your identification, gentlemen.'

Thinking he must have been mistaken, Clive produced his security pass. He shook his head. He'd never forgotten a face or a voice before. *Maybe Le Clerc is on strict behavioural orders with the high security level today*, he thought.

Sticking his head inside the roller, the trooper gave Ethan a staring glance and ordered, 'Yours, too, Captain, sir.'

Ethan handed him his Military ID. The trooper nodded, handed it back to him and said, still in his muffled, formal, military tone, 'Good to see you, Clive. You can go now. We'll talk later. Great module, that.'

'I knew it!' Clive turned to Ethan. 'I never forget a face or a voice. You big tub of lard,' he said, laughing.

As they approached the Great Hall building itself, Ethan

looked up into the sky and saw that the sun, sending bright light all over the land just moments before, had suddenly become almost blotted out by the sheer numbers of military craft circling overhead. Sky trains; attack, passenger and auxiliary choppers; hovercraft and armoured personnel-carrier modules crowded the air space, turning daylight into night, making everything look menacing and eerie.

'You OK, Ethan?' Clive felt compelled to ask again.

'Holding it together, Clive.' It seemed to him that they had gone to a whole lot of trouble for one little meeting.

'That's my man. We'll be off the transport corridor any minute now.'

The Great Hall building was an awesome sight, protected heavily at the best of times. As they approached, it was swarming with military personnel and hardware. Ethan was not surprised at the admiral's warning of what to expect.

Taking a sudden sharp right-hand turn, Clive guided the Roller into an opening that appeared in a flash in a large, blank wall. It seemed to swallow them up in full flight, causing the Roller to come to a sudden halt. Ethan, taken by surprise, feared that the contents of his already-fizzy stomach might become splattered and strewn all over the Roller's spotlessly clean interior.

Clive noticed Ethan's cheeks billowing and, horrified, quickly offered him the convenience of a plastic barf-bag. Ethan grabbed the ergonomically-designed chunder receptacle with a gulped, 'Thanks, Clive,' but the feeling soon passed and he was able to hang on to his meal, which still bubbled furiously inside his stomach. He remembered what his instructors had taught him about the dangers of eating greasy food before the rigors of flight.

'I guess we're here.' Ethan breathed the unnecessary words out in relief.

'Yep. It might be a good idea if we both got out of the Roller for a bit of fresh air, don't you think?'

Ethan offered no argument. He hopped out of the Roller, straightening his collar and tie in the process.

Two slick-looking operatives with expensive suits and official mannerisms walked towards Ethan, talking into hands-free communication microphones conveniently attached to the collars of their designer dress shirts. They were packing hardly-concealed nine-millimetre Stechkin automatic handguns, the hand-grips sticking ostentatiously past the lapels of their pinstriped suit jackets. They were both about the same size and physique and looked remarkably similar to each other.

One, whose hair was a shade lighter than the other's, snapped out the words, 'Captain Knight?' Without waiting for a response, he proceeded, 'I'm Security Agent Tibor Links. This is Agent Marty Fieldmore. It is our responsibility to get you to the meeting safely and on time.'

Agent Fieldmore, speaking in the same crisp, official manner, turned to Clive. 'We can take it from here, Mr Van der Poel. You get back in your module. We'll escort him as far as the first checkpoint. Be certain that you operate your module according to the protocol you received this morning. Don't stop for any reason whatsoever, even if it appears to be a matter of life or death. Intelligence reports confirm the need for security at the highest level of awareness.'

Ethan leaned towards Clive and whispered, 'Thanks for everything, mate. You be careful on your way home. I need you to pick me up on Saturday night. I won't accept any other driver in your place.'

Security Agents Links and Fieldmore quickly whisked Ethan off without giving him a chance to wave goodbye. It was about time for him to stand on his own two feet without support from anyone.

The agents escorted Ethan across an exposed courtyard to a solid metal door in the middle of a long, high, reinforced-concrete wall. A complex control panel jutted out of the wall next to the door.

Agent Links produced the same titanium activation pin, calibrated with Ethan's iris pattern, that had scanned his right eye the night before at Admiral Gazers' house. The admiral's security staff had transported it via an armed courier team to the security unit overnight. Agent Links then held the pin up to Ethan's eye and took a reading. The light at the pin's base showed green. It was a match, all right. Then he immediately placed the pin in a slot in the control panel, where a laser, programmed with Ethan's iris pattern by a separate secure digital transmission, scanned it. The light by the slot glowed green: another match.

Then Ethan had to stand on two foot-shaped tiles on the ground. A cranial-logger headset extended automatically out from the control panel, sensed the location of his head and gently closed in around it. He didn't have to put it on or even adjust it for fit. As he thought of the series of fifteen numbers that he'd memorised at Admiral Gazers' residence, the headset retrieved them directly from his memory waves. He remembered what Willis had told him about the technology's sensitivity and delicacy and started to sweat.

Ethan always perspired when under pressure, and, as he stood there, wearing the cranial logger, streams of sweat started running down his back, soaking his shirt, making him feel uncomfortable. It took almost ten minutes of making slips that resulted in amber lights, followed by seemingly endless seconds of waiting while the instrument reset itself before giving him the white start-again lights, before he completed the silent series of numbers in a manner resulting in a green light.

Well, at least I didn't produce any red lights, he thought, with a sigh of relief, as he pressed the release button and the cranial-logger headset disengaged from his head and disappeared back into the control panel with a hiss.

Finally on the other side of the door, Ethan found himself standing inside a room in stark contrast to the wide-open courtyard between the outer and inner walls in which he'd stood a moment earlier. The room was something out of the Dark Ages, primitive and unrefined, producing within him a little shock of the unexpected.

In the middle of the room stood an old-style television set and against the wall a two-door refrigerator. There was also a fully-laid antique dinner table and chairs, as if suspended in time after the last meal had been eaten on it maybe forty to fifty or even more years before; probably from the nineties.

Ethan was at a loss as to why this room had been preserved. Nothing seemed to make sense. Agent Links entered the room and asked, 'Is the décor to your liking?' in a flat, emotionless voice that gave nothing away, reminding Ethan of Willis.

They must send these blokes to classes to teach them to talk like that, he thought, but what he said was, 'Quite interesting, isn't it? What's it all in aid of? Such an old façade, reminiscent of bygone days,' in a voice mimicking interior designers he'd seen on TV.

'You'll find out soon enough, Captain. Be patient. Try to remember everything in the room,' the agent suggested, adding, 'Try to see what you don't see.'

Chapter Nine

What does he mean? thought Ethan, deciding to be co-operative and to go along with whatever Agent Links had in store for him, reckoning that he was about to have his mental awareness and ability to concentrate tested.

A face – a bland, forgettable, superficially good-looking announcer's face – appeared on the old-fashioned TV screen and announced that the meeting was now in progress, filling Ethan with a mixture of excitement and nerves, as he was already consumed by trying to resolve Agent Links's riddle. He continued to look around, asking himself, *What haven't I seen?*

Agent Links arrived to collect him, asking, 'Are you ready to meet the honourable and illustrious World Ministers?'

'Now is as good time as any. I'm right behind you.'

Suddenly, without moving a centimetre, Ethan was standing in the middle of an entirely different room, feeling as if he were part of an old-time pre-digital film movie, moving frame by frame. *What's going on?* Ethan thought, confused, resisting the temptation to scratch his head. The room was now full of technology; visual life screens and various forms of controls and flashing multi-coloured lights filled its space. Variously-sized and shaped digital plasma visual-display screens cast light into the slightly darkened room, highlighting a couple of dozen people in uniform scurrying around in a beehive of activity. It was similar to the communications room that Ethan had accidentally seen at the admiral's home. It was so different to the old-fashioned room into which he'd first stepped upon entering the Great Hall that he was beginning to wonder whether that old room had ever existed or whether it had been a figment of his imagination, perhaps a subconscious reaction on his part to the stress of the moment.

Disoriented by what had happened, it took Ethan several seconds to realise that he was standing in front of the entire Grand Assembly, who were sitting at individual desks on a large, horseshoe-shaped raised platform encircling the communications and information-technology centre. Only Supreme Ruler Landon's desk, in the centre of the horseshoe, was vacant. He snapped to the reality of it only when he heard Agent Links announce, 'Captain Knight, I believe you have already met Admiral Harlius Fonce Gazers.'

Ethan took a moment for a surreptitious deep breath to compose himself, and then responded, evenly, 'I'm honoured to say that I have.' He saluted Admiral Gazers. 'Sir.'

Acknowledging Ethan's salute with a relaxed return salute, the admiral gave a slight, informal smile, which helped to settle the boy down a touch.

A clipped, military-sounding voice over hidden speakers intoned, 'Captain Knight, meet World Minister Malik, Commissioner for Children's Welfare.' The light around Malik immediately became a shade brighter. The intellectual type, Malik had unimposing looks; the thick-black-rimmed spectacles adorning his face were its most prominent feature. His soft, mild speaking voice gave the impression that he wouldn't hurt a fly even if his life depended on it.

Malik smiled at Ethan in a warm and friendly manner and asked, 'What do you know about the late twentieth century, Captain Knight?'

Ethan returned the smile and, not knowing why Malik had asked such a weird question, replied, 'Only what I have read in books, sir.'

'Thank you, Captain Knight. We'll speak later, my boy.' Still smiling, Malik leaned back in his seat.

Ethan wondered about the emphasis on the late twentieth century since his arrival, and about what he was missing. *Why did Malik ask me that question?* It was almost pointlessly general and vague, and the Assembly must certainly have already known the answer to it if they'd wanted to, anyway. And then, why hadn't Malik followed up with a more pointed question after his general and vague answer?

Next, the voice over the PA and the lighting introduced Minister Biker Reed, Commissioner for Space Travel, Exploration, and Events. He was one of Ethan's living heroes. Ethan had followed Biker's career fanatically since he had been very young, and still did. He knew the strategic and tactical details of every battle Biker had fought and won back during the Resource Wars, and had often taken on the role of Biker in simulated battles with Ralph in his bedroom – in his much younger days, of course.

Biker was going on forty. His rugged, mischievous-looking face sported a short, greying goatee beard, a huge handlebar moustache, deep laugh lines framing piercing blue eyes, and the ruby red cheeks and purple-veined nose of a social drinker.

'So, tell me, Captain,' he said, from beneath his moustache; 'tell me what you know about antiques, especially artefacts from the 1990s.'

'I'm not an authority on that subject, sir. I liked my art classes at preparatory school, but there's not much I can really tell you about antique artefacts of that period: only what I have seen in books, old photographs and in other people's homes.'

'Thank you, Captain Knight. I'd like to catch up with you later, if I may.'

'I'll look forward to that, sir, and that's an understatement.' Seeing Biker had been the highlight of what had been a strange day up to that point. He wanted to ask him about the reasons for the Nineties Room illusion and the questions referring to the 1990s, but he remembered Admiral Gazers' caution about speaking only when spoken to and realised that trying to do that would not be on.

He thought, *What am I missing? Where's the clue? What's all this got to do with my mission? I need to find the answers.*

The voice from the speakers and the lighting next introduced Minister Orlando Sung, Commissioner for Domestic Order. Orlando looked exotic enough, with his Brazilian-Chinese ancestry, but his imposing, immediately powerful personality projected the image and the immediate understanding that he was just a tough cop. He was, after all, the boss of every tough cop in the world. His face muscles seemed to be always relaxed and under control, his eyes hard, watchful and distrustful, and his body language relaxed but ready.

He spoke with a quiet, clipped, chillingly hard voice in a bland, mixed accent Ethan couldn't place. 'Captain Knight, I'll make this brief and to the point. Please tell me what you know about significant crimes of the 1990s.'

Of course! thought Ethan. *Another nineties question*. He thought for a moment before answering. Orlando Sung's eyes were not ones to which people easily gave inaccurate information, let alone told lies. 'To tell you the truth, sir, just about nothing reliable. My courses at the Academy did cover the more significant terrorist attacks and war crimes, of course, but what I know about murders and robberies and things like that all comes from movies and TV, and I couldn't be sure what's history, what's based on history or what's pure fiction.'

'Thank you for your co-operation, Captain. That's all from me.'

The introduction system next directed Ethan's attention to Minister Frikker Linns, Vice Consul of the Grand Assembly and Minister for Northwest Europe. As vice consul, he had a direct influence on the final decisions made. He had a pointy, sharp-featured, weasel-like face, which he pointed at Ethan, with unpleasant seriousness in his gaze, before asking him another mysteriously ridiculous question. 'Captain Knight, what is your favourite old twentieth-century televisual programme?'

'I've always liked The Jetsons, sir. It is an old-process visual animation programme with silly ideas about what they thought life would be like now. It makes me laugh, sir.'

'Thank you for your co-operation, Captain,' Frikker said, in a dismissive manner.

The announcer next called the name of Minister Meena Ramakrishna, Commissioner for Food Allocation and Prime Minister of India. Meena projected the image of being the world's steely grandmother: caring, but not to be trifled with. She had steel-grey hair (some said to match her will) tied severely back into a bun at the nape of her neck, and she wore a colourful, mostly purple-and-red sari. She took off a pair of rimless glasses and fixed her large, expressive eyes on Ethan.

'Good morning, Captain Knight.'

'Good morning, ma'am.'

'You ate well at breakfast this morning, I trust?' Meena was well known for her campaigns to assure all human beings a sufficient amount of food and had been known to speak out about the dangers of wasteful food luxuries. She was Crystal's hero.

Ethan was determined not to show the guilt she made him feel for his luxurious breakfast, answering, 'I am indeed privileged.'

'A good answer, Captain Knight. Tell me, what do you know about the history of the world's problems over the past sixty years or so: since the end of the Cold War, let's say?'

Another historical question! 'Well, ma'am, I got an "A" for the Modern History course at the Academy, which covers just that period, but it was just a survey course and I don't know how deeply it covered the problems.'

'Thank you, Captain Knight.'

Ethan was still wondering what all this had to do with his mission, but somehow the penny started to drop. He focused on Agent Links's instructions to look for what he had not seen in the nineties room. This was the clue.

'Shall we take a short recess and stretch our legs?' Admiral Gazers said this more as a command than as a question. 'Ethan, would you like some refreshment?'

'I would like to get some fresh air, sir, if that would be OK?'

'Fifteen minutes, then, but not outside. Take your break back in the nineties room. Agent Links will accompany you.'

In a flash, Ethan was back in the nineties room again with Agent Links. He could not help but be amazed by how bizarre the contrast was between what he saw there and the Great Hall Auditorium with all its technology. Then the thought flashed through his head: *I've got it! The picture of this room is in an old twentieth-century book, but I can't remember which book, or where in the book it is.* He racked his brain, but remained unable to put his finger on it. Fifteen minutes seemed to fly by in fifteen seconds, and Agent Links reappeared to escort him back into the auditorium.

Chapter Ten

Standing in front of the Grand Assembly again, Ethan continued to piece the puzzle together in his head.

Not waiting for Ethan's silent mental processes to resolve themselves, the voice from the speakers introduced Senior Minister Miningra, Commissioner for World Security. Miningra was a mountain of a man, over 210 centimetres tall, who obviously took regular weight training seriously. His large, black eyes looked out from his mahogany-coloured face with a keen intelligence. In his manner as well as his appearance, Miningra was an imposing person.

He leaned back in his seat and placed his long, strong fingers across the back of his head, his elbows back: clearly a habitual gesture and one that made him look a bit like a giant mahogany cobra. He seemed to look through Ethan with his piercing eyes. 'Tell me, Captain,' he enquired, his voice a deep, hard, rumbling sound, 'do you like to collect old postcards from the 1990s?' Then he lifted his massive eyebrows to indicate that he was ready for an answer.

'I've never really been into that, sir.' As with Willis, Ethan neither warmed to Miningra nor disliked him.

'I see. Thank you, Captain.'

These questions, thought Ethan, *they all seem designed to try to prompt my memory for some reason… but why?* Then, instantly, he knew. He had seen the scene in the nineties room illusion in a photograph from an old box of dusty photographs, postcards and personal effects packed away in the attic over his home in Kingstonia. They had been up there for years and were probably still there. He'd never felt the need to enquire about to whom the box belonged, having just assumed that it belonged to his parents or was, perhaps, the property of an old friend of theirs.

His award-winning memory was now in full flight, and he remembered seeing writing on the back of the photo in red ink, reading, '*Seth's last resting place, 1998*'. He'd thought at the time, back when he'd been about ten, that it had been an odd thing to write on the back of a photograph, but he'd put it back in the box with the other photos and cards and had forgotten all about it until that moment.

Why was this picture so important to the Grand Assembly? Ethan decided that the moment had arrived for him to assert himself about this, thinking, *They've clearly gone to some trouble to confront me with this, so they must be expecting my active participation in what they're doing*.

He stepped forward, saluted and announced, 'Please forgive my probably insubordinate intrusion into the Ministers' deliberations, but, if the programme you have prepared for me this morning has been designed to jog my memory, it seems to have worked.'

'Go on, Captain.' Admiral Gazers' voice was grave, but his eyes were twinkling and he seemed on the edge of a little smile.

'I remember where I have seen the room in that old-time illusion before. It's the exact replica of a photograph in a box of old stuff that's been up in my family's attic for years.' He noticed several of them nodding. 'Please understand, but I have to ask: why is this photograph so important to the Grand Assembly?'

'I can answer that.' The Supreme Ruler, Ziekiel Landon, said this as he entered the auditorium, surrounded by a dozen of his elite-guard SOF troopers.

Landon had taken to rarely appearing in public by that time. Ethan felt honoured to be in the same company as him and held his composure as well as any man twice his years could.

Landon strode to his until-now glaringly vacant station at the centre of the horseshoe. The other ministers rose out of respect, and then sat back down again as he eased himself into his chair.

'I have been waiting in my office just outside the auditorium today, hoping that you could help provide a breakthrough in solving a fifty-year-old mystery,' Landon told him, then paused for effect. 'Back in 1998, a young amateur astronomer living in Kingstonia, far ahead of his time in the techniques of gravitational micro-lensing, hit the headlines with the revelation that he'd discovered a new planet: a perfect replica of Earth, potentially suitable for human colonisation. However, something happened to that astronomer on the same day as the announcement: before any governmental department or academic astronomers could meet with him and secure his vital data, he was robbed and murdered in his own home. The appropriate authorities sealed off the area, looking for clues to the whereabouts of the planet. At the time speculation and suspicion ran rife. Many thought that certain organisations had planned the robbery in order to steal his information, but these suppositions proved to be unfounded. To this day, the location of the planet remains lost.'

He paused again for a moment before continuing. 'The last piece to the puzzle is an article placed in the local *Kingstonia Gazette* newspaper and a single photograph taken of the crime scene by a photojournalist named Jimmy Jones. Unfortunately, twenty years ago, a deliberately-lit fire ravaged the newspaper's archival vaults, destroying nearly everything inside. After painstakingly sifting through what was left, we managed to retrieve a portion of the article, but the picture is very badly damaged, with only half still remaining.

'Unfortunately, the photographer died of old age three months ago, never having the negatives to the original picture; he'd sold them to the *Kingstonia Gazette* all those years before. Our agents were able to meet with him at his rest home before he died. He believed that relatives of the astronomer have a copy of the picture in the article, completely unaware of its importance. Also, these relatives have a connection with one of the military academies in Nevulae.'

After giving this a chance to sink in, he continued, 'This is what you and the old room have in common. You don't mind if I call you Ethan?'

'Not in the least, sir. I would be honoured.'

'After meticulously piecing together parts of the badly-damaged photograph, our technicians visually simulated and reconstructed as much of the 1998 room as possible. It was a long shot, designed to enable us to jog a memory or two, but it is all we have to work with; we're taking desperate measures. At the same time, we have set about undertaking the arduous task of trying to locate the whereabouts of this important photograph, if it really does exist.

'In the last three months, we have investigated the family lineage of all cadets who attended any of the academies over the last fifty years, looking for a cadet with a distant relative named Seth Stevens. We monitored every up-and-coming military cadet in the Capital Territory and its surrounding province, our agents conducting all enquiries with the utmost of discretion and secrecy. We drew a blank all around.'

Ethan's heart beat loudly as he remembered the name written on the back of the photograph in the box and realised that Seth Stevens was a distant relative.

Landon went on, 'Only four days ago, our investigations finally led us to your door. The Grand Assembly called on Senior Minister Miningra for a full report on the Knight family history and your military record. We decided we should call this meeting after your graduation ceremony, realising that until then all your thoughts would be entirely focused on that. Arranging for Admiral Gazers to speak at your graduation enabled us to make contact with you informally. We needed to know if you could handle standing in the line of fire. Inviting you and your family to his home, the admiral took the opportunity to examine your strength of character and that of your family. You did a good job of convincing him that you are well up to the task.'

Speechless and dumbstruck, Ethan could not get his head around what had just happened. Realising that all this information would be hard to absorb, Supreme Ruler Landon gave him some more time to breathe and take it all in.

Carrying on, Landon explained, 'The visual simulation of the room in the old photo was an attempt to prompt any memory you may have had of the photograph, if indeed you had ever seen it. Psychologists designed the questions the Ministers asked you this morning. You see, the photograph is the last crucial part of the jigsaw. It will add the other part to the room and, we fervently hope, bring the fifty-year-old secret to the light of day. I don't have to tell you how important this is for all of humanity. It has taken years of dedication to get to this stage; it's still a very long shot, but the photograph could hold the key.'

'Tell me about the photograph, Ethan.' Miningra's deep voice grabbed everyone's attention. He was leaning forward with his elbows on the desk before him and his chin in his hands, his eyes as piercing as ever. 'Can you remember anything else from the photograph that isn't in the old room?'

Ethan recalled his instructions to 'try to see what you can't see'.

'It's been a long time since I saw the picture, sir, and I was only a child when I did see it, but I do remember a couple of telescopes in the corner of the room, facing out of the window, and a stack of those old-fashioned, clunky computers with a big, old vacuum-tube monitor.'

'What side of the room?' Miningra's voice had softened without losing its tone of authority.

'I think the same side, next to the old fridge – no, on the right, definitely on the right.' He recalled from the nineties illusion room that they only had the left-hand side of the picture.

'Anything else? Think about it, Ethan: anything, anything at all.' Miningra's voice, although softened almost to a purr, remained compelling.

'Why don't we go and get the photograph? We can travel to my family home in Kingstonia, where it is. I do hope it's still in the old box, but there's no reason why it wouldn't still be there; no one has been up there for years, as far as I know. We could pick up my parents on the way.'

'The sooner we get the photo here,' Landon observed, dryly, 'the sooner our forensic scientists will be able to examine every millimetre of it, and we can follow them on the auditorium's screens. There's a very good chance the position of the planet may still be registered digitally on the telescope's dial or the screen of the computer monitor, frozen in time.'

All co-ordinate positions in astronomical technology had for years had back-up anti-knock safeguards, which ensured that positions could never be lost before being recorded, should the apparatus fall over or be knocked over.

Miningra smiled at Ethan. 'Your plan won't be necessary, Captain. Security agents are entering your house right about now, with instructions to search the attic for the photo. Don't worry; my agents do not damage locks. In fact, no one who doesn't know about the photo will be able to tell that they've been there at all –

and let's just leave your family out of it for now. The less they know, the better for them.' Miningra was speaking as the Commissioner of World Security at that moment.

Chapter Eleven

Within less than half an hour, the photograph arrived back at the Great Hall locked safely in an armour-lined attaché case carried by a security agent; a second agent carried an identical attaché case as a decoy. Two more agents, who had acted as guards, came into the auditorium, paused and positioned themselves by the door, near some of Supreme Ruler Landon's Special Operations troopers.

The agent with the photo unlocked the attaché case from the reinforced bracelet on his wrist and handed it to Miningra, who raised an eyebrow at him. The agent nodded and said, loudly enough for Ethan to hear, 'The photograph was still exactly where and as the Captain had reported it would be, but under a little more dust.'

A team of scientists had entered the auditorium a few seconds behind the special agents. Within what seemed to Ethan to be half a minute or less, the scientists were looking at the photograph through powerful, state-of-the-art photon multi-magnifiers, which transmitted their images digitally for display on the twelve-metre, high-resolution plasma screens that had descended from the ceiling around the auditorium. This definitely made it easy for everyone to see.

The initial display failed to show any position registering on the digital dials of the optical prismatic astrolabe telescope and the primitive viewscreen of a radio-electron telescope. One of the scientists, a youngish fellow with a ginger beard and long hair, operated the controls of an instrument, which started to zoom in on one dial. A photon multi-magnifier could enlarge an image up to one million times without pixilation.

It was an arduous task for them. No one knew what to look for. The multi-magnifier scanned back and forth, up and down. The computer screen in the picture displayed a number of oscillograph readouts and, while a murmur of excitement rippled about the auditorium, several scientists examined the graphs and figures on the screen to see if they would lead to the planet's location.

'Well?' asked Landon in a pre-emptory tone, after a few minutes.

'Sorry, sir,' said Dr Ranatunga, one of the scientists, in a Sri Lankan accent, 'but the figures on the screen refer to a planet that would be far too large.'

The sound and mood of disappointment filled the large room. The magnifier continued its painstaking scan. The minutes ticked by without any result, and some of the ministers began to show signs of impatience. Some disappeared for brief periods to use the toilet facilities and then returned.

Noticing a slight disruption to the paintwork at the bottom of the wall next to one of the telescopes, Ethan called out to Miningra that it seemed clear to him that something was scratched onto the wall and that, it being a black and white photograph, the marks had been highlighted a bit.

The marks were so faint that it was difficult to make out what they were. Miningra asked the ginger-bearded scientist if he could isolate that part of the photograph, blacking out the rest of the picture.

The fellow chirped, 'No problems, chief,' in an Aussie accent and manipulated the controls to enlarge that specific area and bring it into focus. As he did this, it seemed that the faint marks were just that: marks. A murmur of exacerbation and dejection followed the anticipation of what could have been. The science lab became deathly silent; no one knew what to do or say next.

Miningra seemed mesmerised, with his eyes transfixed, staring at the photograph. 'Wait a minute; let's not give up. It's got to be here. What if we look at the picture from different angles? Say, left to right or upside down, for instance.'

'Hey, that's right,' Ethan agreed. 'Try back to front.'

As the scope started to scan the photograph, the tiny marks and indentations started reading numerically. 'I knew it,' Miningra exclaimed.

Excitement spread among the people present. Ethan was beside himself; he recognised the significance of what was unfolding before his eyes: his life was about to change for ever. It appeared that, even though Seth was close to death, he was still able to disguise the co-ordinate and lateral marks and scratch them onto the wall in the dying seconds of his life. Thanks to a fifty-year-old photograph and a sixteen-year-old's memory of Seth's discovery and last dying legacy, the human race could have possibly found its way to the brink of a long-awaited miracle.

The scientists immediately keyed the co-ordinates into a large radio-electron telescope on the roof of the main building and wiped its computer's memory of all previously obtained data. Everyone in the room seemed to be holding their breath as a stream of data that really only the scientists could understand started to flood onto the overhead screens.

Finally, Dr Ranatunga spoke softly into his microphone. 'Of course, we'll have to confirm these readings with gravitational microlensing sightings from other telescopes in other parts of the world, but this does appear to be what we've been looking for.'

After initially wanting to shout 'Hooray!', Ethan felt unusually subdued, as his mind came to grips with how it must have been for Seth to be dying and still be looking out for his fellow human beings. *He must have been a hell of a man*, he thought. Even Admiral Gazers lowered his head in awe. Miningra took a drink of water.

Walking towards Ethan, Landon reached out his hand, and said, 'Well done, young man. The world owes you a huge debt; if there's anything I can ever do for you, just say the word.'

Ethan knew right away what he wanted and came right out with it. 'Yes, sir, there is something. I would like to lead the first expedition to the planet as my first mission, and I would like to take a fellow officer from the Academy with me. Admiral Gazers knows of him. In fact, they share something in common that is otherwise unique. The officer is Lieutenant Ralph Baxter, sir.'

'Ah, the young man I presented a distinction to yesterday at the Academy,' the admiral recalled. 'Yes, a real academic, that boy. Loves his dad, doesn't he?'

Landon, however, hadn't been prepared for such a huge and specific demand, and, lost for words, he turned to the admiral for support, as if to ask, *Help me out here, Harlius*.

'Ethan Knight has already been hand-picked to command his first mission upon graduation,' the admiral announced. 'Dependent upon his achieving Honours at the rank of Captain, which he's surpassed, he's also graduated as Top Gun, as an added bonus. There is no better flyer in the Elite Fleet than Captain Ethan Knight, and he's a natural-born leader. As for Lieutenant Baxter, he finished Dux of the whole Academy – something he and I have in common – and his instructors regard him as a bit of a genius when it comes to astronomic computer data. I don't have any problem with including Baxter in the mission.'

Ethan thought, *Yes, it's on – and Ralph's coming with me!*

'Well, all right!' Landon decided. 'It's settled, as far as I'm concerned, but the conditions of the motion authorising the mission require that the Assembly formally convened has to take a vote. All those in favour?'

It was unanimous.

Ethan could contain himself no longer; he clenched his fist up by his chin and let out an entirely too loud, 'Yes! Yes!' He quickly regained his composure and proceeded to thank everyone in the room, including Vice Consul Linns, whom Ethan could hardly recall seeing since shortly after he'd asked him his question.

Welcoming him to his team, Landon wished Ethan well on his most important mission, adding, 'All of us will be waiting with bated breath until you return home safely with all the answers the world is waiting for. I'm sure you can handle the huge responsibility we are placing on your shoulders.'

Wanting to savour the moment and feeling like a national treasure, Ethan straightened his back, adding a few extra millimetres to his already 183-centimetre frame, a ritual he enjoyed in moments of triumph. Landon adjourned the meeting formally and asked the admiral and Consul Linns to join him for an unofficial beverage, then suggested it would be a good idea if Miningra's agents would escort Ethan back to his hotel.

'You can take Air Force 9. My personal pilot is waiting to fly you there.'

As he made his way to the helicopter pad, Ethan thought about Seth and why his parents had never mentioned him, his being a relative and all.

Chapter Twelve

Ethan arrived back at his hotel in Landon's state-of-the-art helicopter, landing on the hotel's rooftop helipad. The flight had been an awe-inspiring experience. Landon's pilot, Skeeta, had been great; Ethan now knew how to operate all the advanced aircraft's controls, thanks to his explanations and demonstrations. Bidding Ethan a good day, he took Air Force 9 straight up and, with a trademark thrust, lurched the chopper dramatically to the right in a fine display of flying technique. Giving Ethan the thumbs-up, he quickly disappeared into the gathering haze.

Ethan could hardly wait to catch up with his dog. Jack had escaped from his enclosure when Bella accidentally left the front door slightly ajar and was waiting near the scenic elevator with his ears pricked and saliva dripping from his mouth, watching his best pal walk up the hallway towards him, confused that he was not arriving in the lift.

They both ran to greet each other. Jack skidded twenty metres past him on the highly polished marble floor: an activity they both enjoyed until one or the other gave in.

The hotel suite's door was still ajar from Jack's exit a minute before. He zoomed back through it, showing Ethan the way, and made a beeline straight to the bedroom, where he flew through the air onto the bed, landing like a torpedo. Only then did he realise that he was in the wrong bedroom. Taking the path of least resistance, he had gone through the only open door, resulting in his cannon-balling into Connor, who had been napping until the moment of impact. Jack squealed with surprise; Connor released a wordless shout and swung an arm in the dog's general direction.

Instantly awake, Connor started shouting something about sending Jack to some country where people ate dogs and took another swing at him, but he was already off, escaping the room as if he were jet-propelled. Outside, in the lounge, he took shelter between Ethan's legs.

Seeing Ethan come into the room, home from his meeting, Bella instinctively put the kettle on.

Connor emerged from his rude awakening, rubbing his tired eyes and asking, 'How'd it go today, son? Tell us all about it and try not to leave anything out.'

'Dad, Mum; it's been a pretty awesome day at times. So far. Whew! I wonder what'll come up next. Here, let me quickly change out of my uniform, and I'll tell you all.' He undid his tie as he strode into his bedroom. His uniform still looked as crisp and tidy as when he'd put it on seven hours earlier, despite the back of his shirt having been soaked with sweat.

'Wait till I tell you about what happened today,' Ethan called out through the closed bedroom door. 'It'll rock your socks off.' He usually dreaded having to endure his parents' interrogations, but that day was different. He quickly changed his clothes to keep them from waiting too long.

Already up at the table, Connor was waiting in anticipation. 'Come and sit down next to me, son; take the weight off those tired feet.' His manner was perhaps more solicitous than it might have been if he hadn't been after information.

Quickly into his stride, Ethan told them of the day's events. His parents listened intently, firing questions at him in turn. It was the sort of bunfight inquisition he had expected, knowing his parents as he did, as Connor and Bella wanted to know everything.

Forgetting to mention the previous night's events gave Ethan a bit of a breather. He hoped, he feared in vain, that they would be so distracted by the day's news that they would forget about it and not ask, but he knew it was probably too much to expect a miracle of that magnitude. Still, he pressed on, hoping for the best.

When he got to the part at which he'd figured out what the clues had been about, he paused and asked his parents, 'Before I tell you that, though, which of you can tell me about Seth Stevens?'

Connor was clearly surprised to hear Seth's name; he took a deep breath and obviously needed some effort to compose himself. 'Why do you need to know about Seth, son?'

Completely confused, Bella looked from Connor to Ethan and back again in stunned silence.

Ethan read his parents' reactions and waited for an honest answer, but, after about ten seconds, decided that he was waiting too long and asked, crisply, 'What's the big secret?'

'No secret, son. I'm just surprised to hear you ask about Seth. I haven't thought about him for years. What does he have to do with your puzzle, anyway?'

'Pretty much everything.'

'Well, of course I'll tell you about Seth.'

Bella, up to put the kettle on again, was listening intently.

'We're going back about fifty years at least here, son. I was only very young myself.' He paused and looked up, willing back ancient memories. 'Seth was an older distant cousin of mine. My grandmother and his grandmother were sisters. He was apparently a scholar of some ability. Anyway, according to my dad, he always seemed to be buried in some book or another or studying something academic on-line, and he spent quite a bit of time in the local library. He didn't have many friends and never really mixed with the family. He was a solitary soul and liked his own space. I only met him once, and, like I said, I was little. I don't really remember him or what he looked like.'

'OK Dad; what happened to him?'

'He developed a fanatical interest in astronomy – sort of like your mate Ralph – and actually built his own telescopes out of cast-off parts he'd salvaged from old twentieth-century observatories. Apparently, he was, all by himself, years ahead of teams of the world's top astronomers in the techniques of sighting and understanding gravitational microlensing, even with those primitive computers that he had to work with back then. The story goes that Seth was murdered trying to protect information about a new planet he had just discovered. No one knows if it's true or not, but it created a great deal of interest within the government agencies concerned with space and security. They never tell you just who they're working for, and the identification and warrants they flash at you don't give much away, either – or so my dad told me. They dismantled the house Seth lived in brick by brick, looking for clues to the discovery and the murder.' He sighed. 'As far as I know, they never found anything and never caught the killers.'

'Where did he live, Dad?'

'Seth lived in Kingstonia. You know, it's funny, isn't it? Seth lived just a couple of kilometres from where we live now in my parents' old home, yet we hardly ever saw him, apart from the time I told you about earlier. The first we knew of his death was when my father read about it in the local newspaper. I do remember, though, that everybody regarded it as quite a poignant story at the time. I just remember my father being given some of Seth's personal effects at the funeral and putting them up in the loft. They could still be up there in an old shoebox somewhere, probably hidden under years of your mother's old rubbish.'

'Rubbish?' exclaimed Bella. 'That's my life's story up there. All of those things will come in useful one day for Ethan, when he flies the coop and marries that Aurora girl. Pays to keep things, you know.'

'Mum!' Ethan, blushing, sounded just like an embarrassed sixteen-year-old boy.

'He won't need those minging things, babe. They've probably gone all mouldy after being up there all these years.'

'OK, can we get back to the story, please, folks?' Ethan clearly wanted to get away from the topic of his mother's saved treasures.

'Well, that's about it, really.' Connor crinkled his brow in thought. 'You know, I don't think I've ever looked inside that box myself.'

Stopping his father, Ethan said, 'I can tell you what's in the box. The shoebox was still in the loft. I found it years ago when I was exploring up there one day as a nipper.'

Bella thought, *Yeah, all those tears ago*.

'I don't remember much about the stuff in it, apart from an old photograph, which turns out to be the original of one that featured in the newspaper article.' Ethan went on to tell his parents about the rest of the day's events, including a mention of the World Security agents' visit to their home and the safe removal of the contents of the box.

'The Grand Assembly sent agents into our home?' Bella sounded as if she wasn't sure that this was a good thing.

'It saved the time it would have taken me to go get it, even using Supreme Ruler Landon's Air Force 9. You see, that photograph's the key to finding the whereabouts of the planet Seth discovered all those years ago. Scientific examination of the photo today revealed a secret set of co-ordinates and lateral marks Seth scratched on the wall moments before he died. The scientists are convinced these relate to the position of the new planet. They're checking it out now. This discovery could be vital for humanity's survival. Seth has virtually come back from the grave and could wind up receiving the credit for being the saviour of our species on this planet.' Ethan was visibly excited as he continued, 'We could rehouse the world's population overflow! Earth will be able to breathe again. We could all breathe normally again, allowing us to let our natural resources flourish and grow and renew themselves sustainably, as they did for all those thousands of years before we exhausted them.'

He paused to give his parents a chance to absorb all of what he'd been telling them, then continued, 'I'm sorry that we retrieved the picture and the contents of the box today without your knowledge, really, but Senior Minister Miningra decided that immediate and discreet action was called for, and I couldn't argue.'

After giving all this a few moments to sink in, Connor started to grin. 'Who would have believed it, eh? One of our distant relatives may be responsible for saving the planet, immortalising the family name in history. Unbelievable! Good old Seth.'

'And that's not all,' Ethan added. 'As you might have figured after our visit to Admiral Gazers' house, they've chosen me to lead the first expedition to the new planet, and Ralph will be my astronomy-computer officer, although he doesn't know it yet. We got the "Yes" vote from the Grand Assembly at the meeting today. As soon as Ralph finds out, he'll be swinging from the light shades. I think I will put a call in now to Ralph's personal portable digi-screen.'

Ralph's mother appeared on the screen in a flash, as if she had been sitting right on top of it. Before Ethan could ask, 'Where's Ralph?' his friend appeared on the screen, fighting to get his mother out of the picture, but she wasn't giving up that easily.

'Oh, come on, Mum; the call's for me,' pleaded Ralph. 'I've been waiting all day.'

She knew very well that the call was for him; she was just in a playful mood. Ralph's incessant background whimpering wasn't her idea of fun, however, so she finally gave up the position.

'How did it go, Ethan?' were the first words out of Ralph's mouth.

'Very well; very well indeed!'

'Well, what's the crack?'

'Military protocol will not allow me to divulge anything that was said at the meeting; it was all Top Secret.'

'You can trust me, Ethan; we never have any secrets.'

'This is different, Ralph: I could lose my stripes or even get court-martialled if the information I told you fell into the wrong hands. It could even be very dangerous.'

'Get real; it's just you and me here. Remember, I am supposed to be your surrogate brother.'

Ethan was stringing his pal out and enjoying every minute; it was payback time for last night. 'You don't know who is surfing the airwaves; there is such a lot of espionage going on these days. I'll tell you what: come 'round to my hotel, and we can have a more secure conversation.'

'Give me five minutes.'

Ralph rushed out the door so fast that he forgot to shut off his communicator, and Inger's face appeared again on the screen.

'Cripes, I have never seen that boy move so fast. I suppose I should log off for him. Take it easy on him, Ethan: he has been waiting all day to see you; he has no fingernails left.'

'Yes, you were a little naughty to Ralph, son.' Bella scowled gently, making her point.

Taking no notice of the beautiful décor, Ralph zoomed for the stairs like a roadrunner, bypassing the scenic lift on the way, then backtracked and came flying back down the stairs as he remembered his pal was on the thirty-third floor and wisely opted to ride the scenic lift instead.

Ralph was soon banging on Ethan's door, and in no time Ethan opened it up, giving Ralph the thumbs-up before he had even stepped inside. Ralph jumped in the air, shouting, 'Yes, yes, yes – you pulled it off! You little ripper! Where are we heading? And what's my capacity?'

'All in good time, Ralph. Let's go down to the lobby and have a melonesto; we can talk there.'

'Lead the way, Commander.'

'Captain, if you will.'

'No, they will have to make you commander, for sure, if you are going to lead a mission.'

'We will see, but I wouldn't bank on it.'

'Boys, remember we have a long journey ahead of us tomorrow,' advised Bella. 'We plan to leave very early in the morning, so don't make it a late night, please!'

'Don't worry, Mother; I'm not long for this world. I am plumb tuckered out. I've had enough excitement to last me a dozen lifetimes.'

'And there's heaps more to come,' Ralph piped up.

Chapter Thirteen

The morning following the long, arduous journey home, Ethan just lay on top of his soft, goose-down quilt, contemplating everything. He looked around his room and noticed things for the first time, although they had been there for ever, such as a family portrait and an old baseball bat from his younger induction days. Rays of sunshine beamed through his bedroom window. He caught his breath and thought about how lucky he was and how good it was to be alive. He saw things differently after his recent experiences in Nevulae, without the insulation the Academy had provided, and felt content just to breathe the fresh country air.

Stretched out next to him on the bed, Jack was snoring away, dead to the world. Neither of them wanted to make a move. Ethan couldn't resist tickling his dog under the chin with his own tail. In ecstasy, Jack stirred and raised his head, then suddenly pounced on top of his pal, licking him all over his face. Ethan played with his dog for a few minutes before getting up and putting on his favourite old cargo jeans and t-shirt. Then he said, 'Come on, then, boy – walkies!' Jumping off the bed, Jack did somersaults with happiness. They left the house before anyone else was up.

Early mornings had always been special for Ethan, especially with the turf still glistening with dew. He loved being out in the woods with his dog, watching him having fun exploring and sniffing the countless things that dogs seemed to enjoy smelling, piddling where he thought the aroma of his pee would mix well with other odours on the ground or the shrubbery, and chasing whatever wildlife or cats he spotted without a chance of catching anything. Following all this had always been good therapy for Ethan.

He sat on a rock to enjoy watching Jack and to take time out to reflect on his unexpected meetings with Aurora. Just thinking about her brought an instant grin to his face. He thought about how things could not have been better for him just then. He had graduated with the recognition he had earned, met Aurora, been assigned on his first mission – a supremely important one – with his best friend, and he had Jack with him there and then.

Only three days to go until I see Aurora again, Ethan thought, and he started counting down the hours until then.

At the family home in Corona, Ralph was still face-down, fast asleep. He had arranged to catch up with Ethan that morning and go fishing, but, as the morning rolled by, it became clear that he was going nowhere. His mother gave up trying to wake him, thinking that it would be easier to wake a hibernating bear in the middle of winter than to budge Ralph right now, so, after her last attempt in mid-morning, she just shrugged and left him to it, deciding to get back into bed herself with a cup of hot tea.

At his office in the Great Hall, Miningra had learned that news of the discovery of the matching-planet's location had leaked out to the press. The evidence was before him on his computer screen the ready-to-be-printed front page of an infamous tabloid called the *Sarantio Echo*. Miningra was sure that the *Echo*'s unprincipled editor, Tiny Tracker, had a direct inside link to large-scale organised crime around the globe. Miningra's security agents had never been able to pin any hard evidence of this to Tracker, however, even with clandestine access to the *Echo*'s computers.

Because of the extreme security measures undertaken to keep the discovery of the matching-planet's location a secret, it was obvious to Miningra that Tracker had obtained this information from an inside source. Now that the story was out, Miningra knew, his job and his life would become enormously more difficult. His people were already at the *Echo*'s offices, blocking the story's publication, but keeping the digital version from circulating on the net would be just about impossible. The dissemination of this information was bound to attract the attention of those criminals ambitious, audacious and ruthless enough to try to exploit the situation to their own advantage, with dire consequences for the future of the human race and the Earth itself. Miningra knew that some would treat this information, once they found it out, as an open invitation to extortion.

Miningra touched some controls on his desk's console and

spoke briefly into a mini-microphone sewn into the collar of his shirt. Within seconds, Tibor Links, on duty at the Security Command and Control Centre, was reviewing all the digitalised security records from the previous day's meeting, from throughout the Great Hall and compound, and regarding all the ministers, scientists, technicians, agents, troopers, pages and catering staff who had been present when the information had been aired. Within three minutes, five other agents had joined him and had started sharing the workload equally. It was a huge task.

At just about the same time, less than four minutes after Miningra had issued his orders, two of the agents who were detailed to mind the Knights reached Ethan, where he was relaxing with Jack in the woods. They displayed their ID badges and one of them, Nui Ormsby, said, 'Sorry to barge in on you like this, Captain Knight, but apparently some manure has just hit the tiller and we have orders to get you ready to be picked up by a chopper in about ten minutes to take you to a more secure location. Where that is, Agent Langley here and I don't need to know. One of our colleagues is now in your house, helping your parents get your kit packed. Let's go.'

At that exact moment, two other agents were shaking Ralph awake with the same news. The chopper would be by for him right after it picked up Ethan. Inger was simultaneously trying to get her rudely-awakened mind around what was going on and focusing on packing Ralph's kitbag, while exerting all her will to avoid going into hysterics.

When Ethan returned to his home with Agents Flint and Langley, he barely had time to hug his stunned parents, scratch Jack behind the ears and hurriedly ingest a glass of milk and a buttered roll with jam before the sound of the rotor blades of the Security NH126 helicopter descending meant it was time for him to grab his packed kitbag and head out with the agents. He barely had time to take a deep breath before striding through the front door. They rushed together towards the village green, which was about sixty metres from the Knights' house and the only place nearby where the NH126 could land.

Almost everybody in the neighbourhood came out to witness

the event. It wasn't every day that a mysterious helicopter landed on the Kingstonia village green and one of their neighbours was hustled into it by two men who were obviously World Security agents.

Chapter Fourteen

The reports coming through to Miningra on his viewscreen were all negative. His agents, along with a couple of dozen of Orlando Sung's police and Domestic Order troopers, had closed down the *Echo* to keep it from publishing the story, but they had so far been unable to find Tiny Tracker anywhere, and the evidence on Miningra's screen told him that the page of the *Echo*'s website with the story on it had received 15,837 hits before his agents could shut it down. He hadn't yet received the figures on how many times it had been forwarded and forwarded again. All the resources at the disposal of the Grand Assembly weren't nearly enough to plug a leak that size.

Highly-trained and skilled security interrogators were interviewing every member of the *Echo*'s staff, but not one of them had any idea of where Tracker was or how he'd got the story. Several suggested where he might be, but security agents had already searched those well-known haunts and had found no sign of him. Other agent-and-interrogator teams were calling on his family and known associates, but so far they had found nothing. Miningra felt it was likely that he had taken a new identity and fled far away.

Miningra checked his screen to make sure that his order to put the highest level of protection on everyone with knowledge of the matching-planet or the mission to it, and on their families, had been carried out. This had meant working with Orlando Sung, who commanded an enormously larger number of police and Domestic Order troopers than Miningra had agents. He didn't like working with Sung. The man, as far as he was concerned, was a brutal thug with no finesse and only minimal discretion.

Vice Consul Linns sat in one of the visitors' chairs in Miningra's office. He was, to Miningra's mind, about as helpful as a fart in a space suit. He didn't offer much help or support, seeming to be mostly content just to sit and listen, and Linns was listening. As he did so, he rested his hand under his very pronounced chin and wore a blank look.

Miningra leaned back, put his hands behind his head and closed his eyes. Before he was able to gather his thoughts, the sound of the touchtone code of Admiral Gazers' personal security module activating came from his console and the admiral himself started to appear on his main screen.

'Miningra.' The digitalised and encrypted-then-decrypted process transmitting his voice and image did nothing to remove the complex web of emotions in his voice and face.

'Harlius Fonce,' replied Miningra, shaking his great head slowly with sadness and shame.

Admiral Gazers held up a copy of a printout of the *Sarantio Echo* website, with the headline Miningra already knew all too well: '**We Are Saved. Young Flying Ace Solves 50-Year-Old Mystery – The Planet Has Been Found**.' 'Do you have any idea yet how this could have happened?' he asked, his voice now all business.

'First of all, my friend,' Miningra responded, 'I want you to know that, from my perspective, this should not have been able to happen at all. As you know, our security systems and procedures are robust, thorough and sophisticated. I am responsible for their operation, which makes me ultimately responsible for this breach. I have been inadequate.'

'Oh, cut out the self-pity, man! What are you doing about it now?'

Miningra quickly briefed him about his immediate operations in regard to Tracker and the *Echo*, and to the personal security step-up for those who were suddenly much more greatly at risk. 'The next step, of course, really needs to have Assembly approval, but I'm about to take what measures I can.'

'I'm with you.'

'Right. Since our immediate review of all systems confirmed that physical and electronic security barriers have not been breached, we'll obviously have to monitor and investigate everyone we're protecting…'

'And, in some cases, that would be politically disastrous without the ministers' go-ahead. So you do think, as I do, that it's an inside job.'

'With the information I have, that seems the only likely explanation, yes.'

'So, how are we going to find this traitor?'

'No one is beyond suspicion now, Admiral; not even I!'

'You are one of my oldest and trusted friends, Miningra, and I would consider you as much beyond suspicion as myself,' Admiral Gazers assured him.

'It's going to have to be a process of elimination, Admiral, and it's not going to be easy. There were 237 people present at the meeting, and, as you know, all of us – and this includes scientists, agents, troopers and computer, sound and lighting technicians, as well as pages, secretaries, tea-servers and ministers – passed stringent screening processes before being cleared to enter the building. Even we will have to consent to the scrutinising process; hopefully; our example will serve as an example to others. No one will be exempt from the procedure, no matter what his or her rank.

'Still, someone has managed to slip the net. Since the security systems themselves weren't breached, the traitor must have passed the information to Tracker after leaving the compound yesterday afternoon or evening. I've started investigations of the movements, activities, and contacts of everyone except the ministers; I'll call a Special Emergency Assembly Meeting for this afternoon and get that cleared,' Miningra promised.

At this point Vice Consul Linns, who had remained completely silent, smugly uttered the words 'Kang-Lee. Mind, if I sit here for a while, chaps?'

Miningra cringed at the sound of that name.

'It's obvious; let's face it: he's the only man for the job. You seemed to have made a right pig's ear out of things so far, Miningra. Well, am I wrong?'

'I hate to say this, my old friend, but I agree with Linns: not about the pig's ear remark, but about Kang-Lee. He may have just come up with the solution we have been looking for.'

'How do you mean?' Miningra asked the admiral.

'Well, as we all know, Kang-Lee is the commander of the elite Black Berets, the most feared and ferocious battle-hardened soldiers on the planet. His special forces can only be redeployed in a Code Red situation, and only on Ziekiel Landon's orders. Once active, martial law will instantly be in force; even our Supreme Ruler cannot intervene until the mission has come to a successful conclusion, and to this day Kang-Lee has an unrivalled 100 per cent success rate. Commander Lee and his army have been stood down for over a decade now. To be precise, Admiral,' Vice Consul Linns continued, 'Kang-Lee was declared a national hero and retired, after emphatically defeating the irregulars at the Inter-Secular Area Revolt in '39. He was so badly injured during that epic battle! He is now a captive prisoner of his victorious exploits and of our harsh environment, living under the crucial protection of a specially-designed and engineered body suit that keeps his flesh and body organs away from Earth's polluted atmosphere. A simple miniscule droplet of rain could immobilise him instantly, and, without medical incubation and the immediate administering of specially-cultivated protein enzymes, it could prove fatal. However, this affliction has in no way affected his ability to enforce the law; in fact, he is even more menacing than ever.'

'If I remember, that was a very one-sided bloody battle; nearly 15,000 soldiers fell on a single day,' Miningra recalled. 'Is that the kind of example and history lesson we want our siblings to be taught at preparatory school? I, for one, don't think so.'

'I am aware of how you feel, Miningra, but this may come as a shock to you: I was one of the co-ordinators responsible for the implementing of the fight plans during that particular battle. I can tell you, I have had many a sleepless night because of that altercation.'

'Forgive me, Admiral; I was not casting aspersions of any guilt, but, if I am reading this right, you want me to hand over all security matters to a loose cannon so that Kang-Lee can apply his legendary heavy-handed tactics to all and sundry. I cannot see the need to adopt that kind of radical action.'

'Miningra, this is not personal and I feel no offence, but you must see that, without martial law, our hands are completely tied. We have to abide by Assembly guidelines. Kang-Lee will implement his own regime; he will have the ability to cross any boundary. It seems to be our only logical option.'

'Unless you have a much better idea, Miningra? Linns asked. 'I thought not. I guess that's it, then?'

'I will recommend our plan of action to Ziekiel Landon immediately,' said the admiral. 'Linns, you will secure any outside links and advise them of our plan and of Kang-Lee's involvement; that will shake the cobwebs out of a few ministers' behinds.'

Chapter Fifteen

Aurora was a bit perturbed by having both Willis and Lopez riding in the front of the Roller along with Clive, but she understood that there had been some sort of security alert, for some reason nobody would tell her, and that there was nothing she could do about it.

She was on her way to her meeting with the Children of the Underground at Glebe Hall. She glanced down at her pocket computer and went over the lesson plan she had prepared on the scientific method and its application to popular superstitions, thinking of how important it would be to these children's lives to be able to think clearly when confronted by nonsense presented as truth, and not to be taken in by it.

Clive eased the Roller down onto its tyres right in front of Glebe Hall. After telling Aurora to stay put until they returned, Willis climbed out of the limo with Lopez and they went into the hall with their instruments to give it a good security sweep.

'Oh, Clive,' Aurora complained, 'I do wish we didn't have to go through all this security folderol. It's – it's unnatural!'

'Ah, if only we had a natural world to live in, Miss Aurora. But, in unnatural environments, people must use unnatural-seeming methods to survive.'

Aurora looked about, up and down the block. It appeared to her that there was a greater-than-usual number of troopers about, and several of them seemed to be doing nothing but guarding the approaches to the Roller. 'Security is an illusion, anyway,' she sulked. 'I do know the limits of our geological understanding, after all, and, as far as anybody knows, there could be an earthquake or something in the next few seconds that would kill us all. That would at least be natural.'

Clive chuckled. 'It would indeed. All Willis and I can do is protect you from unnatural dangers, and we will at any cost. It is a strange world we live in.'

Willis appeared in the doorway to Glebe Hall and sent Clive a hand signal while speaking into his collar mini-mike, telling him that the coast was clear. Clive climbed out of the Roller, locking his door behind him, and then used his remote to open Aurora's door. As Aurora emerged from the back of the limo, another agent seemed to materialise out of nowhere to help Clive escort her into the hall. Aurora rolled her eyes and sighed. All three went to the Roller's boot to get the cartons of food Aurora had brought for the children.

Half-a-dozen children were already in the hall, waiting for her, when she, Clive and the agent who had escorted her from the Roller to the hall, whose name was Payne Samuels, came through the front door, carrying the crates and cartons of food. Aurora greeted each child by name.

Willis, Lopez, and Flint made themselves unobtrusive near the doors: Lopez and Flint by the double front door, Willis by the rear side door. Only Clive stayed with Aurora.

The children helped Aurora and Clive put the food out on a long trestle table, which already held stacks of clean plates and piles of clean cutlery that the children had already brought out from the cupboard. None of them made any move to eat any of the food. They were in the habit of waiting until everyone was present and ready.

Over the next ten minutes, the rest of the children arrived, either singly or in groups of two, three or four. Many were ragged, but others wore sturdy clothing that Aurora had provided. Most wore clothes that were more or less too small for them, as they had begun to grow more quickly than before, thanks to better nutrition. All of them were reasonably clean. Most came in through the back door, which led out into a rubbish-cluttered alley. They cleared the rubbish away from behind the hall once a week, but more always seemed to appear there within a day or so.

The children didn't seem to have an organisation or leaders, but some of the more mature ones had taken on responsibilities and informal roles. Two of those who had already been at the hall when Aurora had arrived were a boy and a girl named Houtchins and Sylvia. Few of the children knew for sure exactly how old they really were, but Aurora guessed that these two were eleven or twelve. Sylvia and Houtchins had a keen interest in knowing what was going on – and which way the wind was blowing – in the complex societies of gangs, extended families, tribes, clans and sub-groups that coexisted in various ways in the crowded undergrounds of Nevulae and Sarantio. Other children looked to these two sometimes for guidance in steering a more or less safe path through their world.

Houtchins and Sylvia had much that they wanted to tell Aurora and Clive about that morning as they set the food out. A large and powerful criminal organisation called the Bang Gang had been more active than usual over the past few days, making life more difficult for the Children of the Underground in particular.

Sylvia told them that she'd heard that 'a couple of their hard-boys had grabbed little Donny near his kip and were asking him all kinds of questions about what goes on at Glebe Hall. They were hitting him and kicking him to make him talk. Mereline and Satira saw the whole thing from their hideout, only about three metres away. They'll tell you. Then the Bang Gang hard-boys hauled him away, and nobody's seen him since. This was yesterday.'

Clive said, 'Excuse me for a moment,' and he walked over to the back door to relay this intelligence to Willis, who took out his pocket computer-communicator and started talking into his collar mini-mike.

Houtchins, not wanting to be outdone in the serious information sweepstakes, said that he had also noticed something interesting. 'Yeah, little Mickey and some other bloke I talked to told me it's been going on for a while, but I've only seen it myself over the past couple of days…'

'Oh, get to the point, Houtchins,' Sylvia snapped. 'If you don't give it to Aurora straight and without all the lead-up fluff, then I will.'

Clive returned from giving the word to Willis.

'OK! OK! I was just stalling until Clive got back.'

Clive said, 'Thanks, Houtchins, my man,' and started slicing tomatoes.

'Anyway,' – Houtchins was now ready to get to the point – 'there's blokes about recruiting people for what they calls a militia, which sounds like kind of a private army?'

'That's what a militia usually is,' Aurora confirmed for him.

'They're recruiting kids, too; they don't care. And they're paying people good money to join. They make a big deal outta having a big bankroll; they say that Someone Big is behind it, but they won't say who.'

Clive let out a long breath, put down the chef's knife and strolled back over to Willis by the back door. Aurora tried not to feel too anxious. This did not seem to her as if it were just another day at Glebe Hall.

When all thirty-seven of the Children of the Underground, except Donny, had arrived, they gathered around the table with Aurora and Clive.

'We are gathered here together,' Aurora said, in her public-speaking voice, 'because we are a real and true family, and to eat food to make our bodies strong, and to learn things to make our minds strong, and to do this together, to help make our family strong.' She paused. 'May as well eat now, aye?'

The children all started eating. A year before, when Aurora had first started bringing them food, they had attacked it with desperation. By this point, they were less afraid that they would not have anything else decent to eat for a long time and ate more calmly.

Clive and Aurora stepped back and watched them, feeling good about what they saw.

Then the floor in the middle of the room exploded upwards.

Fortunately, nobody had been standing over the explosion, but, unfortunately, the explosion had been caused by the shell of a Bitsminov-15 compact artillery piece fired up from a tunnel the Bang Gang had dug under Glebe Hall and was followed by a squad of ten hard-boys with assault weapons.

Pulling out his own Stechkin nine-millimetre compact automatic handgun, Willis noted that the hard-boys did not have their assault weapons blazing nine-millimetres rounds all around Glebe Hall. With society spiralling out of control, the Grand Assembly had given up on enforcing gun control underground, but Miningra had come up with the idea of severely limiting the production and distribution of gun ammunition outside secure military channels, thus making bullets scarce and expensive for criminals and not to be wasted.

Going into their crouch positions, Willis, Lopez, and Flint managed to put some bullets into an emerging hard-boy each. Three hard-boys, coming out of the hole on the side obstructed from the agents' view by smoke, picked out targets and started firing. Willis, talking urgently into his collar mini-mike, hit the floor flat on his belly, rolled and crawled behind a storage trunk. Lopez and Flint, while each managing to hit another hard-boy on the way down, were hit themselves.

With Willis pinned down on the floor behind the trunk by sporadic automatic-weapon fire, three hard-boys made a move to grab Aurora. Shouting, 'Hold it right there, dolly,' one of them held a gun on her and Clive while two more rushed up with nasty-looking electrical cords.

As soon as they reached her, Clive, using the hard-boys with the cords as human shields against the one holding the gun on him, moved like a lightning-cat to grab the chef's knife off the table and bury it deep within the abdomen of one of the hard-boys trying to tie Aurora up. Aurora herself then brought a knee up into the other one, slammed her boot down onto the top of his foot and clipped him one behind the ear with the heel of her hand. Willis managed to get off a burst of shots in the general direction of the one holding the gun on her, causing him to dive for the floor, just as troopers came pouring in through both doors, ruthlessly shooting the remaining hard-boys.

With Willis shouting, 'Don't kill 'em all! I need prisoners for interrogation!', Clive scooped Aurora from her feet and carried her under his arm like a bag of laundry at a dead run out the front door and straight to the Roller Glider, which was surrounded by troopers, unlocking it with his remote while running at full speed. Clive stuffed her into the back seat, got behind the controls, locked all doors and windows and said, 'Time to go home, Miss Aurora.'

Chapter Sixteen

After the World Security NH126 helicopter picked up Ralph, he and Ethan rode in silence for a few minutes. Ralph was still barely awake and Ethan was stunned.

Finally, Ralph rubbed his eyes a few times, ran his hands back through his truly wild-looking hair and looked around. 'I suppose there's no real point in asking you where we're going.'

'None at all,' responded the agent, smiling. 'I don't have a clue myself. The only ones who know our destination are the pilot and the co-pilot, and, as you can see, they have their heads in those unsociable helmet-headsets and wouldn't hear a word you're saying if you asked them, anyway.' He laughed, and Agent Ormsby laughed cheerfully along with him.

Ralph accepted this in the spirit in which it was given and turned to Ethan. 'Well, mate,' he said, with growing excitement, 'I wish I could think of something cool and memorable to say right now, but it looks like this is it.'

'Yeah.' Ethan sounded less than excited.

'What's the matter, pal? We're off to save the world under your command. You could at least seem to be, well, focused.'

Ethan lifted his chin and turned to face him. 'Yeah, I know. I just wish we'd been off to save the world under my command a few days later, that's all.'

'Oh,' said Ralph, as the penny dropped. 'Aurora.'

'We don't need to talk about it. Listen, Ralph: I want you to swear on your oath as my blood-brother that you won't tell anybody at wherever we're going about me and Aurora. I mean, people may twig on that I've met someone, but who she is isn't something I want out until I'm ready to make it public. Understand me?'

'Loud and clear.'

'Oath as a blood-brother?'

Ralph put his left hand over his mouth and raised his right

arm straight up in the air, then swung his hand, palm-down, first left and then right. He took his hand off his mouth and, with his right arm still in the air, said, 'Oath of blood.'

Agents Ormsby and Flint watched this performance with amazement. Then they glanced at each other, smiled and repeated Ralph's oath together in unison, before they broke up laughing.

Watching them, Ralph said, 'I wonder if there's anything to eat aboard this bucket. I haven't had any breakfast yet.'

Ethan thought about that for a moment. 'Yeah. Me neither.'

Agent Flint reached into a sack and pulled out a handful of energy bars. 'They're not exactly a cheese omelette, but I think they're all we have.' Flint made it clear that he considered a cheese omelette in the morning to be a standard for civilisation.

The NH126 landed about half an hour later on a pad at the huge Universal Defence Fleet base at Elsmere, about fifty kilometres from the other side of Nevulae. There, the agents turned Ralph and Ethan over to an easy-going, young-looking officer, who told them, 'Welcome back home to the military, Captain, Lieutenant. I'm Commodore Yitzhak Abramov, and I have responsibility for secure logistics for this sector. It's my job now to get you secretly and in one piece to your secret base. Follow me.'

He led them into a nondescript-looking concrete-block shed housing the top entrance to a lift. They went down maybe twelve or thirteen metres in the lift and got out in a large underground hangar housing an odd-looking two-layered craft, about nine metres long by three metres wide by five metres tall, set on wide-gauge rail tracks.

'The Pescara Quadro,' Abramov told them, with a melodra-matic sweep of his arm. 'Looks like a couple of panini stacked on top of each other, doesn't it? Let's go.'

The three of them climbed up the fold-down stairway into the Quadro and strapped themselves into seats on the lower level. The stairway retracted into the fuselage behind them and the Quadro immediately started to travel at a fairly rapid clip along the tracks through a series of tunnels, making rapid, high-G turns both left and right. It seemed to Ethan like an amusement-park ride he'd been on when he'd been about five years old.

After eight or nine minutes, they emerged from the tunnel into a short transport corridor set into a remote section of the rugged ranges inland from the base. The Quadro's wheels retracted and it proceeded along the corridor for about 500 metres as a low-level hovercraft as rotors extended from its top section, then it lifted off the ground and flew as a helicopter up and through several mountain passes, emerging over the sea at a remote location.

Fixed wings then extended out from between the Quadro's two levels, a jet engine fired up, the rotors retracted and they flew through grey skies over grey ocean. The Quadro, at least, had facilities for making reconstituted hot meals, and, after eating hot synthetic-beef sandwiches with microwave-baked potatoes and hot mugs of tea, Ethan and Ralph were even able to doze off in the Quadro's comfortable seats. About four hours after leaving Elsmere, they came again into sight of land, barely visible in the low cloud cover and mist. The pilot took the craft straight for the rock wall of a 200-metre high cliff. Ralph and Ethan were certain that there had been some kind of malfunction or miscalculation and that they were going to die ironically in a fiery ball without fulfilling their mission, but, at what seemed the last moment, a giant doorway hissed open in the side of the cliff. The Quadro entered another tunnel, the wings retracted and it began proceeding along an underground corridor on low hover. Then its wheels extended back down and the pilot put the craft down gently, moving forward, on another set of tracks.

What a pilot! thought Ralph and Ethan simultaneously. *What a craft!*

The Quadro took them down a wide-spiralling tunnel deep into the Earth. 'Consider yourselves lucky, gentlemen,' Abramov told them. 'The risk of a security lapse means we only use the Quadro and the cliff door on absolutely top-priority missions. Most of the few people who come to Mount Love Space Base arrive by somewhat less elegant means.'

'Mount Love!' Ethan exclaimed. 'I read about this place in history class last year at the Academy. I thought it was abandoned and deserted.'

'You would, wouldn't you?' Abramov smiled. 'That shows

that we've been successful in keeping it a secret.' He chuckled, rather smugly. 'No one outside the base who doesn't need to know it's here knows about it. The admiral has even managed to hide its budget, which is enormous, from the rest of the Assembly somehow, spreading it out throughout the entire Universal Defence Fleet budget.' He sighed. 'A work of pure genius.'

After descending for what seemed to be a long time, the Quadro finally emerged from the tunnel at the edge of what had to be the launch area, because there was the Eden-II exploration vessel standing proud and tall atop a giant launch booster rocket in the middle of what certainly looked like a launch pad, almost sensuous in its functional perfection.

'Your command, Captain Knight,' Abramov said, smiling.

'It's – it's beautiful,' breathed Ethan.

Chapter Seventeen

After the gruelling events of the day, Admiral Gazers thought he would have Clive drive him to the Carlton Club for a well-earned nightcap. He suspected that a few of his fellow ministers would have had the same idea, especially Biker and Miningra.

Biker, as predicted, was holding the floor, surrounded by fellow officers, acting out one of his famous animated adventures. Admiral Gazers silently guessed that it was the battle of Klintok Ridge.

'Still on the ridge, Biker?' he laughed.

'All right, Admiral, but the kids love it; besides that, it's a really good story and one of my best.'

His audience agreed wholeheartedly.

Miningra joined the admiral and quickly advised him that there was a strong contingent of heavily-armed soldiers milling around both inside and outside the club, but he hadn't spotted Kang-Lee's presence yet.

Admiral Gazers answered, 'He's here; I can feel him. I can feel his penetrating eyes.'

To Miningra's astonishment, he had just spotted Kang-Lee positioned high on the mezzanine floor, looking him straight in the eye.

'You are right, Admiral: he's here. Something must be going down. I can hardly breathe with all the muscle and weaponry in this room.'

By now, Kang-Lee had descended from his perch and was in the process of making his presence felt. The whole crowd parted like the Red Sea for Moses to let him through, such was the extreme effect that his intimidating persona had on people.

'Come on, Miningra, let's make a move. I cannot be doing with such overkill.'

'I am with you on that one, Admiral; shall I lead the way?'

Outside the club, Miningra noted that armed troopers were

lining the tree-shaded footpaths along the Carlton Club's quiet street. Being head of World Security, he thought this was ridiculous. He felt an impulse to approach Kang-Lee and tell him to back off a bit with the strong-arm tactics, but he was far too tired.

He was about to join Admiral Gazers in the back seat of the Roller when a nondescript black vanguard came screeching around a corner of the street, entirely too fast, and rammed the admiral's Roller Glider. A crew of armed men in balaclavas leapt through the limo's one open, and therefore unlocked, door. One clubbed Clive over the head with some kind of cosh and tried to take over the driver's seat. Five others knocked Miningra to the ground – no small achievement, considering his size – and started pulling the admiral out of the vehicle.

Within moments, Kang-Lee had the situation under control, his troopers restraining the would-be abductors and he himself issuing orders to seal off the area, as if this were what he'd expected to happen all along.

Miningra's adrenaline had made his tiredness disappear, but he decided to leave the business of securing the scene and in general completing the job to Kang-Lee, who was doing it anyway. Orlando came strolling out of the club and stood off to one side of the scene, observing Kang-Lee's performance with hard eyes but saying nothing.

Biker, hearing all the commotion going on outside, raced to get a glimpse of what was happening. He was shocked to see the admiral's Roller Glider pushed up against a concrete lamppost, badly crumpled, with troopers climbing all over it. He tried to approach the Roller, but one of the troopers stopped him, saying, 'I'm sorry, sir, but this is a crime scene and it is quarantined pending the completion of a forensic examination.'

Why can't these muscle-brained thugs talk in plain language? he thought, before Miningra grabbed his arm and pulled him off to one side.

'What's going on, Miningra?' he demanded. 'Why is Gazers' Roller pushed up against that lamppost? Is he still inside?'

'Kang-Lee seems to have foiled an attempt to abduct the admiral,' Miningra told him. 'That black Ford rammed the Roller and those second-rate ninjas coshed Clive, blind-sided me and grabbed Harlius Fonce.' He gestured at the half-dozen black-clad men in handcuffs, whom the troopers were already loading into a paddy wagon.

'Yeah, but where's the admiral? Is he hurt? Is he OK?'

'I told you, they knocked me over. By the time I got up, there was so much activity going on around here that I didn't see him, and I still haven't. It all happened too fast. Troopers were swarming all over him. One minute he was sitting in the Roller; the next minute, he was gone.'

Miningra noticed Orlando make a gesture at Kang-Lee, who reported to him on the double. Orlando leaned forward and bit off what seemed to be some orders directly into Kang-Lee's ear, so close that Miningra couldn't read his lips at the distance he was from them: about five metres. Kang-Lee nodded abruptly, saluted and returned to his men.

Clive, who had been lying unconscious, with a trickle of blood coming from his scalp, on the front seat of the Roller Glider, started to come around. A couple of troopers helped him out of the Roller. He was rubbing his head and seemed groggy, as if he were in a sort of daze. He started asking the troopers where he was and what was happening. One of the troopers' officers started firing questions at him. He seemed confused and kept saying, 'Get me the hell out of here. I want to go home.'

Admiral Gazers, who had been taken back into the club as a precautionary measure, now returned to the scene, flanked by troopers carrying riot shields. An armoured assault module pulled up outside the club, and the admiral and Orlando quickly climbed inside, with a couple of troopers following behind.

Kang-Lee then looked around and signalled to a sergeant, and, within a minute, a squad of troopers bundled Clive into a waiting armoured surface van, which sped off, leaving heaps of rubber behind. Miningra thought he saw Clive wearing handcuffs, but he couldn't be certain, so he turned to Biker, saying, 'I have to find out what's going on here. Surely Clive isn't a suspect?'

The vanguard carrying Clive had taken off in a completely different direction to that of the armoured vehicle with Orlando and the admiral. Miningra thought this strange. He decided to get back to the security of his office at the Great Hall, where he would be in instant communication with all the far-flung resources of his global agency, to try to resolve what was going on.

Everything was still buzzing outside the club, and troopers were searching every square centimetre when they weren't throwing their weight around. Miningra found all this disconcerting. In his mind, the last thing the world needed was a global police state. That would make a few creeps incredibly powerful and a few more even richer, but it would take up all the scarce resources available and then some, and, with a population the size of humankind's, it would never be completely successful. It would also go against everything he had worked for all his political life. It would be a disaster for hundreds of millions – if not billions – of people. Then he wondered why he was thinking this. He tried to articulate in his own mind what there was about the way Orlando and Kang-Lee operated, and about this whole situation, that suggested this to him.

Biker had managed to commandeer a transporter to get them back to headquarters. Inside the module, Miningra activated his pocket communicator and made some urgent enquiries. He could glean no meaningful news about what had happened either to Admiral Gazers or to Clive. He considered the option of initiating Code Solo, a direct communication band straight to Supreme Ruler Landon, but decided to wait until he got to his command centre.

Miningra felt better once he was back in his office, working with his resources as Commissioner for World Security. Biker, however, was starting to be a pain. He strode up and down in what limited space there was to do so amongst the technological hardware in the room. 'I don't trust that Kang-Lee,' he kept repeating, and, 'The bloke's a loose cannon,' and, 'How did we ever let that Orlando Sung let him have so much power?'

Biker went to lean over Miningra's shoulder to punch in the access code for Code Red, but Miningra grabbed his wrist with a painfully powerful grip. 'Don't be a muscle-head, Biker,' he purred, with that I'm-in-control-now tone in his deep voice. 'This is too important to go off half-cocked.'

'Half-cocked? We're talking about the safety of the admiral!'

'Who just' – he gestured towards one of his screens – 'entered his iris pattern in the scanner at the security gate by Military Vehicle Dock Three and is currently being screened by the cranial logger.'

Three minutes later, the admiral walked through the door, looking tired and drained, followed by Kang-Lee and Orlando Sung, who looked as hard and grim as ever. The admiral looked at Biker and Miningra and said, 'Christ, you two look like hell. Biker, you need a drink.'

Chapter Eighteen

The four ministers and Kang-Lee walked to the lounge in Miningra's suite, two doors down from his office, Biker firing questions of the 'Will somebody please tell me what the hell is going on?' variety and Kang-Lee making 'Hang on a minute, Biker' responses the entire way.

As they settled into their lounge seats with their beverages of choice (a Czech Pilsner for Biker; distilled water through a straw for Kang-Lee; coffee for Miningra, Admiral Gazers and Orlando Sung), Kang-Lee said, 'OK, Biker; it's time for me to make my report to this *ad hoc* security committee of the Assembly now.' He sipped some water through his face-guard before continuing. 'Orlando received a report from the Nevulae Municipal Police that one of their detectives had received a tip-off from an informer, saying that an attempt to abduct the admiral was in the works for last night. He informed me, as the Commander of the SOF, and delegated the job of preventing the snatch to me. I immediately assigned personnel and hardware to cover the admiral's route home from here: all the cross streets, choke points, high ground, underground access and cross-tunnels; Miningra, you know the drill. What I failed to count on was you ministers' – he put a faint but unmistakable touch of disrespect into the word – 'deciding on the spur of the moment to have a drink or three at the Carlton Club. You threw a spanner in my works. Sure, I was able to redeploy personnel and hardware to the club in time, but I couldn't cover all possible approaches immediately. The attackers' module must have slipped into some nearby garage before my cordon was in place.'

He looked slowly at each minister in turn. 'If they got word of the admiral's change in plans at the same time I did, or sooner, they would have to have been given the news by somebody on the inside: either by a minister or a member of his entourage.'

'Now,' – here Orlando picked up the thread – 'the admiral

told me on the way over here that the only people with whom he discussed his change of plans before getting into the car were you two.' He pointed individually at Miningra and Biker.

'Yes,' said Miningra, 'that's right. And I touched in the code to notify Security and Domestic Order of the change in plans, which is how you found out, Kang-Lee, which means the traitor could be someone in one of our departments. I think the presence of a bug penetrating the Great Hall electronic cordon is quite unlikely, considering the number of reviews we've run today.'

'Unless our traitor is involved in the reviews.'

'So,' reflected Admiral Gazers, 'what it boils down to is that either one of us is the traitor, or we have a mole in either World Security or Domestic Order, who could be relaying our private conversations, even this one, to some unknown organisation that seems keen to bring us down – and the human race with us – and our multi-billion-money-unit security system has failed because of it.'

'I would think the latter is extremely unlikely, if not impossible,' said Miningra, 'or our scanners would have picked up on the presence of some unauthorised transmission from this building. All our systems have been on highest alert. A lone operator couldn't compromise all our back-ups and cross-systems. It's just not possible to get a transmission out without its coming to my attention; the technology just doesn't exist.'

'There is, of course, another possibility,' Kang-Lee announced: 'one that I have taken the initiative to investigate.'

Miningra looked at him dubiously and asked, 'What's that?'

Kang-Lee sipped some water through his straw before answering. 'Clive knew of the admiral's change in plans as soon as you got into the limo and told him where to go. He could have sent out a signal as soon as you left the security area. This makes him a prime suspect. Until we can safely eliminate him from our enquiries, he will remain in custody, locked in a secure prison cell, along with the other perpetrators.'

'You can't be serious!' exclaimed the admiral. 'Clive is one of the family. I trust him with my life, and, more than that, I trust him with my daughter's life. He risked his life to protect her yesterday, killing a gangster in the process, and he risked his life trying to protect me at the Carlton Club, sustaining what could be a serious injury in the process. That doesn't sound like he's one of them to me. Clive needs to be commended for his bravery – not locked up!'

'Let me ask you this,' interjected Miningra quickly: 'have you found a bug on Clive's person or in the Roller? You have done a forensic on the Roller, haven't you?'

'It's ongoing now. I could call the lab to see if it's done yet. Of course, he could have disposed of the bug some time between when he sent the signal and when you left the club. Nobody was watching him. It would've been easy. And, if he did, it could be anywhere between the Great Hall and the club.'

'Which proves nothing. Without a bug, all you have is supposition and yeah-well-maybe-technically-possible. Where's your proof?'

'The investigation is proceeding. I'll keep you informed.'

'Clive will be climbing the walls,' observed Biker. 'Look, it's just not possible, Kang-Lee. It's absurd. What planet are you on, for goodness' sake? Clive wouldn't hurt a fly – unless the fly seemed likely to harm one of the Gazers.'

'I am only doing my duty,' Kang-Lee said, blandly. 'I'm sorry that you feel the need to question my actions. Intelligence reports show a different side to Clive's supposedly squeaky-clean existence; there's a much darker and sinister side to the story.' He paused for another sip of water, more for effect than for thirst, before continuing.

'Clive is one of a pair of identical twins. When he was fourteen, his parents, his brother Clarence and he had to flee Cape Town for Toza, a province far up the coast. My reports indicate that his father, Phoenix van der Poel, had made some dangerous enemies within the devolutionist movement, who put out a contract on his life. Phoenix quickly became prominent in the coffee trade, upon which Toza's economy depends, and then basically bought himself a seat in Toza's Congress and began to bleed the system dry. Within two years, the family had become extremely wealthy and Phoenix had established an extensive network of corruption and politically-protected crime. Clive's mother, Cecilia, managed to send the twins to boarding college so that they wouldn't get mixed up in their father's criminal activities.'

After sipping more water, Kang-Lee continued. 'Then, while on summer camp somewhere in Borneo's dense jungle when he was fourteen years old, Clarence mysteriously vanished without a trace. Word came back to the family that headhunters may have been responsible, even though they hadn't been in the area for over sixty years. Phoenix took the news hard. He became a recluse and never appeared in public again. The arrogant criminal Phoenix had been bad enough, but the erratic and mentally disordered version was more than Cecilia could deal with. She finally divorced him and took Clive to Tikata, well away from Toza and Phoenix. Phoenix eventually died, pretty much from self-neglect. Cecilia still lives in Tikata and works as a missionary.

'In the mid twenties Clive joined a local militia during the Corporation Wars and quickly became known as "The General", leading his band of labourers and subsistence and tenant farmers to startling victories over battle-hardened professional mercenaries. After the wars, Clive got elected to Toza's Congress with some eighty per cent of the votes in his district, but, immediately after the election, he announced that he was not going to take his seat in Congress and promptly disappeared from public view, without a bank account or any other appearance in public records except for his driver's licences.'

Kang-Lee sipped some more water before concluding, 'And then he surfaces, after all this time, conveniently installed within the sanctuary of your own home, Admiral, as a man with no past. I think it's quite plausible that Clive could be our mole.'

Miningra leaned back and locked his hands over his head. He narrowed his eyes and seemed to be trying to stare through Kang-Lee's face-guard. 'So?' His voice, although extremely quiet, as they were in a small room, had razor edges all over it. 'So Clive was once highly regarded as a military and political leader in Africa. That's not a crime. I must say, though, that your dossier arouses my curiosity on a number of points. Yes, I would like to know why he abandoned his public career and has kept it secret. I would also like to know how you acquired such a thorough historical dossier in the short time since you arrested him.'

Orlando interceded on Kang-Lee's behalf over this. 'We in Domestic Order are a particularly competent, resourceful and energetic team, Minister. I take it that your people in Security would find this level of performance unusual?'

Miningra grunted, his face showing that he was enormously unconvinced.

'Listen,' the admiral said, leaning forward and pointing with his finger as he talked. 'My daughter Aurora loves Clive dearly, and nothing really escapes her. I mean, her powers of observation, analysis and judgement are extraordinary – and this isn't just a proud papa speaking. Her achievements in many fields are not only recognised by leading academics and researchers; they're also well documented in the public record. If I have to choose between her judgements, based on close observation over an extended period of time, and your suspicions, based on a flimsy dossier prepared over the space of an hour, Kang-Lee… well, there's just no competition, as far as I'm concerned.'

The admiral started to sit back, having had his say, but, within about a second and a half, another thought occurred to him and he leaned forward, jabbing with his forefinger again. 'And, anyway, what's so bad about being modest and humble? So he used to be a military and political success and doesn't want to talk about it; so what? Maybe he experienced things in battle and in politics he'd much rather forget. I can understand that entirely. Maybe, instead of arresting him on this information, we should recognise him as a world hero!'

'Yeah, I don't buy it,' added Biker. 'There's no possible way he's a traitor. I'll stake my life on it. We all have our little demons to contend with: good, bad and indifferent. I'm sure as hell still dealing with my own, but that doesn't make me a bad person, either.'

Orlando and Kang-Lee took this defence in silence, unmoved. Orlando's face gave nothing away; Kang-Lee's face-guard hid any feelings he may have had. They appeared to be waiting for something with fine patience.

'And another thing.' The admiral was still leaning forward. 'Your dossier contains at least one factual error. Clive didn't "surface, conveniently installed" in my household. He came to me, highly recommended, from the employ of a trusted friend and former colleague of mine, Captain Nash Cousins. Your red-hot, convict-on-sight dossier missed that easy-to-obtain fact. Nash was being transferred to a remote base and couldn't take Clive; my long-time driver Hugo was retiring; Nash approached me about taking Clive on as a replacement, giving him the highest – well, "praise" would be more accurate than "endorsement" or "recommendation"; Nash's recommendations had always proved justified in the past. End of story. That was twelve years ago.'

'This is all quite informative and touching,' Kang-Lee said, sounding somewhat intentionally insincere, 'but I still have my duty and my responsibilities, and, until or unless I can eliminate your chauffeur from my enquiries, he will remain in custody.'

Admiral Gazers took a deep breath. They were getting deeper into the wee small hours. 'OK, then: take me to his holding cell. I want to see him.'

'Indeed,' added Miningra. 'As this involves my portfolio, I need to talk with him as well.'

'I can't let you do that,' said Kang-Lee, in a very authoritative manner.

'What do you mean?' Biker suddenly shouted. 'How dare you take that tone with the Admiral of the Universal Defence Fleet? And with the Minister for World Security! Who do you think you are?'

'I can speak for myself, Biker,' the admiral snapped. 'Thank you very much.'

'Sorry, sir. I'm tired. But it miffs me when someone is disrespectful.'

'This is not a matter of respect or disrespect.' Orlando seemed to bite off each word as if it were a meatball. 'It's a matter of law. Order 0/48-DOWS118.09.04 clearly empowers the arresting authority to hold suspects in terrorism, assassination and special-operations cases incommunicado for interrogation for ninety-six hours with no recourse except to the accountable minister: in this case, me. I understand that interrogation of the suspect has not yet been completed. Let's all go home and get some sleep. I'm sure you'll see things more clearly with a rested mind.'

'It's Clive, Godamn it!' shouted Biker. 'And he's been injured. He's a human being!'

'Is Clive being held at Sarantio Pen?' Despite having gone almost twenty-four hours without sleep, Miningra was, as usual, calm, controlled and seeking information.

'No,' replied Kang-Lee: 'he's at Castle Rock, along with the other prisoners—'

'What the—?' Biker's outrage was reaching the point at which he seemed in danger of throwing a punch at Kang-Lee: something that would not have been a clever thing to do. 'You can't be serious! That hell-hole? Why? It's for convicts – not suspects – and convicts of the worst order! What's happened to the legal principle of innocent until proven guilty?'

'I refer you to World Order 0/47-DOWS—'

'Oh, shut up, Orlando!' Biker interrupted.

'It's the most secure, impenetrable fortress on the planet,' said Kang-Lee, 'tailor-made for traitors. And this is a case requiring the highest degree of security. Incarceration there serves as a constant deterrent to all would-be perpetrators of crimes of this magnitude.'

Miningra was about to point something out when a small melody started to play on Kang-Lee's pocket communicator. He pressed a key on it and an image came up on a large screen on one wall of the lounge. There was the face of a police inspector-captain, who said, 'We've tracked it down, sir,' before the image of a digital photo filled the screen. It showed Clive in full battle dress, without the insignia of any Grand Assembly or World Minister-approved force or militia.

Kang-Lee suggested, 'Now, maybe we should take a short break and be careful not to trip the wire on this very delicate situation. It's been a very long day, and there's no need to be at each other's throats.'

Kang-Lee's communicator played its tune again, and more images flashed up onto the wall screen. Kang-Lee let out what sounded like a yelp of relief. 'That's it. We can all go home now. We're done. I now have enough evidence to convict Clive, along with the other prisoners.'

The screen now displayed a series of colour images of a not-very-much younger Clive in full military kit, sitting astride a commandeered assault vehicle with four other men, all of them holding heavy assault weapons above their heads, posing for the camera.

'Is that conclusive enough for you now? It seems cut-and-dried to me,' snapped Kang-Lee.

Miningra said, 'I congratulate you and your people for getting a job done once again, Kang-Lee.' He seemed gracious enough.

'I need to talk to Clive before you let your dogs loose on him, Kang-Lee,' said the admiral, who was visibly upset. 'After living under the same roof with this man for over twelve years and trusting him with the life of my daughter, I need to satisfy myself and ask him why.'

'And,' pointed out Miningra, evenly, 'despite my esteemed colleague Orlando's clever attempt to sell us a dummy and make a run around the wing with his claim to be the only one with authority over Clive's investigation, Assembly Order 0/48-DOWS118.09.05 clearly empowers me to accept accountability in cases I deem to involve world security.' He smiled extremely coldly. 'Kang-Lee, take us to Clive.'

Kang-Lee looked to Orlando, who shrugged slightly. Kang-Lee nodded and said, 'My job is to produce the facts, and I've done just that. I don't let personal sentiment cloud my good judgement and get in the way of justice. What you choose to believe is entirely up to you, but, as far as I'm concerned, your precious Clive is going to be living out his life at Castle Rock, and, Castle Rock being what it is, that won't take much time at all.'

Chapter Nineteen

As Orlando took out his Lexus communicator and started barking out orders for transportation to Castle Rock and security clearance from Minister Jaywe's Department of Corrections, the admiral turned his thoughts towards Aurora, recognising that she might have been worrying about him. It wasn't just that he'd stayed out all night, which did happen from time to time, but that she was accustomed to messages from him at regular intervals when he did, and the night's extraordinary security measures, both at the Great Hall and at their home, had made this impossible. He decided to make contact with her straight away.

He and Aurora shared a rare genetically-predisposed capacity to communicate through thought-wave interaction. When he could tune out extraneous stimuli from other wave forms, the admiral could send thought waves through the atmosphere directly into Aurora's brain, and vice versa. Both needed to feel each other's presence and be on the same wavelength for it to work effectively.

Aurora had often used this gift while she'd been away on research or discovery-training expeditions and had been in need of some reassuring TLC from her papa, sometimes making him smile at the most inopportune moments. She liked to refer to the process as 'riding the waves with her special man'.

Needing to find a quiet location to start the ball rolling, Admiral Gazers recalled Aurora's occasional impromptu visits to see him at the Great Hall and how much she'd loved sitting in the main reception atrium, sometimes spending hours daydreaming, immersed in the sweet smell of the garden there.

He excused himself from the others and, bearing Clive's crisis in mind, quickly made his way to the wooden garden bench where Aurora usually sat. Easing himself down onto it, he felt her presence everywhere. Utilising his yoga training, he put himself into a semi-trance and, with his eyes closed, soaked up everything present that could lead him into contact with her.

Sure enough, Aurora had had the same idea, as they made contact simultaneously. Immediately, the admiral's ashen, fatigued face regained its colour. Aurora was safe and well.

Admiral Gazers sat quietly on the bench, his facial expressions those of someone on the wrong end of a hiding, and it was obvious that Aurora was giving her father a right good rollicking for not getting in touch sooner. After a few moments, though, all was forgiven, and the admiral was smiling as they signed off. He had been careful just to check in and not to provide her with information, such as about his own kidnap attempt and Clive's arrest, as he didn't want her to become unduly alarmed. One thing he certainly didn't want was for her to decide to fix things herself.

Settling into the Domestic Order Sikorski patrol helicopter that Orlando had arranged, Admiral Gazers was all business, turning to Kang-Lee with, 'I need dates, times, and places. I mean, just give me everything you've got. I want to be able to watch the expression on Clive's face when I put this information under his nose. The Clive I know can't lie to save his life, and it may well come down to that. Once I've spoken with him, I'll know the truth.'

It took them close to an hour before they approached their destination, Miningra the only one on the chopper to take the opportunity to doze off for forty minutes or so.

Hidden thirty kilometres deep inside some mangrove swamps, Castle Rock fortress was in an area known as the Devil's Bracelet, referred to by those who had to work there as the backside of beyond.

In the early twenties, the then-provincial Department of Corrections released a genetically engineered species of croco-diles, known as killerparthians, into the swamp to deter inmates from trying to escape. The Castle Rock experience seemed to be worse than death to many inmates; from time to time, the most desperate had tried to escape, fancying their chances at avoiding the killerparthians over a life worse than death inside. Every escape attempt had resulted in more scattered, splintered bones washing up along the edge of the swamp.

Reaching over nine metres in length, killerparthians patrolled up and down the mangroves in packs. They had special heat-sensitive glands that allowed them to home in on prey from over eight kilometres away, and reached water speeds of over fifty knots, or ninety-three kph, with rapid acceleration. They could survive for little more than forty-five seconds out of water. Biologists believed that over 500 killerparthians inhabited the swamp by that time, a quarter-century or so after their initial release.

Obviously, the preferred method of travel to Castle Rock was by air. As the Sikorski carrying Kang-Lee and the ministers started descending into a murky fog that hung over the swamp, thoughts of the killerparthians crossed each man's mind. Then, through near-zero visibility, the somewhat ghostly eighteenth-century façade of the Castle Rock fortress appeared.

'Take a look at that,' said Biker. 'So unwelcoming. I don't like this place at all.'

Kang-Lee instructed everyone to remain seated until the jailer arrived, then got on the Sikorski's communicator to contend with various security issues that had to be settled before they disembarked. Within a minute or so, the exit hatch slid open and an obese, untidy hulk of a figure appeared out of the fog on the landing pad.

'What the bloody hell's the bloody Assembly doing coming here and disrupting my routine this early in the bloody morning, anyway?' The figure spat the words out, literally, through rotting teeth that stuck out from gums covered with green calculus.

'Ah, Biggin,' Kang-Lee greeted him warmly. 'Good to see you. How're my prisoners?'

'Cold, wet and miserable – and in need of a good doctor,' Biggin replied, with a bellowing belly laugh, spraying a slimy gunge in Kang-Lee's direction. 'Only joking. Let's get you all inside and me out of this grotty, miserable weather.'

The five men hurried down the stairway out of the helicopter, then followed Biggin across what seemed like a walled courtyard paved with large, now-slippery stones and into a stone-walled gatehouse. All the architecture was forbidding grey stone neo-Gothic. Iron bars graced all windows.

'Let me introduce you guys to a living legend,' said Kang-Lee, once they were in the gatehouse. 'This is Master Jailer Mr Biggin Bollack, Commander of the Rock, the angriest man on the planet; even the killerparthians avoid him.'

'Don't overdo it, Kang-Lee. You're the angriest man on the planet. I'm just the meanest.' Biggin chuckled obscenely. 'Only joking, again.'

'Are you two going to exchange pleasantries all day?' asked Biker. 'I don't wish to spend more time than is necessary in this creepy place. Wouldn't it make good sense to get out of this awful gatehouse and do what we're here for?'

'Who's Mr Gloom?' asked Biggin.

'That's the famous Biker Reed – or should I say infamous? You couldn't see it, Biker, but I smiled when I said that.'

'Ah, the flying ace,' said Biggin. 'I've read about you in the papers; they say you're up for retirement soon. You don't look that bad for a wrinkly old pensioner. Only joking.'

'This is Admiral Gazers, and the big fella is Senior Minister Miningra, Commissioner of World Security,' said Kang-Lee. 'You've met Chief Sung before, I think.'

'You've received a briefing over an encrypted band about why we're here,' Orlando reminded him.

'Oh, yeah – the General. He's locked up in B Tank over in the West Wing, along with the other traitors. It's good and damp there, and the rats are as big as tomcats. That's to your liking, isn't it, Kang-Lee?'

Kang-Lee rolled his head around on his neck: a habit he'd picked up, since people couldn't see him roll his eyes. 'On that note,' he said, 'I think we should get going and see for ourselves.'

Inside the fortress's stark central hall, Biggin proudly pointed out the collection of medieval torture implements displayed around the neo-Gothic stone battlements. Even the cobwebs looked as though they had hung undisturbed for hundreds of years and had been abandoned by their occupants long ago.

'I just can't believe that such a disgusting place needs to exist in our advanced technological age,' said Miningra. 'Sometimes, I wonder at what goes on in Jaywe's mind to allow this sort of rubbish. Let's be as quick as we can and leave this place as soon as possible.'

'Oh, the hell with that; what say we crack open a keg and take the chill off our bones?' suggested Biggin, farting as he bent down to warm his hands in front of an open fireplace. 'That bloody dog, Barka,' he muttered, apparently referring to the pong that had emanated from his nether regions. 'Must be the mutton bones.'

'I need to be taken to Clive van der Poel straight away,' ordered the admiral.

'As you like,' Biggin shrugged. 'I'll drink for the two of us, then. Cheers.'

'Biggin,' said Orlando, in his tough-cop voice, 'I realise that you report through the Department of Corrections chain of command to Minister Jaywe and that you are not directly under the command of the Universal Defence Fleet, World Security or Domestic Order. Now, it may or may not be because I may or may not dislike the atmosphere here – who can say? – but, if you don't stop farting around and comply with whatever directions any of us World Ministers give you, you may find yourself the victim of an unfortunate and unexplained accident in the very near future – and find that nobody listens when you call for help.'

Biggin gave Orlando an extravagant salute, with flourishes, then turned to Admiral Gazers. 'Follow me, your highness – oh, slip of the tongue – I meant, "Admiral". Beg your pardon!' He produced a huge bunch of keys, rusty and otherwise, and spent the entire walk to B Tank in the West Wing trying to sort out the one that opened it.

'It's a bit of a walk,' said Biggin, as he sorted through the keys. 'My legs don't work as well as they used to, so you'll have to be patient with me and walk slowly.' He scurried up the dark, dingy corridor, dragging his slightly long trouser legs behind him. Admiral Gazers walked impatiently beside him, followed by Orlando and Kang-Lee. Miningra and Biker covered the rear flank.

'Are they claw marks on that wall over there, Miningra?'

'Where?'

'Over there.' Biker pointed to a huge, heavy chain with leg shackles attached.

'Stupid, gruesome and unnecessary,' Miningra pronounced judgement.

'Aha, that's where old Captain Willie Maikette was tortured for reasons that were classified as highly sensitive,' Biggin explained. 'They say he went mad after that, and that he still roams the corridors at night looking to escape, even though he's dead. His cousin "Noah Didn't", still occupies a cell here and has for twenty years. I was only a young man then, and Old Dangar was the chief jailer: a real mean, ugly son-of-a-pit-bull, not an amicable, handsome type like me. Into all sorts of medieval torture contraptions, he was.'

Not looking where he was going, Biggin nearly tripped over a huge rat looking for its next meal. Instinctively kicking it against the wall, he said, 'I'm right for dinner tonight. Look out for one for yourselves; they're great pan-fried in lard with onions.' He licked his lips.

'Wow! Did you see the size of that?' The admiral was impressed. 'I thought it was a dog at first, Biker.'

'I noticed no one tried to save Biggin from falling flat on his face altogether,' said Biker, 'Shame! Don't lag behind, Miningra. Old Dangar will get you.'

'Put a sock in it, Biker.' Miningra was not amused. 'What happened to Old Dangar?'

'That nutcase? He's in the Secure Chronic Unit of the Oakridge Mental Health Facility – although why they can't come right out and call it the Loony Bin is beyond me.' Biggin chuckled, the lines crinkling around his beady eyes. 'He turned into a real nutcase after he got attacked by an inmate who bit off his tongue and ate it, helping it down with a pint of his own blood, so the story goes. He must be all of eighty years old, at least – if he's still alive at all. This is it. Welcome to Devil's Doorway,' he said, with a huge grin, finally finding the right key to open the huge, fortified wooden door to the cell.

The door was too heavy for Biggin to push open on his own. He coughed and sputtered, making hard work of it.

'Mind, out the way. Let me have a go,' said Miningra, who enjoyed having opportunities to show off how big and strong he was.

The huge door emitted a piercing creak as it began to open, causing Biker to cringe. 'I hate that sound,' he whinged.

Inside the cell was a scene out of nightmares. The room was tiny, less than two by one-and-a-half metres, and seemed to have at least eight occupants squeezed tightly within its walls.

Biggin took a whip from inside his grubby, tattered jacket and started to hit the prisoners with it, shouting, 'Make way, you dirty varmints!'

'Give me that, you sad, sadistic water rat,' the admiral snapped. He snatched it from Biggin's hand and swiped him across the face. 'Hurts, doesn't it? Hit them again and, so help me, you'll wear your guts for garters.'

'Go for it, boyo, and let's see how far you get,' retorted Biggin, his bloodshot eyes bulging out of his head.

'So help me!' The admiral's face was turning red with anger. He raised his hand.

'Leave it, Harlius,' Miningra cautioned him, noting the interest Orlando and Kang-Lee were showing in the incident. 'That piece of scum's not worth it.'

'Thanks for the compliment,' Biggin sneered. 'I like you, too.'

Chapter Twenty

Clive was lying in a corner shivering, bunched up in the foetal position in a pool of stagnant water mixed with urine.

Admiral Gazers stepped over some of the others to get to him, calling out, 'Clive, are you all right? Are you hanging in there?'

Biker turned to Biggin and snarled, 'I've got your measure, you evil mongrel. Your turn will come. These people aren't animals; they're human beings.'

'Get real, Biker,' Biggin sneered. 'This is a prison, not a holiday camp. These vermin are traitors to the world. They belong on death row. What they don't deserve is any consideration.'

'You don't deserve the right to lock people up by being just as nasty a criminal as they may be. You're just two sides to the same coin – and Clive's worth any hundred of your sort!'

'Oh! Aren't you ever the noble saint, Biker, and how many people have you killed playing toy air-soldier, anyhow?'

Clive, his hair still matted with the congealed blood from the gash he had received during the abduction attempt seven or so hours earlier, looked up at the admiral. 'Damn, I'm glad you're here, Admiral! I'll be all right now,' he said, wearily letting out a long sigh. 'Am I going home? Why am I in this awful place, locked up with these… these criminals?'

This pricked a few ears amongst his cellmates, most of whom were dangerous to be around under the best of circumstances.

'Let's get you out of here and cleaned up,' Admiral Gazers said. 'You'll feel much better with some hot food inside your stomach. We'll talk about it once we've got you feeling more alive.'

'Sorry,' Biggin whined obstinately, clearly not sorry at all, 'but I can't let you take the prisoner out of the cell. I have my orders from Jaywe. He'd have my agates.'

'Just you try to stop us,' said the admiral, glaring menacingly at him.

'If you do try to stop us, it won't be just your agates you'll need to worry about,' Biker warned him.

'I think,' said Orlando, 'that this is a matter best settled amongst ministers: people of the same rank.'

Biggin, who had shown no respect to Biker, seemed to feel that Orlando posed a greater danger. 'If you're gonna be like that, I wash my hands of it. And don't think I'm scared, either.'

Miningra helped Clive onto his feet. 'Come on, mate; your bad dream's about to be over,' he assured him, but he thought, *How can I say that to Clive? He could be inside – somewhere else – if not here for ever.*

Back in the reception hall, Kang-Lee reminded them, 'I think this is about as far as we go now, gentlemen. This man is still under arrest and has a case to answer.'

'Yes,' agreed Orlando; 'we have to follow correct police procedures. I couldn't stand silently by and allow a legally-detained suspect to be released without due cause just because he has a few powerful friends.'

'This man needs dry clothes and a good meal,' the admiral insisted. 'He can't possibly answer questions in his condition; it's a matter of natural justice.'

Bewildered, Clive thought, *What am I supposed to have done? I'm just a chauffeur, for heaven's sake.*

Kang-Lee looked first at Clive and then at Admiral Gazers, then at Orlando, who nodded ever-so-slightly. 'OK, ten minutes, then. Biggin, bring some hot soup for the prisoner.'

'Hot soup? Where am I going to get hot soup?' shouted Biggin. 'Pull it out of my butt?'

'Stop being insubordinate, Biggin,' Orlando warned. 'Just do it.'

Grunting, farting and protesting, Biggin did as he was told.

'And bring a basin of water and some towels,' added Biker. 'We need to clean him up some, too.'

All Biggin felt it was safe to do in order to express himself was to spit into the basin of water when nobody was looking.

Hot soup and a bit of a wash brought Clive around enough for them to get down to business.

'I think,' said Kang-Lee, 'we should use a proper interrogation room.' He led them through a door.

The brilliantly-lit room's stone walls were whitewashed and windowless. Kang-Lee led Clive to a straight-backed wooden chair in the middle and told him to sit, then took his own seat on one of several comfortably-upholstered chairs in a dimly-lit area against the wall and said, 'All the recording devices are now operating. Go ahead.'

'Are you ready?' asked Admiral Gazers, stepping into the brightly-illuminated part of the room so Clive could see him. 'We need to ask you important questions, Clive. Please think about your answers very carefully before you answer. Do you understand?'

'I can only tell the truth, Admiral,' answered Clive, squinting painfully into the lights.

'I know that,' the admiral told him. 'Just take your time.'

Kang-Lee pressed a button and a screen descended from the ceiling. The colour image of Clive in warrior's gear filled the screen.

'OK, Clive,' said the admiral. 'Please explain.'

Clive looked at the image for a while in amazement. He shook his head, then leaned forward, peering at it closely, and cried out, 'That's my brother, Clarence! He's alive!'

'Crap. He died years ago,' Kang-Lee interrupted. 'That's you.'

'Give him a chance to speak, man,' Admiral Gazers ordered. 'Go on, Clive.'

'Well, sir, I can't say that this is a complete shock to me, seeing Clarence again after all these years. I knew he was still alive – identical twins know these things – even though he was presumed dead. I never really believed that story blaming headhunters myself, but my parents did, and it destroyed them. I haven't heard a word from Clarence since then. It must be now, let's see, thirty-eight years?' He licked his lips. 'Could I have a glass of water, please? I'm really dry.'

'Biggin, a glass of water, and be quick about it,' ordered Kang-Lee.

'Jeez, what did your last slave die of, then? Overwork, I'd bet. What's wrong with a little common courtesy? A simple "please" would be nice,' Biggin muttered, as he went to fetch the water.

After taking a long drink, Clive continued. 'Clarence fancied himself to be an expert on survival and very skilful with his Bowie knife, always telling me that, if we ever got marooned on an island, we could last for years; we could hunt animals together and live off the land. That was him: always wanting action and danger. He often told me he was going to run off and be a soldier of fortune.' He coughed, or laughed; the others couldn't tell which. 'Seems like he's done just that, judging by that image. A five-star general of some kind, to boot.'

'Our information, Clive,' Orlando said, in a quiet but hard voice, 'is that your brother Clarence is dead. You have presented us with no credible evidence that you are not the person in that image, and I have yet to see any evidence that you aren't concocting this whole far-fetched story just to save your skin.' He stepped out of the shadows and into the glare, then snarled, 'Why don't you just admit it so we can all go home?'

'That is Clarence. I can prove it.'

Miningra said, 'How on Earth are you going to do that, mate, short of Clarence actually walking through that door?'

'All you have to do is examine both the image and me closely; you'll see a key difference,' Clive explained. 'On one of Clarence's first got-to-prove-myself adventures, when he was really just a little kid – I think eight – he was crawling through a swamp, when he encountered some pathogens to which he was unusually sensitive, causing an optic imbalance in his right eye. He underwent delicate experimental corrective microsurgery at Kinhassee General Hospital. You should be able to come up with some documentation for this; the procedure was the first of its kind ever performed and was well reported in both the popular press and in medical journals. They removed his right pupil entirely and implanted opal optic fibres as a substitute.'

'So?' asked Kang-Lee.

'Look closely. Clarence and I were both born with two brown eyes. He came out of the operation with one brown eye and one green eye. You can see that very clearly in the visual image, if you'll look closely enough. My eyes are still both brown, as you can clearly see.'

Biker ran to stand directly under the image, then shouted, 'He's right. He's flipping right. Over and out. Stick that in your pipe and smoke it,' and did a celebratory Irish jig around the room.

Miningra just raised his eyebrows in amazement.

'Can I presume,' Admiral Gazers said, smiling, 'that you will concede graciously and release Clive without further notice, Kang-Lee?'

'Hold your horses, Admiral,' responded Kang-Lee. 'Let's be careful here before doing anything precipitous. Let's consider, for a moment, the possibility of some kind of deception involving contact lenses.'

'That's OK,' said Clive. 'Yes, I am a bit short-sighted, and I have worn contacts for over fifteen years, but clear ones. Anyway, the ones I had on last night got knocked out somewhere along the line and I'm not wearing any now. Take a look.'

The admiral stood up. 'I think Clive has proven his innocence without a shadow of doubt – and has suffered enough. Don't you?'

'Thank you, sir, but excuse me if you don't mind,' said Clive, 'but please tell me what the hell is going on here. OK, it seems that my brother Clarence has reappeared and is somehow responsible for my predicament, but what's the crime? All I can remember is collecting the admiral outside the Carlton Club, another vehicle colliding with the Roller and pinning us tightly up against a lamp post, people running around shouting, and me getting a knock to the head while trying to pull a couple of guys off the admiral. Then I woke up, covered in blood, getting pulled from the front seat of the Roller, manhandled, handcuffed, bundled into a waiting van and held in the dark until getting thrown into this awful place.'

'Yes,' said Admiral Gazers, 'there is plenty to tell you, but I think it'd be best to get you out of this hell-hole and back to civilisation right away. That head wound looks like it needs treatment as soon as possible; it's probably infected. No telling what nasties you can pick up in this disgusting place.'

'Uncivilised?' Biggin was somewhere between disgruntled and outraged. 'Hell-hole? Disgusting? What do you expect: wine and roses and the Sports Channel, maybe? A personal maid, perhaps? Get real!'

'I hate to say this,' Miningra said, frowning, 'but Clive still hasn't been legally released from custody. Kang-Lee?'

'Until I can investigate all the facts, I will entrust Clive to your custody. He will remain under close supervision while we continue the investigation and be prepared to appear in court when so ordered. If, for any reason, the situation changes, believe me, Clive will be back in here quicker than you can say "killer-parthians". I can promise you, it will be far worse the second time around. Right, Biggin?'

Chapter Twenty-One

Mt Love Spaceport had been the centre of most of Earth's initial voyages of discovery back in the mid-thirties, after Professor Pushpinder Prasad's discovery of hyperspace and the parabolic-spiral means of accessing it in 2029. The base itself had housed over 2,000 UDF and support personnel, and a small but thriving community had grown around its fringes. Then, in '38, an exploration spacecraft had returned contaminated with an alien species of virus, which doctors named the 'coxikillie'. It had wiped out Mount Love's entire population, earning it the nicknames of 'Mount Jinx' and 'Death-Camp'.

The UDF had immediately put the entire area under quarantine and had made every effort to make it appear from the outside as if it were totally abandoned and desolate. Meanwhile, however, Helen Grussgott, then the leader of the newly-formed Grand Assembly, put Admiral Harlius Fonce Gazers in charge of secretly rehabilitating the base. It took two years for his researchers to find a vaccine for the coxikillie, and, once that had been accomplished, almost three more years to decontaminate the area so that reconstruction of the base – and the construction of the Eden II – could begin.

Even though tests had repeatedly shown that the decontamination had been successful, all new arrivals were still immediately vaccinated, as Ethan and Ralph somewhat painfully discovered. As soon as the vaccination was over, Commodore Abramov took them to their quarters to clean up and get into uniform before they met the base commander, Rear Admiral Obidinga Olansinju.

'You have ten minutes,' Abramov told them. 'I'll be waiting in the galley at the end of the hall.'

Their rooms were both basic, windowless cubicles, with narrow beds; wardrobes with built-in double drawers just large enough to hold their kits; desks with monitor screens, keyboards, control panels and swivel chairs; toilet cubicles off to one side, and small bathrooms, each with a sink and shower stall, off to the other. The two young officers showered, shaved and dressed quickly and efficiently. Their training at the Academy had prepared them well.

They met Abramov with a minute or so to spare. He led them along a seemingly endless series of corridors to an office with five armed guards in UDF uniforms sitting at desks. They all leapt to their feet to salute him, and he returned their salutes with a smile, saying, 'Let the commander know we're here, Langley.'

A female guard, wearing chief warrant officer insignia, touched a button on her desk and said, 'He's expecting you, sir. Go right in.'

Abramov walked up to a door, which used an electric eye to scan his iris, then slid open. With a sweeping arm gesture, he indicated that Ethan and Ralph were to precede him through the door.

Wearing a basic working uniform without all the regalia to which his rank entitled him, Rear Admiral Olansinju was seated in a comfortable-looking chair in his office overlooking the Eden II. He seemed at first glance to be relaxed, his long, gangling legs stretched out in front of him and crossed at the ankles, a brilliantly white smile spreading across his deep-forest-brown face as he saw them. It was only when he stood up to take and return their salutes that the stress clearly showed around his eyes and the edges of his large, sensual-looking mouth.

'Welcome, gentlemen; welcome. Do fall out. Yitzhak, you may return to your regular duties. Carry on.' He and Commodore Abramov exchanged salutes. Then, as Abramov did an about-face and headed out the door, Rear Admiral Olansinju turned to Ethan and Ralph. 'Do take a seat.' His voice was surprisingly high and reedy, rather like an operatic tenor's.

Ethan and Ralph looked around the office. A viewscreen, keyboard and control panel were all that was on the desk, which faced a large window overlooking the Eden II. Three identical chairs and a sofa, all upholstered in a light-grey fabric, surrounded a glass-topped coffee table. The carpet, also light grey, was short and seemed like artificial turf. The office had no decorations or personal objects whatever.

'I suppose we'll find out all we need to know in due course, sir.'

'Well, let me give you some news, gentlemen: due course is going to come a whole heap faster than you may have anticipated. Thanks to that woo-woo security scare, those nervous Nellies at the Grand Assembly have been sending me hints that not only have they moved you here a month early for security reasons, but that they have their knickers in such a twist that they're probably going to demand an early take-off, too. That's what happens when politicians make decisions properly left to technical experts. You two are going to have to get up to scratch on your respective duties for this mission in record time, and I'm afraid there just may be a chance that you'll still be learning your jobs at take-off.'

He paused, giving them all of four seconds for this to sink in. 'So, it's been lovely chatting with you, but I'm not going to invite you to stick around for a cup of tea. Captain Knight, you're off for the Eden II control simulator. Lieutenant Baxter, I expect you to start getting acquainted with the Eden II's astronomical-hyperspace computer navigation systems immediately.' He stood up; Ethan and Ralph followed suit. 'CWO Langley will show you where to go. Dismissed.'

After arriving discreetly back at Headquarters, after earlier having declined an invitation to join Admiral Gazers and his daughter for an impromptu late supper, Miningra immediately headed to his office for a little midnight mayhem. In between travelling from Castle Rock to headquarters, he had developed an insatiable hunger to expose the traitor personally; he was so consumed by the prospect of saving face that his judgement was in danger of being impaired.

To his astonishment, he caught Consul Linns in his office, sifting through the masses of papers that were strewn all over the floor. Vice Consul Linns was so preoccupied with what he was doing that he hadn't seen Miningra entering the building over the security monitors.

'What's happening, Frikker? Can I help you find what you're looking for?'

'Heavens! Miningra, you startled me. I thought you'd still be at Castle Rock with Admiral Gazers and the others.' Frikker could feel his face turning scarlet.

'I didn't know that it was broadcast.'

'Nothing escapes my attention, Miningra; you should know that. Being vice consul of the Assembly, it's my job to keep one step ahead at all times. How was the excursion? Meet any killerparthians?'

'You could say it was quite an experience, Linns; one I don't wish to repeat soon. It was truly amazing. That Biggin character was the icing on the cake of hell.'

'Yeah, I've heard about him. Just the sort of bloke you'd want to take home and be one of the family, eh?'

Miningra looked at Linns suspiciously, wondering why he was being so chatty. Those who knew Frikker generally had him pegged as a starched-shirt who only voiced his opinion when pressed. He was also fiddling compulsively with his gold cuff-links, which was something Miningra couldn't recall seeing him do before, although it could have meant nothing. He made a minimal noise in response. 'I was brought up to honour my father and mother.'

Linns allowed himself a thin smile. 'Yes, I guess it all depends on how much you like your family.'

Miningra managed a grunt in response to this, thinking of some of his cousins on his mother's side. 'So – I don't want to sound as if I'm doing my job or anything, but what the hell are you doing in my office?'

'Well, after I heard of the failed attempt to snatch the admiral and your exit from the Great Hall, I exercised my powers as VIP to have your people keep me updated on the situation by the minute. I felt it was my duty to do what I could to manage key security objectives until your return. Tell me: you're back from Castle Rock, right? What's the state of the investigation into the admiral's personal chauffeur, that Clive character?'

'You seem to know an awful lot already, Frikker.'

'Nothing recent about Clive. I haven't seen anything on him coming in since they got him there. However, the other four prisoners caved in after a bit of, um, gentle persuasion, and told us about getting instructions from Ringo Bang himself, surprisingly without implicating Clive.'

'Surprisingly?'

'Kang-Lee was absolutely positive Clive was high up the food chain with the problems that've come up, in particular the kidnap attempts. He has inside knowledge and all that. He went after Clive with all the resources that Orlando could make available to him, and he scored fabulously, for just a few hours' digging, with that dossier and those photos. He was skiting about how on top of it he is, but I put it down to luck.'

'Luck, eh?'

'Listen, you know that Kang-Lee likes it all his own way and detests the thought of being proven wrong. He got it into his head – I don't know how – that nicking Clive was the key to success in this case, and went about things in his relentless way.'

'It would be interesting,' Miningra observed, more to himself than to Frikker, 'to find out how he got it into his head.'

'So, tell me, Miningra: what has happened to Clive?'

'When we got him out of that sickening hole he was in and had him cleaned up and interviewed him, he provided us with both information and hard, physical evidence that the stuff Kang-Lee came up with on him is as worthless as teats on a bull. Kang-Lee took the news as best he could and did a bit of strutting to save face, but Clive left Castle Rock with us – in our custody, according to Kang-Lee – and he's in hospital now for observation.'

'What about all the evidence Kang-Lee had against him? What was wrong with it?'

'I'll tell you, when I saw it, I began to have my doubts about Clive, to be honest. I can't let feelings or anything else get in the way of doing a professional job as Commissioner of World Security. I always go on what facts I have and stay honest with myself about what I know and what I don't, y'know. I did take into account Harlius Fonce's and Biker's close affection and friendship with the man, but I kept an open mind: something Kang-Lee seemed to be having some trouble doing. Anyway, without going into details, Clive's twin brother Clarence is apparently alive, after all, and up to heaven knows what – but I'll find out.'

Frikker was still playing with his cufflinks, twirling one around vigorously, which caused it to ping onto the floor.

'Damn. Did you see where my cufflink went?'

'It flew under that filing cabinet. There it is; I can see it.'

'Thanks, Miningra. My father gave them to me just before he died. They're not really worth a lot, but the sentimental value is priceless.'

Retrieving his prized bauble, Linns showed dismay at finding it broken. He took off the other one and put both links into his trouser pocket for safekeeping.

'When did your father die, Frikker?'

'Two years ago to the day, on his sixty-fifth birthday. He was in his prime: miles too young to go.'

'Wasn't he a decorated war hero?'

'That's right.'

'How'd he die?'

'Why the sudden interest in my father, Miningra? What's it to you?'

'Sorry, I didn't mean to pry. With such a famous father, I thought you'd be proud to talk about him. I would be myself.'

'Well, I'm not you. I appreciate your interest, but my father's demise is my private business. Please respect that and leave it alone.' He fumbled with his link-less shirt cuffs for a moment, and then decided to roll up his sleeves. 'Now, where were we?'

Miningra immediately noticed a prominent tattoo on Frikker's right forearm. It was a multi-coloured depiction of two golden eagles, facing each other, within a circle of vine leaves. Miningra recognised this straight away as a symbol of a now-defunct fanatical neo-fascist movement known as Power Against Parliament, or PAP, which had acquired a dangerous amount of power and influence about a quarter-century earlier by using heavy-handed tactics to bully the more weak and corruptible parliamentarians of the day into supporting its philosophy that the strong had a spiritual obligation to dominate the weak and to crush those who resist. The movement's leader, a charismatic but mentally unstable former businessman who was obsessed with the Roman Empire and who called himself Augustus Maximus, was found murdered one morning on the steps of Parliament, slashed to ribbons by, the coroner reported, thirty-eight knife wounds. Without its leader, the PAP disintegrated.

Staring at Linns' tattoo with fascination all over his face,

Miningra disingenuously asked, 'The tattoo on your arm, Frikker: has it any significance? When did you get it?'

'Oh, the stupid things you do when you're young. I was a victim of my own callow foolishness. It has no real meaning; it's just a tattoo.' He sheepishly and unconvincingly pulled his shirtsleeve down to cover it up.

'See you, then, Vice Consul, sir. Oh, just one other thing: who was that fanatical political leader back in the twenties, assassinated on the steps of Parliament?'

'How should I know? I really wasn't interested in politics at all back then. Why do you ask?'

Miningra smiled. 'No particular reason; put it down to curiosity if you like.'

Sitting with her father in the Relaxation Zone, Aurora sipped at a cup of hot tea, watching her father settle into his favourite chair with a heavy, cut-crystal glass tumbler two-thirds full of his favourite single malt. A string quartet by Mozart, the admiral's favourite music, caressed them from the sound system.

Deciding that the time was right, Aurora put her teacup on its saucer on the table beside her. 'Dad, where's Clive?' she demanded, softly but sternly.

'We had a minor altercation shortly after the meeting. Unfortunately, the Roller sustained some damage, and Clive came out of it with a slight injury and had to be admitted to Sarantio General Hospital. He's going to be OK, though, so don't you worry; it's only a precautionary measure.'

'What about you, Dad? Are you all right?'

'Just a little tired, that's all, kitten. It's been such a long day; I can tell you, it's super-good to be home with my favourite girl.'

Aurora's eyes narrowed. She clearly wasn't going for it at all. 'And what else?'

'Nothing else, but I do have some very important issues to attend to later in the day. Unfortunately, we can't share dinner this evening. Sorry.'

'Are those issues something to do with Willis not letting me go out and meet Crystal for coffee at lunchtime? Are they something to do with the large contingent of troopers around the house? There must be millions of them.'

'You could say that. After all, some thugs did try to put the snatch on you, y'know; but we're getting things all under control, and there's nothing for you to worry about.'

'Dad, that's the second time in five minutes you've told me not to worry. What is it? What's happened? Don't forget, I can read you like a book, so no horse-feathers, please.'

'I'm all too aware of that, my sweet.' He took a long sip of his Scottish elixir and sighed. Then he put his glass down on the Bauhaus table by his chair and rubbed his eyes with his knuckles. 'OK, I give up.' He stood and moved himself and his drink to the large maroon-plush sofa. 'Come over here and sit by me. Signal Riley for more tea, if you want to, and maybe some snacks. It's going to be a long journey. Please let me finish what I am about to tell you before asking questions; everything will make sense as I go along, all right?'

Going through the events of the previous twenty-four hours, Admiral Gazers was painfully but determinedly honest with his daughter and left nothing out. 'There you have it, my sweet: the whole unpleasant story,' he announced, when he got to dropping Biker off at the Commodore Club, a rather seedy dive the old pilot favoured. He seemed relieved not to have any more secrets from her.

'Dad, this isn't over yet, y'know.'

He nodded sadly. 'I know.'

'What happens when they try again? It could be you lying in hospital seriously injured, or even worse. I couldn't bear it if something happened to you.' She failed to stifle a sob.

'Listen, they've shown their hand now too many times. There's bound to be a trail now, and I have full faith that Miningra and World Security will be picking up on it, probably today, if they haven't already. And I wouldn't be surprised if Orlando Sung's police investigation also comes up with things we can use to nail this down.'

'The way they came up with things on Clive?'

He rewarded her insight with a sour little smile. 'That's why I have to be ready to take action when the time comes. We may need to be a tad careful for a day or so, but I'm confident that we're the hunters now, not the hunted. Hey, nothing's going to happen to me, sweetheart. I promise. You trust the Admiral of the Fleet, don't you?'

'I'm scared, Dad. There are still a lot of troopers camped around our home, and I'm not going to feel comfortable until they go away.'

'I won't lie to you. This is a key moment in history, and security is something we have to pay close attention to until the coast is clear. As I told you, it seems that, for some reason, somebody on the Grand Assembly has decided on being a traitor to the human race, and, until we sort out what he or she or they are up to and put a stop to it – well, we'll just have to remain vigilant.'

Riley appeared at the archway leading to the hall and coughed discreetly. He carried a covered tray.

'Yes, Riley?'

'You did ask me to have Tokita prepare some snacks?'

'Just put them there, thank you.'

'Smoked fish with cream cheese and tomatoes on fresh buns, sir.'

'My favourite. Horseradish sauce on the side?'

'Of course, sir.'

'That'll be all, Riley.'

The admiral and Aurora both helped themselves as Riley departed. They munched away contentedly for a minute or so, the admiral smiling in the way he did when he ate what he called comfort food. Then, after wiping his mouth with a linen serviette, he continued, 'We're bringing the voyage of discovery's lift-off forward as much as we dare, and it's our top priority. It has to go ahead on schedule at all costs. All our hopes for a liveable future are riding on the success of this mission.' He took another bite, chewed and swallowed, and took a last, short sip of his single malt. 'So far, we've kept the location of Eden II secret, but we don't know for how much longer we can do that unless we find who's leaking secrets, y'know?'

'And Ethan?'

'Sorry, my sweet: this is going to hurt. It's going to have to be a rain check on dinner Saturday night. Young Captain Ethan is already at the secret base. He is leading the expedition, you know.'

'So soon?' Aurora sounded somewhat dismayed and somewhat angry. 'I don't suppose he looked too disappointed when he was informed our dinner date would have to be postponed. It doesn't bother me much.'

'I believe you, kitten, Oh, by the way, I forgot to mention that Lieutenant Skip Slider will be junior surface-explorer pilot on the flight.' He waited for her response.

'Skip who?' she asked, rolling her eyes.

'OK. Enough said. It could turn out to be quite interesting, though, couldn't it?'

'Um, maybe a little harmless rivalry might prove useful. I'd love to be a fly on the wall when he and Ethan discover they have a common interest: little old me!' She chuckled.

Chapter Twenty-Two

Miningra bent over the screen of his principal monitor, using his laser mouse to scroll down the reports that his agents were sending him in a steady stream.

Local police in Castleton, the nearest town to Castle Rock, were investigating reports of a crashed private helicopter, apparently armed with rockets, on the edge of Castle Rock Swamp, but they were reluctant to investigate too closely, due to the presence of killerparthians near it. *I wonder*, he thought, *if Clive was being used as bait to get Harlius Fonce, Biker and me to fly into a trap. But, if so, why? And by whom? And did they know that Orlando and Kang-Lee would be going there, too? Are they targets as well?*

Then an intriguing piece of intelligence came up on the screen: Vice Consul Frikker Linns had lost an enormous amount of money from investing heavily in a software company that had all but gone out of business due to almost simultaneous corruption scandals in Houston, Mumbai and Hong Kong. He had secretly sold his mansion in Queen's North Nevulae to pay his debts, but he still seemed to be having trouble paying some of his bills. *Now, there's a motive!* Miningra told himself, and he contacted the agents he had detailed to keep an eye on Frikker under the pretext of protecting him.

He tapped his desk impatiently, waiting for their reply. Finally, it came up on his screen: '*Subject has used unmistakable evasion tactics to give us the slip. Taking steps to pick up his trail.*'

Linns walked through the kitchen of a Chinese restaurant in Discovery Heights, one of Sarantio's older, barely-still-liveable suburbs, looked around, and then slipped out the back door. He walked a short distance down an alley and got into a waiting black ground car with tinted windows. It was an old Lexo, but it seemed well maintained and in good condition. The driver, a silent, thick-necked man with cauliflower ears and a conservative dark suit, took him along several back streets before turning into another alley and depositing him before another back door surrounded by rubbish bins.

Linns got out of the car, walked the few steps to the door and let himself in. He was in the back room of a dark, working-class bar. He looked about himself briefly, allowing his eyes to grow accustomed to the gloom, steadied himself, then walked to a booth in a corner facing both the back door and another door leading to the front of the bar, where he joined the three men who were already sitting there. They were the only people in the room.

The three men were Ringo Bang and two of his most elite thugs. Ringo gave an impression of great physical power, which was enhanced by his slightly humped back. His head, which was too small for his body, was lumpy and almost chinless. His eyes bulged out from his head and were continually bloodshot; his bulbous, purple-veined nose displayed evidence of having been broken several times; three long, jagged scars sliced their way across his acne-scar-cratered face.

'Well?' he said by way of greeting, showing a magnificent set of even, white dentures.

'You amaze me, Ringo,' observed the vice consul, by way of answering. 'How did you manage to stuff up two simple kidnappings in two days? I wonder if you could organise a successful afternoon nap in a retirement home.'

'Don't push it, stuffed-shirt. You still owe me money. Two-and-a-half million money units, to be exact.'

Frikker Linns smiled. 'Pish-tush, my dear fellow. I, at least, know how to do what needs to be done. It's not my fault if your people can't properly use the information I sell you.'

'Two-and-a-half million, rat-face.'

'Would you say that a hundred and twenty digital images of Miningra's top-secret files would be worth that? I'd think it'd be worth more.'

'Depends on what's in them files.' Ringo sounded thoughtful.

'I didn't have time to study them all closely, you understand, but, from what I noticed as I was scanning them, I'd say you'd be getting a bargain – if your people are able to use the information properly.'

'Yeah, and what if I think it's rubbish?'

'You'd be a fool. Look here, how many of your criminal competitors have an asset on the inside of the Great Hall? Let's not pretend that we're both stupid, because we're not.'

'OK. OK. Let's see it.'

Linns reached into one of his waistcoat's pockets and pulled out a mini digi-camera only eighteen millimetres wide: about the size and shape of a thumbnail. Holding it away from Ringo's grasping hand for a moment, he said, 'This makes us even. You want anything more from now on, you're going to have to pay up front.'

'Yeah, yeah.' Ringo snatched it. 'And, if it's not worth what you owe me, you're going to find yourself pushing up daisies – after suffering more terror and pain than you would have ever imagined possible.'

'And then how will you get your information, my good man? I suspect that, for a man like you, having access to the inside dope is – well, like dope. Yes, I'd be very much surprised if I don't have you already addicted.' He smiled sourly.

Chapter Twenty-Three

Ethan and Ralph were discussing the afternoon's progress over a dinner of poached eggs on toast, with roasted vegetables on the side, in the crew's mess.

'I don't know if they're going to give me enough time to prime myself for take-off, hyperspace and surface-exploration modes, not to mention spaceport docking and transition,' Ethan told him, after washing down a mouthful of food with a big swallow from his mug of strong tea.

The discovery of hyperspace and the parabolic-spiral means of accessing it, and the subsequent development of hyperspace technology back in the thirties, had revolutionised the way people conceptualised space travel. Hyperspace referred to the phenomenon of megayottaherz waves which made the universe bend in forms of space-time not visible to either light or electron radio-wave receptors. By operating an exactly-configured (to the nanometre) vessel, called a hyperspace velocitor, through open space at a strictly-controlled level of parabolically changing exponential acceleration co-ordinated with a precisely navigated parabolic spiral, it had become possible to jump across visible space to locations that humans could never realistically have thought of going back to in the days when they had been restricted by the limitations of motion in einsteinium space-time, in which the matching-planet, being 175 light years away from Earth, was just that: 175 years away, if they could have travelled at the speed of light, which they couldn't.

The trick, of course, was in figuring out how to wind up safely in a particular location after going through hyperspace, which involved a precise setting of the parabolic spiral's angle to the solar system and the spiral's overall length, and in being able to get back safely through hyperspace again to the home port. In the early days, back in the thirties, three missions had failed to return, and another one had disappeared in the early forties; their crews had become venerated as heroes and martyrs.

A vessel such as the Eden II was basically an enclosed computer with accommodations for a crew. There, at Mount Love, it was attached to a rocket-powered launch vehicle to take it out of the Earth's gravity and to the top-secret ultra-high-orbit spaceport, called Bifrost Three. After Eden II docked at the spaceport the crews of both the Eden II and the spaceport, would proceed to attach it to the cold-fusion-powered hyperspace velocitor. This had to be assembled at the spaceport, because of the need for the process of fabricating some key components and assembling it to be done in a space-quality vacuum. Inside the velocitor, the Eden II would join a smaller vessel called the surface-explorer (but more commonly referred to as a 'hopper'), which was designed to descend to the surface of the target planet and return to the velocitor, should their trip through hyperspace put them within orbiting distance.

All this required the precise operation of dozens of systems and operations, each providing the hardware, the software, the crew and, especially, the commander with ample opportunities for mistakes and malfunctions, which – even the tiniest ones – could spell disaster. Ethan, had, of course, been Top Gun in all aspects of hyperspace-travel navigation and control, but the top-secret Eden II was far more advanced than anything that he had ever seen, and he had plenty to absorb to the point of being second nature. He wasn't fooling himself.

Even though it was after midnight, as soon as Aurora received word that Clive had returned from hospital, she buzzed for Riley and told him to bring Clive to her.

Riley raised one eyebrow. 'Are you certain, Miss Aurora?' He curled his lip barely more than a millimetre. 'Do you really judge it to be best to receive the chauffeur here in your private drawing room?' Then, remembering the unseemly and inexplicable fondness the young mistress had for that impossible motor-head, he added, 'I expect he'll be wanting to rest initially; after the rigours of his recent experience and injury.'

Aurora smiled brightly at the family butler. 'Riley,' she twinkled, then, switching suddenly to a hard, commanding voice, as her smile, while staying on her lips, left her eyes, 'please bring Clive here immediately. I trust I haven't suddenly acquired a difficult-to-understand accent and that my enunciation is clear.'

Riley bowed his way out of the room, properly chastened, and, a few minutes later, Clive tapped on her door and entered. Aside from the bandage on his head and the ill-fitting clothes the hospital staff had provided him with for the trip home, he looked surprisingly fit, rested and alert.

'Heavens, Clive! Look at you!'

'They treated me well at hospital, Miss Aurora. I must say, the care and medication were excellent. I mean, I feel as good as new – as if I'm ready to go twelve rounds with any gang of thugs – although, I must say,' – he tugged at the sleeve of a shirt that was entirely too tight in the shoulders – 'their haberdashery skills fall far short of their medical ones.'

Aurora laughed. It was her Clive, after all. 'I'll bet you're famished.'

'Right you are there. I chose to give the hospital food a pass, after seeing what was on offer, and wait for something sublime from Tokita, instead.'

She grabbed him by an overly-tight shirtsleeve and tugged him towards the door. 'Come on, then; let's go to the kitchen and get Tokita to whip us up something yummy. Father's had to go back down to the Great Hall in the Eurocopter to meet with Miningra and who knows who else. You're having dinner with me!'

Clive freed his arm and chuckled. 'How 'bout if I meet you in Tokita's domain in a few minutes? I'd like to get some of my own clothes on first.'

An hour or so later, Aurora, Clive and Tokita were sitting around the big kitchen table, very few remains of their excellent dinner left on their plates. Aurora and Clive were drinking tea; Tokita, a medium-sized fellow in his mid-twenties, who was fussy about the styling of his longish black hair, was drinking from a bottle of home-brewed Japanese-style beer, which he insisted was essential for his health.

'Y'know, Clive,' Aurora was saying, 'I think I'll make Dad take me to the secret base to see Ethan, just to make up for having him spirited away before Saturday. What d'you think?'

'I think it'll be a true test of your powers of persuasion, that's for sure… but, if I had to bet, I'd put my money on you, kid.'

Tokita snickered. 'I wonder if they'd give you security clearance to go to such a secret place.'

'That's a thought,' Aurora said, smiling. 'I wonder if I could bribe Willis.' Her pocket communicator announced a call with the sound of her favourite piece of music, a jazz-rock electronic harpsichord piece by the sensational young high-brow Argentine composer Joaquin Jacóbi. She touched the button to answer and said, 'Go for it!'

The little screen showed a badly-lit, dirty little face against a background of old-looking pipes. It was the little boy from the Children of the Underground called Mickey. As was the case with Miningra's agents, Aurora didn't ask him how he came to have an expensive Lexus pocket digital communicator, let alone the money to make calls on it.

'It's you!' he exclaimed. He looked about nervously, and then said, in a hurried voice, 'Houtchins said you'd given him your private number, but I didn't really believe him.'

'Well, it is me, Mickey, as you can plainly see. What's up?'

'Sylvia and Li-Tian are hurt. Some of those new militias bashed 'em. I'm afraid, Aurora. They need your help. You know that the only hospital that takes Undergrounders is Charity Hospital, and the waiting time for emergency help there is eleven hours or more now!'

'What about Doctor Mediatis's Free Clinic?'

'I guess you haven't heard. Somebody burnt it down early last morning. Please, Aurora – they need you! Please help them! Please!'

Aurora decided instantly that she was going to have to shed her protective cage somehow and go to help. 'Where are they? How can I find them?'

'I'd best wait for you around the bottom of the stairway to Fluorescent Park.' Fluorescent Park was a former underground transit station that had been cleared out and kept clean by an interfaith religious mission and lined with bright fluorescent lights, which glowed twenty-four hours a day. They'd fitted the area up like an underground park, with children's playgrounds, basketball and tennis courts, and other park-like amenities. By an unspoken understanding of unanimous consent, all the gangs and clans and factions and families of the Nevulae-Sarantio undergrounds treated Fluorescent Park as a crime-free non-combat zone, as neutral territory: as a sanctuary.

'Now, listen, Mickey: it might take me a while to get there. There are troopers all around my house and stuff after what happened at Glebe Hall, and it's going to take some doing to get past them, but I'll be there as soon as I can.'

The screen fizzed and Mickey's image disappeared. Text appeared on the screen, informing her that the caller's prepay credits had expired.

Aurora looked at Clive and Tokita. 'Well, guys...' Her voice projected a convincing amount of determination. 'It looks like we've got a job to do.'

'We?' cried Tokita in despair. 'What can I do? I'm just a cook. Do you want me to do ninja-movie tricks with my kitchen knives?'

'Maybe,' Aurora said, evenly. 'Clive made good use of one of those knives the last time they tried to ambush me.'

Clive was already thinking things through. 'We're going to have to get Willis on side, or we'll never be able to get out of here and down to there in anything like a reasonable amount of time.'

'Do you think he'll try to clear it with my dad and Miningra, or can we talk him into taking initiative?'

'We'll see. You go hit him with your manipulative best. I've got to go and make sure the Luxor's filled up and ready for the road.'

The Luxor was Admiral Gazers' back-up transporter. It was smooth and luxurious, but didn't have nearly all the high-tech bells and whistles of the Roller.

Tokita looked from one to the other. 'I'll make sandwiches. Those kids're probably always hungry.'

Willis was in the house's communications room, monitoring the images from the external security cameras, suspicious of what some of the troopers might be up to. He noticed that half-a-dozen or so, spaced at relatively regular intervals, seemed to be paying more attention to what they were protecting than to protecting the possible approach lanes for attacking it. *I wonder...*

159

he thought. *Maybe I should contact Miningra over an encrypted secure line and tell him about it.*

A light over the bank of screens he was watching changed from green to aqua. He smiled, swivelled around in his chair and watched Aurora stride purposefully from the hall door towards the station he was using.

'Well, well, well,' he said, smiling as she approached him.

'Let's cut through the pleasantries,' she said, coming briskly to a halt in front of him. 'A couple of the Children of the Underground are seriously hurt, maybe from trying to get information for you people, and we've got to go down there and get them to medical help. It may be a soft-hearted, emotional thing on my part, but those kids are the best eyes and ears you have down there and we owe it to them, so let's go!'

Willis sat silently, looking at her with shrewd eyes, for three or four seconds, and then answered, '"Let's go", Miss Aurora? This sounds like a job for World Security agents: not something I could get away with risking your life over.'

'What you could get away with? Are we talking about saving the lives of kids I call family and you call intelligence assets, or are we talking about covering your butt? You and your agents will never find these kids. They'll only trust me, so I have to be in on the action!' She took a deep breath. 'Listen: you know they say it's always easier to get forgiveness than it is to get permission? Well, we don't have time to get permission!'

Willis stood up. 'I'll inform Miningra of what's going on when we take off.'

'Clive's getting the Luxor...'

'If we're really in a hurry, we should take one of the Security NH126 helicopters parked over in the court of the security wing. Have him meet us downtown. Let's see, who's on duty?' He looked at the screen of his hand-held computer. 'Ormsby and Flint. Good team. Where are we making rendezvous?'

'At the bottom of the stairs to Fluorescent Park.'

'I'll arrange for more agents to meet us there for back-up.' He looked over at the monitor screens for the external security cameras, thought for a split second, and then said, more to himself than to Aurora, 'I think I'll notify Domestic Order for liaison at the last possible moment before we get there – or get Miningra to do it.'

Willis's face, with the background of city lights buzzing by through the window of the helicopter, unexpectedly flashed up on Admiral Gazers' home navigation surveillance screen. Before he could speak, the admiral cried, 'Where are you? I thought you were detailed to stay at my place and control my daughter's protection!'

'Well, sir,' Willis explained, 'half of that's the case at the moment.'

'*What*?' Miningra and Admiral Gazers shouted in unison.

'I'm in control of Aurora's protection, but we're not staying at your place.'

From out of Willis's communicator's visual range, Aurora's voice called out, 'Hi, Daddy!'

The admiral exploded. 'What the hell is going on there?'

Willis gave them a concise report of what had happened with the Children of the Underground, Aurora's reaction and decision, what they were doing and the steps he had taken to protect Aurora during their rescue operation. He concluded by telling them, 'I haven't notified Domestic Order yet. I've observed, over your household surveillance cameras, that some troopers seem to be more interested in keeping an eye on the house than on guarding it – and in what seems to be an organised pattern. After the way Domestic Order handled that business with Clive, I thought it best not to notify them until the last possible moment. Aurora and I both kept our heads down when the NH126 took off, but I'm sure they're making inquiries about it by now.'

'I'll detail an additional contingent of agents to meet you there, and others to infiltrate Fluorescent Park,' Miningra decided, 'and I'll contact someone I can trust in the Nevulae Trooper Barracks to get some loyal troopers there right away. Out.'

'I don't like it,' the admiral announced. 'It's a trap.'

'Of course it is, so we have to be ready. But do you think anybody on Earth could stop Aurora from effecting this rescue when she's this determined?'

Chapter Twenty-Four

Vice Consul Linns sat in his office, breathing deeply and looking at a framed photo of his father on the opposite wall. He closed his eyes, then opened them again when he heard a knock on his door.

'Come in… Miningra! Admiral! Grab some seats. What brings you guys here at this time of night?'

They each found a conveniently-sited chair. Miningra looked deeply into Linns' eyes and smiled. 'We saw on my monitor that you'd returned, and so we thought we'd come by and exchange some more notes on this business of tracking down that leak.'

'Yes, yes. A perplexing and disturbing affair.'

'And then there are the attacks on my daughter and myself,' the admiral added. 'Security's investigations into them seem to bring up more questions than answers.'

'What do you mean?' Linns leaned forward, his pointy face pointing intently at them.

'Well, for one thing,' the admiral mused, calmly, 'there's the problem of motivation. Why were these assaults attempted? Do we have someone on the Assembly with, let us say, a political objective that they hoped to advance by gaining the leverage that taking my daughter or myself hostage would give them?'

'What political objective would doing something like that help one of our colleagues to achieve? Be specific.'

'Exactly our point,' Miningra put in. 'Admiral Gazers, by himself, would not be that useful a prize, given the Assembly's no-negotiating-with-terrorists policy, and Aurora – well, holding her would only bring leverage over Harlius Fonce, not the entire Assembly.'

Admiral Gazers continued this line of thought. 'Even if one of our colleagues had gone mad with the lust for power and was intending to try to pull off a coup, just getting me out of the way – or putting pressure on me through Aurora – wouldn't do the trick. Ziekiel or his son Marlon would seem to be the more likely targets.'

'Yes.' Frikker nodded. 'I see what you mean – and don't forget me. Anyone wanting to take control would have to neutralise me as well, as I'm the next one down the ladder from Landon.'

Miningra leaned back and laced his fingers over his head. 'And then, all that whoop-ti-doo about Clive is suspicious as hell. I can't for the life of me figure out what that was all about, and none of my investigating agents have yet been able to come up with the source of it. So, once again, we're left wondering why as well as how.' He dropped his arms so that his elbows were resting upon his lap and his hands were hanging loosely and negligently between his knees.

'You told me you were following that one as it was unfolding, Frikker. What are your thoughts on it?'

'To tell you the truth, I've been thinking about what you said, Miningra, about the mystery of what put it into Kang-Lee's head that your Clive was so certainly guilty. What I think is that, instead of railroading him, maybe Kang-Lee didn't investigate Clive hard enough.'

Admiral Gazers' face started to turn red, but Miningra's calm voice cut in before he could blow up. 'What d'you mean by that, Frikker?'

'Now, I know that Harlius Fonce is real fond of this bloke and trusts him completely and all, but, from what I've been able to glean from the reports on what happened down in Castle Rock, he really did get away with a cream-puff interrogation, and I haven't seen any reports of any follow-up investigation of his story.'

Miningra leaned back with his hands on his head again. 'World Security is, I can assure you, following all lines of inquiry. I think your mistake here, as was Kang-Lee's, is that you seem to want to follow only one line of inquiry at a time and to throw all available resources into that single suspicion in order to get as much of one side of the equation as possible in as short a time as possible. A proper investigation has to consider all reasonable possibilities; blindly following only one seems to me to be more in the category of witch-hunt than of a professional investigation.'

'What other lines of inquiry are you following, then?'

Miningra looked down at the readout on his hand-held computer's screen and smiled sadly. 'Of the several that we are following, the most promising one is, as is so often the case, about money.'

'Money?'

'Yeah. You know the stuff. It's what people buy things with.'

'No need to get shirty, Miningra. How does money tie in with these attacks on Harlius Fonce and his daughter – and with the leak to Tracker?'

'Please, Vice Consul. There's no need to pretend that all three of us are dimwits. The process of kidnapping hostages for ransom is older than history. All we have to do is investigate anyone within the Assembly who has had unusual large movements of money units into and out of his or her accounts lately. It's an established procedure called "following the money".'

'And have you got anywhere with this kind of inquiry yet?'

'We have some promising leads.'

'Such as?'

At that moment, Supreme Ruler Ziekiel Landon, surrounded by Special Operations troopers, entered the office without knocking.

Linns reacted with extreme surprise. 'Mr Landon!' he spluttered, 'Ziekiel! Sir!' He rose from his seat.

'Stay right there,' Landon ordered him. 'After receiving reports of your financial situation and the movement of money into and out of your control lately – and tonight – and of your contacts and dealings with Ringo Bang, I'm afraid I'm going to have to strip you of your responsibilities as Vice Consul and order you into the custody of World Security pending a full and comprehensive investigation.' He sighed sadly and shook his head. 'There would have been simpler ways out of the predicament your bad investments got you into.' Then, turning to a pair of troopers, he ordered, 'Take him.'

Chapter Twenty-Five

The World Security NH126 patrol helicopter with Aurora and
the three heavily-armed agents aboard descended onto the roof of
a building in downtown Nevulae. All four passengers were now
wearing neokevlar vests and helmets. Clive, with Tokita along for
the adventure with a sack of sandwiches, had left in the Luxor
fifteen minutes before the helicopter had lifted off from the
landing pad in the courtyard of the security wing of the Gazers'
residence, but he was still only halfway there.

A contingent of eight armed and armoured agents rushed to
greet them as they clambered out of the chopper, then immediately escorted them down some stairs to the street as it took off
again. What looked like a full company of troopers, perhaps a
hundred, lined the street and occupied positions covering the
entrance to the Underground.

Aurora, surrounded by the eleven agents, jogged to the entrance
and down the stairs to Fluorescent Park. At the bottom of the stairs,
they were momentarily dazzled by the brightness of the kilometres
of glowing fluorescent tubes covering the walls and ceiling. Children
were playing on swings and slides and other pieces of playground
equipment; young people were playing basketball or flirting with
each other by soft-ice-cream and hot-pretzel vendors; old men were
sitting at benches, playing dominoes, draughts, backgammon and
chess; old women were watching grandchildren playing in a
fountain; young mothers were walking infants in pushchairs. Here
and there, small groups from various clans and gangs, each with their
distinctive hairstyle or tattoos or uniformly-coloured vests or scarves
or hats, clustered together around raucous boom-boxes, smoking
and spitting. These groups spaced themselves evenly about the park,
always giving each other plenty of room. The panorama stretched
out for more than two kilometres in every direction.

Following her instincts, Aurora veered off to her right, towards a spot where some ragged boys were gambling for pennies

by seeing who could toss theirs to land closest to the wall. As she and the agents approached, she heard a familiar whistle coming from the dark, close-by entrance to what had once been a maintenance tunnel, leading off into the depths of the Underground itself. She dashed into the entranceway. Little Mickey, who was maybe eight or nine years old and small for his age, was standing in the darkness of a hollowed-out recess that may have once been a storage closet, not far from the tunnel's entrance.

Aurora stopped and held out her arm to signal her escort to stay back and let her approach the child unaccompanied. Four of her agents had remained to guard the entrance to the tunnel; the other seven were standing on either side of her and close behind her.

She stepped forward to the entrance of the recess. 'Mickey?' she whispered loudly at the darkness.

A little voice filled with tears came out of the grotto. 'Oh, Aurora – I'm so scared!'

'Where are Sylvia and Li-Tian?' Aurora's voice was gentle but urgent, loving but no-nonsense.

'Near Dun Eagan Junction. It's dangerous around there. Follow me, if you're willing to have a risk.'

'That's why I'm here, Mickey.' *Steady as she goes*, she thought. *Steady as she goes.*

He emerged from his hole and started to lead them wordlessly through a maze of variously-sized tunnels. Occasionally they passed Undergrounders who, making note of the heavily armed agents, looked resentfully at them with tattooed or just dirty faces, but who made way to give them a wide berth.

Aurora had always felt like an intruder underground since she, along with her inevitable minders, had first ventured into Fluorescent Park to start recruiting her family. This occasion, despite the undeniable adrenaline rush that heightened all her perceptions and kept her moving forward, was no exception. *These people just want to get on with their lives*, she thought, as always, *and we privileged people just seem to take away their dignity and bring them more misery*.

Willis, with a communication headset built into his helmet, remained in constant contact with the agents who had stayed at first at the tunnel's entrance but were now following them at a discreet distance, with other agents who were infiltrating that area of the Underground, and with the Domestic Order major commanding the troopers who were taking positions in nearby underground stations and starting slowly to close in.

The quality of the air got worse the deeper they worked their way into the maze. In some places, ventilation seemed to be almost non-existent, making dampness and mould the predominant features. The faint odour of urine tinged the air in places. In some places, the light became exceedingly dim; other spots, crowded with people cooking over open fires and working on various small crafts, remained brightly lit and well ventilated.

Mickey signalled for them to stop when they came to a set of rusty iron rungs bolted to a wall. It seemed to Aurora indistinguishable from dozens of similar ladders they'd passed along the way. Mickey clambered up the rungs to an opening about two metres up, with Aurora right behind him. They slipped into a crawl-way, lined with a variety of pipes of different diameters, where Sylvia and Li-Tian were lying, fear all over their faces, dried tears caking the dirt on their cheeks. Sylvia looked as if she had a broken arm; she held it close to her body across her narrow chest, her shirt soaked with drying blood from just below the shoulder down. Li-Tian, a tiny girl of about nine or ten, had a completely mangled knee that looked as if it had been hit by a cannonball. Someone had wrapped it in a rag to stop what had clearly been serious bleeding. The rag was, by this time, entirely covered and caked with blood. Li-Tian's once-dark skin was pale from anaemia.

Aurora, her heart breaking, put her finger to her lips to let them know she didn't need any explanations that might weaken them further. She gathered up Sylvia, her arms beneath her knees and behind her shoulders, and, crawling on her knees, carefully dragged her for a metre or so to the crawl-way's entrance and handed her down to Agent Ormsby, the biggest of her escorts. 'Get this child out of here and to the best medical care there is; I'm paying!'

She then crawled back to pick up Li-Tian and, overwhelmed by how little the child weighed, carried her to the end of the crawl-way and passed her down to Agent Flint, then immediately followed them back down to the floor of the tunnel.

Agents Ormsby and Flint, carrying their light but precious loads, had already taken off at speed back the way they'd come. Aurora, surrounded by Willis and the other four agents still with them, followed. Running slowly and carefully, they came to a hub where seven tunnels came together: the Dun Eagan Junction. The agents, having been selected for their senses of direction – amongst many other things – and trained in maintaining orientation, headed across the fifteen-metre-wide hub, towards the tunnel through which they had come.

Black-uniformed militiamen wearing black balaclavas appeared simultaneously in all seven tunnel entrances, assault weapons at the ready. Shouting instructions into his microphone, Willis forced Aurora to the ground. General gunfire broke out. More agents came onto the scene from several directions, coming into close, hand-to-hand combat with what seemed to be dozens or even hundreds of militiamen.

As Aurora tried to get herself into a position from which she could make a plan to escape the junction, her neokevlar vest took the impact of three bullets, but it did its job and she remained unharmed. Crawling on her hands and knees through the chaos of the mêlée, she managed to take the legs out from under two militiamen on her way to the now-vacated entrance to one of the tunnels. She had almost reached this gateway to freedom when a militiaman who had taken a bullet in the leg fell on her, trapping her under him. He was a big man, apparently overweight, and his writhing and screaming made it difficult for her to move him off her.

Then she felt a pair of strong hands grasp her by the shoulders and lift her up and free, propelling her into a now-clear tunnel. She looked up and cried out, 'Clive!' – for there he was, in his chauffeur's uniform.

He snapped out the words, 'No time for chat! Let's go-go-go!' Running, he led her along the tunnel into the Underground.

Aurora, hearing footsteps behind her, increased her speed to keep up with him. Coming to a fork where the tunnel went off into three different branches, he led her without hesitation into the one on the left. Despite the confusion and her breathlessness from running, Aurora thought, *How does Clive know his way around the Underground so well? How did he get through all the World Security and Domestic Order and probably militia sentries to the battle?* Then she noticed that he wasn't wearing the bandage on his head and the penny dropped.

She stopped and fell to her knees, breathing heavily, pretending exhaustion. Clive, who, she was now certain, was really Clarence, spun around on the dead run and returned to her.

'Here, Missy,' he said, barely breathing hard, 'let me carry you. We've got to get away from here!'

Clive has never called me 'Missy', she thought, and, as he bent over to pick her up, she could clearly see that his eyes were two different colours. Putting all the hours she had spent in self-defence and martial-arts practice while growing up to good use, she planted her hands and her left foot firmly on the ground for leverage and launched a reverse-pivot kick with her right foot to reassuringly solid impact behind his left ear, his head having been moving towards her as he bent over. She saw his differently-coloured eyes roll satisfyingly back up into his head and she shouted, 'Bulls-eye, Clarrie!' as he tumbled face-down onto the tunnel's filthy concrete floor.

Her feeling of triumph lasted about a second and a half before she saw about a dozen militiamen coming around a bend in the tunnel up ahead of her. She scrambled to her feet and, hoping that their surprise at not seeing her in Clarence's control – and her neokevlar vest – would keep her alive, she started running back in the direction of the mêlée.

After taking a moment to get a grip on what the situation was, the militiamen started pursuing her. Some bullets whizzed by her, but the militiamen hadn't been well enough trained to shoot accurately while running, and those who stopped to take aim were afraid of shooting those up ahead of them, chasing after her.

Willis and three other agents came into view and Aurora hit the deck once again to let them get off some telling shots at the pursuing militiamen, who all turned tail and fled.

Turning, Willis almost shouted, 'Let's get some fresh air!' and, taking directions over the headset inside his helmet, led her through the tunnels back to Fluorescent Park, which was by this time deserted, except for hundreds of troopers.

As they climbed the steps up to the street, they had to struggle to make their way against the flow of what seemed like an endless stream of troopers pouring down into the Underground under orders to hunt down the black-uniformed militia and wipe it out. Up on the street, perhaps a thousand more troopers had taken up positions near other known entrances to passages leading underground.

They made their way to a corner, with Willis and the other agents having to display their IDs every few metres to get permission to pass, and finally saw Clive and Tokita standing next to the Luxor.

'Clive,' Aurora said, wiping some dirt from her face, fingering the bullet-impact marks on her vest and squinting into the pollution-tinted sunrise, 'I want to talk to you about your brother when I'm not so tired.'

Tokita looked at the agents surrounding them and said, 'OK, who wants sandwiches?'

Chapter Twenty-Six

Commander Kang-Lee stood in the otherwise-empty gymnasium of the Special Operations Force's Great Hall barracks, slowly going through his Tai Chi exercises. It was just barely dawn, but he had awoken to the discomfort of his affliction more than an hour before and was starting his waking period (the words 'day' and 'night' held little meaning for how he ordered his life and habits) in the usual way. The Tai Chi relaxed him, removed his mind from his pain and reminded him of what was beyond this life of agonies.

His pocket communicator played the opening bars of Tchaikovsky's 'First Piano Concerto', his personal theme music, telling him he had a call. Cursing, he discontinued his exercise routine, took the communicator out and punched in the code for answering it. After several seconds of decrypting and encrypting static, Orlando Sung's face filled the small screen.

'Commander Kang-Lee.' Orlando's manner was formal, terse, and full of authority.

Kang-Lee responded with equal formality. 'Sir!'

'We have received shocking intelligence: information that will require immediate and courageous action. I trust you are ready to follow orders unquestioningly without regard for your personal safety.'

'Sir!'

'It is an historic moment, Commander. The history of the world is about to change, and you are at the heart of it.'

'Sir!'

'Our intelligence overwhelmingly reveals that the traitor is Supreme Ruler Ziekiel Landon. As commander of his elite protective unit of the Special Operations Force it is your duty to arrest him and his co-conspirators Admiral Harlius Fonce Gazers and Commissioner Miningra, and to hold them in custody incommunicado until I can arrive there to confront them with the evidence. Do you understand your duty?'

'Yes, sir!'

'Do you have troopers at your disposal who will follow your orders – I mean, without any question, weakness or emotional wavering?'

'Yes, sir, I do.'

'Very good. You will now proceed to muster them. Prepare them to expect resistance from those guarding Landon now, as those brave men have conflicting orders and know no better.'

'Yes, sir. I know what to do.'

'Oh, and, Kang-Lee: once this operation has been successfully completed, there's a good chance that the new Grand Assembly will elect you, as the hero of the revolution, the new Supreme Ruler of the World.'

'Thank you, sir. But may I say, sir, that I seek no reward for myself other than the opportunity to do my duty?'

'Very good. Well said. Then now's the time for you to do it.'

'Aye-aye, sir.'

'I'll keep in touch.' His face faded from the screen.

Emotionlessly, Kang-Lee touched a key on his communicator. A broad, snub-nosed face with blue eyes and black hair came up on the screen. Kang-Lee said, 'Sergeant Lightfoot!' in a commanding voice.

'Sir!'

'Code One.'

'Sir!'

He touched another key and a long, pale face with dark hair, bushy eyebrows and a large nose came up. 'Major Balagazi!'

Vice Consul Linns sat leaning forward in the most uncomfortable chair in Landon's office at the Great Hall. His head, with its forehead resting on his hands, was almost between his knees. He was crying.

Miningra sat not much more than a metre away, facing him. He, too, was leaning forward, but his head was up and his eyes were ablaze. His deep voice was soft, almost caressing, but without mercy. 'So, you do admit to taking money from criminal elements in exchange for information intended to benefit those elements to the detriment of the Grand Assembly and the welfare of the human race.'

Linns sobbed.

'You do admit it?' Miningra's voice remained gentle but unbending.

'What do you know? You don't know what it's like! You have no idea what I've been through – what's been going on!' Frikker's usually prim and composed face had collapsed from this unaccustomed outpouring of emotion into a shapeless, blubbering, out-of-control mess.

'You're right. I don't. I can't figure out for the life of me why you responded to your personal financial crisis in this way.'

The vice consul returned his face to his hands. 'I just couldn't – the way I was brought up – y'know, go to my supposed peers and ask for help, especially since you peers have obviously never particularly liked or trusted me – you in particular, Mr Landon, sir; you've always treated me as if I'm not good enough for you! I just couldn't come right out and show you that you were right by begging for help! And then, all the time, I kept hearing the voice of my sainted dad, as if he were right there next to me and still alive, telling me that a man takes care of himself and doesn't go snivelling.' Then, as if he were spitting the words out, he repeated, 'My sainted dad!'

'How much did you get for your treason, Linns?' Landon asked this in a cold voice, clearly unmoved.

Speaking to the floor, Frikker mumbled, 'Twenty-one million, four hundred and twenty-seven thousand money-units, more or less.'

Miningra nodded and repeated the words, 'More or less,' with a note of sarcasm in his voice. 'How much of that do you have now?'

'Nothing. I'm flat broke.'

'Well,' said Landon, thoughtfully, 'where you're going after your trial, I doubt if you'll have much use for money, anyway.'

Miningra's computer-communicator started making a beeping noise. He took it off his belt and manipulated its controls, his eyes focused intently on the screen. 'That's strange,' he said quietly, more to himself than to the others. 'Three squadrons of SOF troopers seem to be moving through the building, generally advancing towards this office from three different directions. Did you issue any orders to mobilise additional protection for us, Mr Landon, sir?'

'No, I didn't.' He touched some keys on a control panel mounted on his desktop, and the image of a squad of fifteen armed-for-combat troopers trotting along a corridor at triple-time came up on his big wall screen.

Miningra manipulated his hand-held computer further. 'There was an encrypted message from the Sarantio Police Headquarters to Kang-Lee's private computer about twenty minutes ago, immediately followed by encrypted messages from Kang-Lee to three squad sergeants.' He looked down with distaste at the piece of technological wizardry in his hand. 'Unfortunately, I can't decrypt those encryptions with this little thing.'

Landon touched some keys on his control panel. 'I'll get Kang-Lee on the screen and ask him what's up. That'd be quicker than sending you back to your office to find out.' He touched the keys again and waited for a moment. 'He's not answering.'

Miningra checked the screen on his hand-held. 'They'll be here in less than a minute, anyhow.'

Landon keyed in a different code. The face of the trooper standing outside his office came up. 'Trooper Raoul, there are some SOF troopers we don't know about coming this way. Find out what they're up to, will you? And don't let them in until they tell you.'

'Yes, sir.'

Admiral Gazers shook his head. 'This smells bad to me.' His voice carried a definite feeling of anxiety.

Then, on the big screen, they could see Trooper Nolan's face turn to one side and they heard Kang-Lee's voice. 'Stand at ease, Trooper. You're relieved of duty. We'll be taking over this station now.'

'One moment, Commander. I need to inform the—'

The image on the screen blurred, Trooper Nolan's communicator having clearly been knocked from his hand. The men inside the office heard shouting and several bursts of gunfire from semi-automatic weapons. Then the door to the hall flew open. Kang-Lee and about a dozen troopers with weapons drawn rushed into Landon's private office.

'OK,' Kang-Lee barked. 'Everybody stay where you are! Mr Landon, Admiral, Miningra – you're all under arrest!'

One of the troopers standing behind Landon brought up his nineteen-millimetre Mini Uzi machine pistol in defence and Kang-Lee himself fired the volley from his already-drawn firearm that cut the trooper down. Landon's other bodyguards, sizing up the situation and coming to the obvious conclusion, raised their hands above their heads, palms forward, in the universal posture of surrender.

Kang-Lee and half-a-dozen SOF troopers had stationed themselves, guns drawn, around Landon's spacious office, Kang-Lee standing behind the large, ornate oak desk. At his shoulder, his new adjutant, Trooper Bailey Spragg, stood at attention, a faint expression of uneasiness at the corners of the eyes of his otherwise-impassive face. About thirty more troopers stood guard outside in the corridor and the approaches to the corridor. Everyone's pocket communicators lay on the desk in front of Kang-Lee, switched off, except his own. Kang-Lee spoke into it. 'Yes, sir. I've confiscated their pocket communicators and switched off Landon's desk unit.'

Orlando Sung's voice came quietly through on Kang-Lee's communicator. 'Very good. You will maintain communication with me and me only until I can get there and sort this out. Understand?'

'Yes, sir. Perfectly.'

'Casualty report, please.'

'Four troopers guarding Landon killed: one in the office and three in the corridor. Bodies taken for temporary storage in the walk-in freezer down in catering. Three troopers sustained non-lethal injuries. They are in the sick bay in the brig down in the basement, and the eight Landon loyalist troopers who surrendered are locked up in the brig under guard.'

'Very good.'

'What do you want me to do about Vice Consul Linns, sir?' He glanced, his distaste hidden by his faceguard, at Frikker, who sat on the edge of the desk.

'Don't arrest him. He may prove useful. Keep an eye on him, though.'

Linns called out towards the communicator, 'I'm prepared to be loyal, Orlando, once we've had a talk and understand each other!'

'OK, Kang-Lee. You can tell him that I'll interview him when I get there. For now, though, just sit tight until I do get there. Carry on.'

Kang-Lee turned off his communicator and dropped it into his pocket. Silence filled the room.

Miningra leaned back in his chair and put his hands behind his head, as was his way. His eyes were fixed on where Kang-Lee's must have been behind his faceguard. 'Tell me, honestly: do you know what the hell you're doing?'

Kang-Lee made a little snorting noise. 'I'm following orders.'

'Legitimate orders? After all, Landon is your – and Commissioner Sung's – commander-in-chief.'

'Commissioner Sung, who is my immediate commander, has, as I have already told you, received compelling evidence that our illustrious leader here has been betraying the Assembly. I'm only holding you here until Commissioner Sung arrives to confront him with the evidence in my presence.'

Admiral Gazers, a look of disgust on his face, observed, 'I wonder if this "compelling evidence" is as good as the flimsy tissue of misleading crap he jacked up against Clive van der Poel. Can't you see that Orlando's turned into a loose cannon and that you're disgracing yourself by throwing your lot in with him?'

'I'm a fair man. I'll wait until I can see and evaluate the evidence.'

The sound of a series of explosions rattled a few objects in the room, followed by the barely-audible sound of gunfire.

'Do you wonder what that's all about, Kang-Lee?' Miningra asked. 'I do. I understand why you took our communicators and switched off Landon's desk unit – it wouldn't do to have us calling out for help, would it? – but don't you wonder why Orlando ordered a total communications blackout here? Don't you think it's possible that he doesn't want you to know what's going on?'

'Miningra, if you don't shut your mouth, I'm going to have some of the troopers tape it shut.'

'Kang-Lee,' the admiral said, softly, 'I fervently hope that, when you come around to see things as they are – and I know you will – it won't be too late.'

Chapter Twenty-Seven

Minister Ramakrishna looked on in horror as the waves of black-clad militiamen swarmed into and then all over the Sarantio Food Distribution Depot, which she had gone to inspect that morning before retuning to India. From her vantage point in the glassed-in office of Dawnelle Freeman, the depot's general manager, she could see them shooting the unarmed and unresisting depot workers and the benefit clients who had been queuing up as the depot opened for the day. She was so appalled that she had no idea what to do. Should she make a stand and bravely try to assert her authority, and then surely be cut down? Should she hide? Should she try to escape? The three World Security agents accompanying her didn't wait for her to issue them orders, but kept talking into their collar microphones and listening to whatever responses they were receiving.

A stream of militiamen started running up the two separate flights of exposed stairs towards the office. Her three agent bodyguards took up positions and started firing their nineteen-millimetre Mini Uzi machine pistols, mowing down dozens of invaders, but there were hundreds and, in less than ten minutes, the three agents themselves were dead, as was Dawnelle.

Two of the black-uniformed men, clearly officers, apparently knew who Meena was and took her prisoner, roughly taking her by the elbows, one on each side, and muscling her wordlessly down the stairs to imprisonment in a cool store otherwise filled with all sorts of food supplies. As they hustled her across the main floor towards the cool store, a warehouse for storing cooking oil off to one side was racked with a series of explosions and started burning fiercely.

Having been awakened by an urgent Mayday call over his bedside communicator after barely more than an hour's sleep, Willis stumbled unshaven into the telecommunications room at Admiral

Gazers' home without having taken the time to put on his tie or jacket. The duty agent, a nineteen-year-old West Indian fellow named Desmond Fortune, with fear and even panic showing in his eyes but not in his voice or demeanour, gave Willis a hurried but orderly briefing.

'First, we picked up indications of some kind of conflict between units of the SOF assigned to Landon and the Assembly. Then all communication lines with Miningra, Admiral Gazers, Landon, Vice Consul Linns and Commander Kang-Lee went dead. Nothing. We've been able to monitor images from security cameras that seem to indicate that almost all the SOF troopers at the Great Hall are deployed in and around Landon's office, although there seems to be some activity at the brig.'

'I see.'

'Then the agents in charge of protecting Ramakrishna reported that at least two battalions of the black-uniform militia were invading the Sarantio Food Distribution Depot, which she happened to be inspecting. Then they reported being in a firefight with the invaders before going off the air, presumably killed. Moments later, Ramakrishna's communicator went dead.'

'The food distribution depot, eh? Obviously,' observed Willis, 'the gambit before dawn this morning at Fluorescent Park was a diversionary manoeuvre.'

'Then we picked up communications amongst the second, third and fourth battalions of the Capital Region Domestic Order troopers to mobilise and move to occupy the Great Hall, apparently on the orders of Commissioner Sung. With Commander Kang-Lee incommunicado, Agent Links, our senior man at Headquarters, has taken command of both our people and the line troopers there.'

'Are you in touch with him now?'

'Yes, sir.'

'Hook me up.'

Agent Links's face filled a nearby screen immediately.

'Tibor, what's going on down there?'

'It looks to me like a coup attempt, sir. Kang-Lee has Landon, Linns, Gazers and Miningra captive. Orlando Sung keeps trying to get through to the Assembly's regular trooper detachment, but it looks for now as if Major Fordham is set to remain loyal and follow our lead. The skinny on it is that we have Kang-Lee's boys surrounded, but he seems ready to stay put and wait for reinforcements. It'd be far too risky for us to attack them, so we have a stalemate there.'

'How does it look outside?'

'We can see the food depot burning. It's clear that the police troopers are sitting on their hands about that. We can also see the Capital Region D.O. second, third and fourth taking up positions, but it doesn't look as if their helicopter gunships are ready to chance headquarters' air defences yet.'

'They're probably waiting a bit for Fordham to turn.' Willis looked at information that was keying up for him on another screen. 'But I don't think they're going to wait for long. The D.O. fifth and sixth are reassembling in downtown Nevulae and in Docklands, and Sung's boys almost certainly have access to their communications. Even if they blow up the Sarantio Bridge, the loyal battalions should be able to get there to reinforce you in two or three hours, so Sung is certain to send in two-three-four, with helicopters, before then.'

'Have you picked up anything about Gritchikov and the first battalion?'

Willis studied the readout on the other screen. 'He seems to be waiting to see which way the wind is going to blow. Hold on.' He turned to Rinaldo and said, 'Get me Rear Admiral Lo at the UDF base at Elsmere – now!'

Seconds later, Rear Admiral Lo Ki-Yang's bland, young-looking face came up on the screen. 'What the hell's going on over there?' he snapped, before Willis could say anything. 'We're getting all kinds of mixed-up, crazy news and nobody seems to be in charge.'

'Well, it looks like, if anybody loyal to Admiral Gazers has command and control responsibility right now, it's me, sir. There's a coup attempt on right now. Three rebel D.O. battalions under the command of Orlando Sung, who's turned traitor, are massing to attack the Great Hall headquarters, where the Assembly's legitimate leadership has been taken captive. How soon can you get air defence cover there to take out their gunships and convince them to surrender?'

'They'll be there in twenty minutes; twenty-five at tops. I'm going to issue the orders now, but keep this channel open.'

'Aye-aye, sir.' Then Willis ordered, 'Get one of the agents to review the security camera images from eight hours ago immediately. Note the troopers who are watching the house instead of its approaches and order the other troopers to place them under arrest.'

All the men gathered in Landon's office flinched as the anti-aircraft batteries on the roof started to fire and, a few seconds later, the entire building shuddered as a rocket crashed into one of its outside walls.

Landon, retaining his composure, looked sadly at Kang-Lee. 'Go ahead,' he told him: 'take a peek at my communicator. I promise I won't interfere and I won't give you up to Orlando for doing it.'

The sound of gunfire and rocket blasts outside clearly had Kang-Lee disconcerted. He stared through his visor, first at Landon and then at Admiral Gazers, making a point not to look at Miningra, and then manipulated Landon's computer controls so that he could view the desktop screen but leave the wall screen blank. With his faceguard keeping his facial expression hidden, he keyed a few more commands into the computer and studied the screen a bit longer. The building shuddered again from another hit to the outside walls.

Standing at his shoulder, his young adjutant saluted him and said, 'Sir!'

Severe irritation in his voice, Kang-Lee said, without looking away from the screen, 'Yes! What the hell could you possibly have to say to me now, Spragg?'

'Sir! Yesterday, when you were reminding me of the overwhelming importance of Duty, sir! What do those images tell us our duty is, sir?'

Suddenly, Kang-Lee swung his face around to confront his impudent teenaged adjutant. Bailey did not flinch, but stood impassively and respectfully face-to-faceguard with his commander.

'Our duty,' Kang-Lee answered, even though everyone present knew he didn't have to answer, 'as I told you yesterday, is first of all to Honour.' He turned and looked around at the troopers guarding the hostages. 'All right. That's it. Let's declare this little game over.' He touched a key, looked at his monitor and said, 'Links!'

'Kang-Lee! What the hell do you think you're doing?'

'Opening my eyes. My men are needed to defend the building. Where should we deploy?'

Agent Links paused for only a moment. 'South wall's been breached at Sector Four. Go there.'

Without bothering to switch the unit back off, Kang-Lee left the desk and strode for the door with Bailey at his shoulder, gesturing to his troopers to follow him and calling out in that barking-like, military voice, 'Come on, men, we have a building to defend.' He led them at double-time out into the corridor, leaving Landon, Gazers, Miningra and Linns unguarded in the room.

Moving with incredible speed for such a big man, Miningra was on his feet in a flash and behind Landon's desk, working the controls. The big wall screen came to life, divided into eight images, each from an external security camera and each showing a battlefield scene of horrible carnage and destruction. Armoured personnel-carrier modules, many of them already burnt out, surrounded the fortress-like building, along with at least a dozen shot-down helicopters. A large hole had been blown out of one of the Great Hall's outer walls, however, and troopers, both in armoured modules and on foot, were fighting their way through it, taking heavy casualties from the defenders' gunfire but bravely pressing forward.

Running at the head of his men towards the sound of battle, Kang-Lee fought to focus his mind on the battle at hand and not on the reasons it was being fought or how he had been used by those fighting it. *Honour. Duty. Being remembered as a tough but noble man to be admired*, he thought as he ran: *that's all I've ever wanted; that's all I've ever lived for. I can't die a traitor!*

Kang-Lee could now see where three of the defenders' armoured hundred-millimetre gun modules had taken positions in the open court between the outer wall and the main building in order to cover the ground behind a breach in the outer wall, where he could see signs of close-quarters fighting even at a distance. Signalling to his sergeants where he wanted them to lead their squads, he himself went through a door into the outer wall as one of the gun modules took a direct hit and burst into flames. He ran up the stairs to the top of the wall, Bailey only a few steps behind.

Chapter Twenty-Eight

The former hostages in Landon's office watched the monitor screen as the first attackers overwhelmed the troopers directly defending the jagged hole in the wall, destroyed their light armoured-artillery support and moved inside, to the courtyard between the outer wall and the main building. Then Kang-Lee's SOF troopers came rushing out from four different concealed openings in both the outer defensive wall and the sheer, win-dowless, two-metre-thick, twenty-six-metre-high outer wall of the building itself, all of them firing hand-held mini-rockets in a withering crossfire. Kang-Lee emerged on the rampart of the outer wall, shouting orders into the headset inside his helmet and firing mini-rockets from launchers cradled under his elbows, Bailey crouching at his feet, trying to cover him as best he could with his semiautomatic assault rifle.

A squad of five attack helicopters moved in on the breached section of the wall at an altitude of no more than seven or eight metres, just beneath the angle of the anti-aircraft batteries. The one in front fired a barrage of rockets into the defending troopers' forward position, but, before it or any of the others could get off another barrage, a W.S. NH126 patrol gunship came in low from the northwest and shot down all five attacking choppers with heat-seeking missiles within the space of twelve seconds, then started strafing the attacking troops who were approaching the hole in the wall.

Orlando Sung leaned forward towards his observation, com-mand and control module. Swearing profusely, he shouted, amongst other things, 'Pollari, what's the matter with you? Get your bloody third air support modules over to the battle at the south wall and take out that hotshot there! Shoot that dog down! And terminate Kang-Lee, for pity's sake.'

Led by the SOF, the defending troopers mounted a counter-attack, driving the attackers back in what degenerated into vicious hand-to-hand combat over the rubble at the base of the gap where the wall had crumbled. Losing heart somewhat, the attackers drew back to regroup as heavy guns succeeded in hammering out another breach in the eastern outer wall.

Attacked by another two squads of the troopers' Sikorskis, the W.S. NH126 left off its strafing to peel off into a one-on-ten dogfight, in which it more than held its own. Still more attack helicopters closed in on the battle to support the attackers on the ground. A rocket from one of them scored a direct hit on Kang-Lee, ending his constant pain by blowing him into countless pieces. Bailey screamed, both in protest against fate and in pain from the shrapnel that tore through his right leg.

The attackers, meanwhile, had started to redeploy to concentrate on getting through the eastern opening. The defenders pulled back to stay inside the walls. As the attackers moved in on the new breach, first one, then another squadron of UDF jet fighter-bombers came screaming down on the scene, blasting the attackers and their helicopters mercilessly. The NH126, which had managed to shoot down four of its attackers, disappeared back to the northwest. Soon, dozens of UDF fighters were on the scene, and within a few minutes all of the attackers were either dead, wounded, surrendering or running off in disarray. The battle was over; the coup attempt had failed.

Two weeks after Kang-Lee's death, when calm had been semi-restored, a solemn Biker Reed was going over the 'what-if's' with an equally solemn Miningra. Both were propping up the bar at the Commodore's Club, Biker's favourite watering hole, which was a first for Miningra, seeing that he was usually teetotal.

Suddenly, both Biker and Miningra simultaneously received an urgent encrypted message on their pocket communicators from Admiral Gazers; they had to be ready to leave immediately for a secret location. Biker was certainly worse for wear, but Miningra was still very much in control, such was his resolve.

'That Kang-Lee wasn't such a bad guy, was he, Miningra?' Biker asked. He was mumbling and sort of dribbling at the same time. 'He gave his life for all of us, the poor wretch.'

'Yes, Biker; who would have thought it? Not me, that's for

sure. Now, let's get some thick black coffee down your neck and sober you up before we meet with the admiral.'

Clive, the bandages now gone from his head, pulled up bang on time, as always, and welcomed them both into the back of the roomy and luxurious Luxor. Observing Biker's delicate condition, Clive ordered, 'Kindly use the barf bag in the seat console if needs must, please, Biker. Miningra, I think more strong black coffee is the order of the day; there is a sachet in the insulator container. I think it will be just what the doctor ordered.'

'Thanks for your consideration, pal.' Biker smiled, belching slightly. 'How much longer before your Roller's ready to roll? This is a bit of a comedown; what do you say, old chum?'

Miningra could not stop his top lip from curling slightly at his pal's comical off-the-wall banter.

'Oh, another day or so.' Clive smiled. 'It doesn't matter, though. From what the admiral tells me, I expect you'll be gone until long after that.'

'Really? Where are we going? How far away is this secret location, anyway?'

'D'you think they'd tell me?'

Clive drove them to the Gazers' mansion, where Riley escorted them directly to the security-wing heliport. Admiral Gazers and, much to Biker's surprise, Aurora were already in the back of the Eurocopter.

'Greetings, gentlemen; take a seat in the back with us. Skeeta knows where we're going and you don't. And I won't mention that you're obviously over the limit if you don't give me cause to mention it.'

'Sorry, Admiral, sir. Mum's the word!'

Aurora couldn't help but see the funny side of Biker's predicament although she kept her humour to herself. Even Admiral Gazers turned a blind eye. Biker had fought a battle; some of his close comrades had fallen at his feet.

After they'd taken off and had flown out over the ocean, the admiral said, 'Well, I guess it's safe to tell everybody that we are heading for the secret base camp at Mount Love.'

Chapter Twenty-Nine

Biker was well aware of the chilling history that surrounded the site and sobered up instantly; so many of his then-young friends were still buried there.

Having been stationed at Mount Love earlier in his career, he'd enjoyed his posting immensely at first. The moon had been a true friend, casting its majestic shadow romantically over the snow-capped mountains and making the occasional moonlight liaison quite special. Then, when he'd been posted there years later, the virus had arrived and the whole place had turned sour, and eternal darkness had, in Biker's mind, extinguished the moon's uplifting glow.

He could still remember the distinct smell of burning, de-composing, dead human flesh smouldering on mass funeral pyres, and the heart-rending, agonising cries of his frightened friends and colleagues. Once, he'd held the hand of a promising cadet as the virus gradually ate the life out of him, then closed his young friend's lifeless, staring eyes with trembling fingers at the end, his own life protected only by a gas mask he'd had to wear constantly. The ghastly image of this event had haunted him during the years since. Occasionally, he would still awaken from the middle of deep sleep soaked with sweat, reliving the nightmare.

Upon hearing the name of their destination, Biker was even more surprised by Aurora's presence in the Eurocopter. He turned to the admiral with a fierce look in his eyes. 'Why are we bringing Aurora to this awful place? How can you be so irrespon-sible? Come to think of it, why are we here ourselves? This place is evil. It stinks of death.'

'I can appreciate your concerns, Biker,' Admiral Gazers re-sponded complacently. 'Please trust me on this one. I do realise this place must hold some dreadful memories for you.'

'You can say that again. I vowed never to set foot on its blood-soaked, tainted ground ever again. I cannot believe I'm here after all this time.' He briefly covered his eyes with a hand. 'Forgive me. This is quite an emotional piece of information for me. As soon as I heard you say the words "Mount Love", my heart sank and nearly induced a severe panic attack. I can honestly say that I'm tempted to turn back and go AWOL.'

'All is not what it seems, Biker. Would I willingly expose my daughter to any element of danger?'

'That's just what I was wondering.'

'All will be revealed when we reach the centre dome. This place has changed dramatically over the years, as you'll soon see.'

Aurora had been sitting back and listening to all this with growing impatience. She cupped one hand behind her ear and made a funnel out of the other one in front of her mouth in imitation of some primitive, long-ago radio operator. 'Hello, hello! This is Aurora Gazers, daughter of Admiral Harlius Fonce Gazers, speaking. I am a sixteen-year-old, intelligent, resourceful and – may I add – beautiful young lady, now virtually revered as the heroine of the Underground. Why are you all ignoring me? Obviously, I must be invisible or something, so just keep talking about me as if I'm not here.'

'So cutting, sweetheart. I wonder where you get that naughty trait from.' The admiral made this observation in a dry tone. 'I wouldn't get on the wrong side of that young lady if I were you. She's not on a mission of mercy today.'

After more than six hours in the air they landed on a high pass far up Mount Love. Climbing out of the Eurocopter, they noticed that the pass was devoid of roads, land vehicles or hover modules.

Biker, who remembered the place from fifteen years before, knew about the single footpath, hidden amongst a maze of similar tracks, that led down hundreds of metres along the slippery narrow ledges into the Dome, but he lacked enthusiasm for showing the others. 'I hope we don't have to walk down this cursed mountain,' he grumbled. 'It'll kill me, with my arthritic leg.'

The admiral smiled. 'Some things have changed for the better over the years, Biker. Fortunately for all of us, the access down is one of them.' He produced a hand-held remote-control unit. 'Watch this, and be prepared to be amazed.'

Admiral Gazers keyed a code into the remote, and immediately two large boulders swung apart to reveal a state-of-the-art mountain hopper specially designed to scale sheer mountain slopes quickly and safely.

Biker walked over to it and examined it closely. 'It seems to be attached to flimsy wires or something.'

Admiral Gazers laughed. 'That's the concept, Biker. There's a control panel inside the canopy, which, once activated, disengages the safety braking system. This allows the hopper to begin sliding slowly down the tungsten-steel wire stays, gradually picking up speed in stages. It can travel at speeds of well over forty kilometres an hour, only slowing approximately fifty metres from the base of the dome. There's a huge safety net at the end.'

'Oh, yeah? What's the safety net for?' Biker seemed increasingly doubtful about the hopper.

'Just a back-up precaution in case the wire snaps during the descent. It's designed to catch the hopper before it goes over the edge of the mountain and kills us all. Ingenious, isn't it? Don't worry, Biker; we can control our speed of descent manually at any time if the need arises.'

Aurora asked her father the most obvious question. 'How do we get back up the mountain, then?'

'We just throw the hopper into reverse and ride the mountain all the way to the top. Those tungsten-steel wires act as giant winches; all we have to do is sit back, relax and enjoy the breathtaking scenery. It's perfectly safe, and it takes half the time to reach the summit that it does to descend to the base – and the views are truly amazing. It's a piece of cake, trust me.'

'It's me that I don't trust, Admiral,' Biker whined. 'You wouldn't like to see a grown man cry, would you, Aurora?'

'Come on, Uncle Biker; it's not going to be all that bad,' Aurora said, laughing. 'I'll hold your hand, if you like.'

'Oh, thanks, you darling girl. I think I can manage to build up enough courage with you holding on to me.'

'Are we ready? Then climb aboard. Watch your head on those metal bars over the hatch, sweetheart. OK, then; see that lever there in front of you, Biker?'

'This red one?'

'Can you see another one?'

'No.'

'That's the one, then, isn't it? Take the safety latch off and throw it into forward gear, all in your own good time, if you please.'

The craft immediately started to creep, creak and groan forward and downward as the brakes released.

'Here we go! Hold on to your hats, folks; we're in for the ride of our lives! How was that, Biker?'

'Um, not bad; not bad at all,' he replied. 'You forgot the white knuckles!'

The hopper started travelling sedately through the first tunnel along the initial, almost-level track. It then started gradually to build up speed and the speedometer indicated they were travelling at just over fifteen kilometres an hour, which seemed a lot faster than that inside the canopy. As the craft neared the mountain's edge, Biker casually and confidently remarked, 'What a surprisingly comfortable and easy ride this has turned out to be.'

A moment later, the hopper dropped unexpectedly over the corner of a ledge and they began hurtling though the clouds towards the ground head-first, dangling on a piece of wire, leaving their stomachs still at the top behind them. The ride seemed to last an agonising eternity, but in actual time, not anguish time, it took only thirty seconds from 'go' to 'whoa'. Biker hollered an unsavoury word the entire distance down.

The three of them sat silently for a full thirty seconds after the hopper had come to a halt.

'Excuse my language,' apologised Biker, still holding Aurora's hand, which she feared she may have had to have surgically removed. 'The sudden drop took me a bit by surprise. I need to retrieve the remains of my stomach some time later, when we have a moment. I seem to have lost it somewhere near the top.'

The admiral unhooked his safety belt and sprang to his feet. 'What a fantastic ride!' he exclaimed. 'The icing on the cake is that we have the return journey to look forward to. That'll be even more awe-inspiring!'

Biker looked at him with a sour expression. 'With all due respect, sir – stuff it.'

The view from the craft was exactly as Biker remembered it. Nothing seemed to have changed at all. He looked about through the Perspex window. 'This place still looks as dark, desolate and cold as the last time I saw it – only now it's full of memories of my comrades' last moments of life. I said back then that I doubted if the moon would ever show its face again on this barren, angry terrain, and it looks as though it never has.'

Admiral Gazers looked at him sadly. 'I asked you before to trust me, Biker. I uphold that request just for a few moments more, please.'

Aurora was looking out her window as well. 'Dad, where is everyone? This place looks deserted. Dead. I mean, there's no sign of life out there: only dust blowing about.'

'That's the whole idea, Sweetheart; it's just a façade designed to deter would-be snoopers. If we can continue to fool people into thinking that this is still contaminated ground, then they're more than likely to stay well clear. We deliberately left this scene exactly as it was all those years ago to ensure as much secrecy and security as possible. Remember, even Miningra didn't know we'd cleaned it up and reactivated it, and I'm glad we've kept that information from Orlando, too. Oh, and, for your information, Biker, we exhumed all our fallen comrades and secretly gave each one of them a full military funeral.'

'All of them? But how could you co-ordinate such a huge evacuation without raising questions within the Assembly? What about the poor souls' relatives?'

'Let's just say that we have always been extremely careful and discreet.'

'And you kept it secret from us?'

'This was a difficult decision for Ziekiel Landon and myself, but, in the end, we decided that it was in everybody's interest to do it this way. Hiding the budget was a challenge, but, as it turned out, it was a challenge we had no trouble meeting.'

They finally took off their safety harnesses and started getting ready to leave the hopper. The admiral continued to explain. 'Over the years, a small, hand-picked group of scientists volunteered to work tirelessly, isolated from all other human contact, within the confines of this base. We were careful to eradicate all traces of their previous existence from all public records. Only their immediate families knew they were still alive, but they didn't know where they were.'

He continued his tale as they climbed out of the hopper. 'The scientists, code-named the "Chosen Few", had to be single and without personal ties. Some of them were, dare I say, conveniently orphans. They came from every continent to volunteer to be part of the programme. I must say that Ziekiel and I feel a certain pride in having – as far as we know – achieved our objective of rebuilding this base beneath the ground in complete secrecy, and of maintaining that secrecy.'

'Dad,' Aurora interrupted, 'how have these people here managed to avoid going bonkers with cabin fever? Don't they have any desire for contact with the outer world?'

'Several of the scientists managed to develop a radical new technique for brain reprogramming early on in the piece, which, to this day, has proven very successful. The workers and support staff seem to be content with the little world we have created for them, and, of course, with digital satellite multimedia telecasts: read-only, of course.'

Biker was aghast. 'The knowledge of how to do that would be catastrophic if it fell into the wrong hands! Hell, I don't think I could even trust myself with it.'

'Biker's right.' Aurora sounded as worried as she looked. 'Here we are, upholding your moral right to govern against the likes of Orlando Sung and his gang, and what we've been doing flies in the face of the principles you've claimed to be upholding – and for which poor, foolish Kang-Lee and so many other brave troopers and agents have died!'

'I'm sorry.' Admiral Gazers cast his eyes downward to his boots. 'All I can say in our defence is that we made the painful decision that it was necessary, and destroyed all records of it once our objective was accomplished – although the knowledge still exists inside the heads of three scientists at the base. Most of the personnel you will see and meet here today have undergone the reprogramming procedure successfully and are as dedicated devotees of our mission as they were twelve years ago – oh, apart from the flight crew and some key UDF scientific staff on the ground, of course. In every other way, they're normal human beings, just like us.'

Aurora thought, *Thank goodness for that last bit about the crew! I wouldn't want to marry a zombie, even if it was Ethan – oh, maybe I would – oh, I don't know*.

Leading them to a spot of dusty ground that looked like all the other spots of dusty ground, the admiral said, 'Now, let me show you around the city and you can absorb our amazing achievements to date. It's bound to leave you all speechless.'

A group of four people emerged from what seemed to be no opening at all in the sandy, barren ground. They were standing on a circular platform. All were dressed in basic working UDF uniforms. One of them had a face which was more than just familiar to Aurora. She was Dr Gertrude Golly: a renowned physicist and geologist, and a good friend of Aurora's from the university. Aurora held an Advanced Doctorate of Physics, Geology and Geophysics, which made her, although only sixteen, technically just as qualified as Dr Golly, but there had never been any jealous rivalry between them. Each regarded the other highly for her abilities and accomplishments.

Chapter Thirty

Biker, to his delight, recognised another of the four as First Lieutenant Miles Mahoney, a long-time flying mate from back in the early forties. The last time they'd seen each other had been five years earlier in the Middle East, flying reconnaissance together during the Resource Wars. Biker had heard rumours that his friend had been officially reported missing in action. That was obviously, he thought, one of the admiral's little deceptions.

'Well, blow me down, Miles, you old tart! What are you doing way down here? The last I heard, you were lost somewhere in the desert.'

'It's true, Reedy. I had to ditch old Bertha in the desert east of Damascus. She was a tired old tart and close to retirement anyway; still great loss, though. I miss her badly.'

Aurora politely asked, 'Is Biker's friend talking about his airplane or a woman?'

Her father gave her a knowing smirk. 'His airplane, I hope.'

'I was stranded in the middle of nowhere, almost out of water and with a broken collarbone, suffering from extreme exhaustion and exposure, crawling desperately through the scorching sand, covered in huge painful sun blisters, ready to give up the ghost, roll over and call it a day. Then, all of a sudden, I saw a small rock formation. I thought, "Miles, m'boy, there's some shade and maybe a spring." It turned out to be the entrance to a cave, which led me to a lost city populated by a tribe of Amazons who kept their men as love slaves, if you catch my drift. It was bloody hard work, so, after a week or so I managed to escape and found my way back to the surface, where I got picked up by a camel caravan smuggling gold into Baghdad, where I made my way to freedom.'

'OK, Miles,' Biker said, laughing, 'now tell me what really happened.'

'Would you believe I crash-landed two hundred yards from a friendly Bedouin village and safety, with only a tiny scratch on my finger, and I returned to base riding pillion with a seventy-year-old blind Mongolian on a lame, deaf donkey, holding a cup of water and a stale biscuit?'

Biker clapped his friend on the back. 'Well, you're sure as taxes really Miles and not an impostor, that's for certain.'

Then the two of them both broke down with laughter.

'Old Bertha has gone to greener pastures, though,' reflected Miles solemnly. 'She was a good old bird to us, wasn't she?'

'We did some miles in that old crate and shared some exciting adventures, didn't we? It's really great to see you, mate.' Biker said this with emotion.

'Can we continue the reunion down below, Biker?' suggested Admiral Gazers. 'I'm sure you'll both have plenty of time to rekindle the spirit.'

'Good idea, Admiral,' Biker conceded. Then, to Miles, 'Does this hotel happen to have a social club that sells alcohol or, better still, gives it away?'

'Not only a great social club, Biker, but one that's well frequented by the female of the species as well. It's one popular watering hole: they like to party and, if you like to drink it, they've got it in quantity.'

'You're talking my language, pal, but how many ladies?'

'Biker, give a bloke a chance. Would you believe two grannies and a cat with the mange, then? No, seriously, we have masses on the base and a host of townies.'

Dr Golly rolled her eyes. 'May I suggest, gentlemen, that, even though I realise that your banter may have some entertainment value, it's time everyone gets into gear. All three of you new arrivals will need to receive your precautionary inoculations to immunise you against the coxikillie virus before boarding the Mole Train, which is the only transport, apart from the chute, in and out of the Dome's centre.'

'Inoculations?' Biker asked, with a tremble in his voice.

'It's a simple, painless, safe precautionary procedure. It honestly doesn't hurt a bit.'

'Thank you for the reassurance, Dr Gertrude,' responded Biker. 'Will you give me a sweet if I'm brave? You don't mind if I call you Gertrude? Doesn't your lovely name mean "breath of fresh air"?'

'Not in the least, Biker. You remind me so much of my lovely old granddad, who's got more front than the Sarantio hydro-electric dam.'

'Wasn't I even close?'

'No. It means "strong spear".'

'But I like "breath of fresh air" – it suits you – and, hey, a little less of the granddad business. I'm not as old as I look, Gerty. I've just had a few too many late nights lately, that's all.' He stopped and thought for a moment. 'Oh, I don't think that came out right.'

'I think it would be quite prudent to cut your losses, Biker, and stop digging a deeper hole for yourself.'

'That will teach you not to wander out of your depth,' Miles whispered to him. 'Next time, take some friendly advice and make sure your feet are firmly planted on the ground before you go plunging straight into the deep end, looking like a grade-A wally!'

'I guess you're right. She likes me, though. I can tell. I'm now her patient, Miles. I was only fooling around, having an innocent laugh; bit embarrassing, though.'

'I'm only getting you at it, pal. So's Gerty. She's the life and soul of this place and loves to get down and boogie. She's a real bloke, but she isn't a Doctor of Medicine: only a Doctor of Geophysics.'

Admiral Gazers interceded at this point. 'Sorry to rain on your parade, Biker; I'm afraid the social club is off limits until further notice. I need you to have all your faculties until the briefing's finished, and even after that it depends on the outcome.'

'Please, no! Admiral – Sir! Anything but that! Just one to wash the dust out of my throat. I'm dry as a nun's cellar.'

'We have nice, cool, natural mineral water, straight out of the ground. That'll do the trick, and it's easier on your stomach than all that fizzy stuff.' Dr Golly said this with a huge, merry smile.

'Oh, if that's what the doctor orders, then who am I to argue? Make mine a double with a twist of lemon, would you? Shaken and not stirred.'

One of the other members of the welcoming party, who had kept silent until then, pointed out, 'We have a tight schedule to keep. Let's go.'

'So sorry, Agnes,' apologised Dr Golly, 'and you too, Taylor. Admiral, can I belatedly introduce my colleagues, Chief Flight Engineers Agnes Gantts and Taylor Grimes? They're responsible for making sure that every item of hardware on the Eden II, down to the last screw, is ready for the expedition. The lives of the crew and the success of the mission are in their hands as much as anybody else's, even the commander's.'

'I'm proud to have you both on the team,' the admiral told them. 'I'm sure you realise the importance the success of this mission has on our future. Let's go.'

Dr Golly led them to a point on the wasteland, close to where they had been standing. It turned out to be a concealed platform, which descended into a white-walled room staffed by a group of cheerful paramedics in white uniforms with waiting syringes of vaccine. After the immunisation process, Dr Golly instructed Taylor Grimes to page the transport, to take them to the next level.

'Thirty seconds to arrival, Doctor; we should move to the platform and prepare for boarding.'

'Yes, Taylor; if you would all fall in behind me, the entrance to the starting platform is through that yellow doorway to our right. We will have to remain in single file to board safely; there is not a lot of room for manoeuvrability. You will see when we get to the platform.'

Chapter Thirty-One

The Mole Train fit snugly into its tunnel without a millimetre to spare anywhere. As they belted themselves in, Agnes went into an introduction in the voice of a tour guide. 'It has been known for the Mole to reach speeds of over 145 kilometres an hour. We travel vertically straight down into the Earth's crust, so, if anything goes wrong, we'll most probably bury ourselves in the rock at the bottom of the tunnel and some archaeologist will discover our fossilised bones in a few millennia, frozen in time, so I hope you're all wearing clean underwear.'

Within minutes, the Mole came to a soft landing at the Dome Centre, a huge spaceport city built deep inside the earth. As they stepped out, they saw that it was buzzing with activity.

Admiral Gazers signalled for the others to gather around him. He spoke intently as he issued them orders. 'You're all to stick together with me and not wander off anywhere without authorisation. Any breaking of electronic security monitors will prove extremely painful to whoever does it. Understand?'

Biker gave him a salute. 'I hear you loud and clear, sir.' Then, looking around, he observed, 'I don't see any sign of a launch pad, Stargazer.'

'That's because it's a further 2,300 metres below the city. Most of the people you see milling around here have undergone the reprogramming procedure; they're dedicated workers and highly skilled at what they do, and, as technology advances, so will their capabilities.'

'We'll take our leave now, Admiral, if you don't mind,' Dr Golly announced. 'We've been longer than anticipated. Time is always on the move in this city. Oh, and you'd better take these.' She gave the admiral a couple of communications modules. 'My code is 9911 if you need me. Lieutenant Mahoney will accompany you for the remainder of the journey.'

Lieutenant Mahoney saluted the admiral. 'Sir! Shall we take the chute or the Mole Train to the launch pad?'

'Let's take the chute; it'll be quicker. I have a young lady on a mission here, and if she doesn't see that young lad of hers soon she's likely to explode.'

Lieutenant Mahoney's eyebrows shot a good distance towards his hairline.

'What's the chute?' asked Biker.

'The chute,' explained Admiral Gazers, 'is an elevator pod designed to travel at the speed of sound. We can reach the launch site in exactly fourteen seconds. I myself have been fortunate enough to play some part in its development.'

'It couldn't possibly be mechanical, Admiral,' Biker said. 'Nothing could propel an elevator from a standing start that quickly, not even a rocket.'

'That's right, Biker. We have designed and developed an engineering masterpiece. Our technology is simply fuelled on natural gravity, the same as the Mole Train. We hope we'll be able to adapt the concept and make regular expeditions beneath the Earth's crust one day, and a couple of our scientists are considering exploring the possibility of travelling back through time.'

Lieutenant Mahoney's communicator played his attention tune. He checked it, then saluted Admiral Gazers. 'Sir, the chute is arriving at its station. Should I reserve a position in the pod?'

'That would be a wise move, Lieutenant, thank you. One thing I did omit to mention – this could affect your aspirations, Biker: after we reach the launch pad, the chute has to recharge its energy cells. The regeneration cycle can take up to four hours to complete. Since we're taking the chute, the Mole Train will stay docked at its station, so, once at the launch site, we'll be stuck there for most of the evening.

'Is there a bar in the area?' Biker asked, crossing his fingers.

Miles gave him a wry smile. 'Afraid not, sir; it's completely teetotal in the launch area. I'm sorry. You can understand that.'

'Drop the formalities, Mahoney. It's bad enough I can't get a drink around here, let alone having to put up with military protocol from my pal.'

Lieutenant Mahoney shepherded everyone into the chute. It was a tight squeeze. Biker accidentally stepped on Aurora's toes and incurred the force of the release of her pent-up anxieties, as her mind had been entirely on meeting Ethan again and what might or might not happen when she did. 'Get off my foot, you clumsy – person.' She'd wanted to say 'oaf', but her good-heartedness had not allowed her to.

Before Biker could apologise to Aurora for his clumsiness, the chute was on its way to the launch base. For the first-timers, the sensation was amazing. The ride was smooth and silent and, once they got going, took just eight seconds, which averaged out to about 288 metres per second.

Hidden well inside the extinct volcano of Mount Love, origi-nally known as Mount Ettabola, the spaceport's launch area hit their eyes as a startling technological masterpiece. The majestic profile of Eden II, standing poised atop the launch vehicle's giant booster rockets in the middle of the crater, dominated the scene. Thousands of metres above her nose cone was the exit point; natural light filtered down through the mountainous rock formations. Biker was so entranced he wanted to hold on to the spaceship's skirts and ride the Universe along the Hallelujah Trail.

Rear Admiral Olansinju was there to greet them. After a brisk exchange of salutes and greeting, including a kiss on both of Aurora's cheeks, he pointed out a few of the visible features for the benefit of Aurora and Biker, Admiral Gazers being a relatively frequent visitor.

'And now,' he concluded, 'I don't know how to put this with the proper delicacy, but I do need to confer with Admiral Gazers privately about some classified matters...'

'No problem, Obidinga.' Admiral Gazers clapped him on the shoulder in a fraternal manner. 'Biker has full security clearance, and my precious daughter has other fish to fry.' He winked. The rear admiral chuckled knowingly.

Aurora felt herself flushing a bit, but thanked the rear admiral for his warm greeting and headed towards the control zone. She kept her eyes peeled for any sign of Ethan in the beehive of activity. Following a footpath around the corner of a large shed, she heard a voice shouting her name and her heart rate escalated. Her first instinct was to run and hide. She closed her eyes and took a deep breath just to steady herself in readiness for the magical moment when her Prince Charming held her in his arms and whisked her away into Paradise. Her innocent, never-been-kissed lips subconsciously puckered up and practised on the cool breeze in anticipation – a poor substitute for the real thing, she imagined.

Opening her eyes to experience the full impact of this most special moment in her life, Aurora was surprised and disappointed to see that it wasn't Ethan who stood before her, but Skip Slider.

He threw his arms enthusiastically around her and planted an uninvited, wet, slobbery kiss firmly on her lips. 'Hey, Princess, what are you doing way down here? It's great to see you.'

Aurora had always hated it when Skip referred to her as 'Princess', a privilege reserved only for her father. In addition, Skip's kiss had rather grossed her out.

'You look surprised to see me, Princess. Are you disappointed?'

'I'm sorry, Skip. I was expecting someone else, that's all. One thing, though: could you please refrain from calling me "Princess"? You know it really grates on me.'

'Who else would you be expecting way down here?' Skip's agile mind produced the answer for him before Aurora could say a word. 'Hey, wait a minute! It's that young captain, isn't it? What's-his-name – Eton Day Glow – no, Ethan Knight! That's it! Ah, what an idiot! You're the beautiful, wonderful, fantastic, unbelievable angel he bores everyone to tears about. It hadn't registered until now; how stupid I am not to have twigged on to it! Is it serious?'

Aurora's silence was Skip's true answer. She didn't want to stir up any further speculation amongst the ranks, just in case she was misreading what Ethan was up to, but she had noted that he did seem to be continually sending out all the right signals, though.

'I suppose you'll want to know where to find the boy.' Skip made a big show of being nonchalant about it. 'This place is massive and full of little hideaways. Ethan's usually beavering away at preparing for the mission, usually at the pit. He's probably there right now.'

'What and where is the pit?'

'The pit is the centre where we have our flight simulators. Ethan is totally fanatical about being on top of every tiny detail of all three modules that make up the Eden II – and about the Bifrost space station as well. He's always got his head down, buried in some flight manual. Sometimes he just sits in the cockpit, fiddling about with the instruments. Each to his own!' Skip took a deep breath and looked off to one side. 'I can take you over to him personally, if you like.'

'Thanks, Skip, but just point me in the right direction, if you wouldn't mind. I need the extra time to get over my initial disappointment.'

'Oh, thanks for the kind compliment, Princess.'

'You know what I mean, Skip. No disrespect intended, but I have been psyching myself up all day to see Ethan, and then what do I see when I open my eyes? Your ugly smiling face. I know it wasn't your intention to steal his thunder, but unwittingly you did – and stop calling me "Princess".'

'Ugly? Now, I draw the line at that.'

'Can we drop this awkward, one-sided conversation, Skip? I really need to see Ethan.'

'OK. But I'm not going to let it drop, though. Now, you see that No Entry sign about fifty metres on the right, next to that safety-orange oxygen tank?'

'The blue one?'

'Yes, that's the one. Well, that's off limits; if you go into there, you'll get into serious trouble.'

'Skip!'

'All right. Head for the red door twenty metres on the right and chuck a left just past it. You'll see a spiral staircase in front of you; don't go up the stairs.'

'Skip! Honestly, I'll hit you!'

'No, I mean it. Bypass the stairs and go through the double doors into the main Operations Complex. Then take the first corridor on the right, which will take you into the pit. It's a bit of a walk. I can drive you there in the cart, if you like. I promise to behave.'

'No, thanks. I like to walk. Helps keep me fit.'

'OK, then. Follow the blue-and-silver striped arrows on the floor and on the signs. See you next month.'

Chapter Thirty-Two

Skip had been right. It was indeed a long walk along the military-grey-painted corridors. She amused herself as she walked by watching the personnel scurrying in and out of doorways like mice in a cheese factory. The base struck her as being like a fortress. It had no windows or natural light, and it was cold, damp, and impersonal.

The never-ending maze of guide arrows led her through endless corridors that seemed to go on for ever. Finally, the arrows stopped and she found herself standing outside the door that was supposed to lead her into Ethan's arms – unless Skip had deliberately misled her, which was something Aurora would have rather not thought about.

Still waiting outside the door, expecting an invitation to enter, Aurora, in all her excitement, had completely forgotten to knock. Scepticism and fear started to create confusion, and subconsciously she took a backward step, thinking seriously about making a dash for it in retreat.

The door opened unexpectedly, taking Aurora by surprise. Her heart started to beat wildly in fright, but it wasn't her man coming out of the room, just a woman warrant officer carrying some documents. Fortunately, the W.O. left the door slightly ajar, and Aurora, feeling extremely charged and nervous, was able to see into the room. To her joy, Ethan was sitting at a computer with his back towards her. She just stood in the doorway, not having a clue what to do next.

Sensing that someone was watching over his shoulder, Ethan reacted instinctively by turning rapidly on his swivel chair to see. The surprise of seeing Aurora standing there rendered him speechless. The well-oiled chair continued to revolve and he fell dizzily onto the floor. Aurora ran to his aid, thinking that he might have hurt himself.

Chuckling, Ethan reached up and pulled Aurora down on top

of him. They were just rolling around on the floor, laughing uncontrollably. They clambered back onto their feet – just in case someone came in and got the right idea – and Ethan at last managed to stutter a few words. 'Why? How – are you here?'

'It's purely to see you before you leave on your mission, Aren't you glad?'

'Glad? I'm over the moon! This is the perfect start to the rest of my life!'

Aurora looked into his eyes. 'When I realised how long you would be gone – a whole six months – it was more than I could bear! I was afraid that I would never see you again.'

'Aurora, since the moment we met I've thought of nothing but you – when I haven't been forced to concentrate on the mission – and when I found out that the mission had to take off ahead of schedule and that our dinner date would have to be postponed… oh, I felt despair I didn't know was possible. I can still see them waving as my helicopter accelerated out of sight. It was extremely emotional, I can tell you.'

'I get the impression from my dad that you may be leaving within the next twenty-four hours.'

'Truth is, the Supreme Ruler Ziekiel Landon and his entourage have already arrived, and, now that your father is here, my guess is that we'll probably leave as soon as tonight. The ground crew are already fuelling Eden II up, and Fleet Command has notified us that we're on standby, which means we're ready to scramble at a moment's notice.'

'Well, let's hope that's not the case, Ethan. I so wanted to spend some quality time together before you leave.'

'One thing I can promise you, Aurora, is that, when I get back from the mission, I'm never going to let you out of my sight again.'

'Y'know, I'd love to be coming with you, Ethan. We'd make a formidable team.'

They were nearly lost in the moment until the inevitable happened and Ralph Baxter walked in on them. Aurora and Ethan looked up like a pair of wide-eyed, guilty, startled rabbits. Ralph was going to have a field day with this one.

'Sorry, folks, I should have knocked.' Ralph smirked, closing his eyes and slowly backing out of the room.

'No need to leave, Logic. Why change a habit of a lifetime? You never knock. This is Aurora.'

'Aha! So I finally meet the elusive, wonderful, beautiful, intelligent, fantastic, fabulous angel you keep talking about, m'boy.' He stepped forward and took her hand. 'Pleased to make your acquaintance, fair lady. We weren't properly introduced that evening outside the Cyber Lounge.' He bowed over her hand as elegantly as he could, which seemed more comical than elegant, and planted a kiss on it. 'I have known all along that my pal wasn't exaggerating, as some around us here have accused him of doing, behind his back. You are indeed truly captivating!'

'Thank you for the compliment, Ralph.'

'You are most welcome, m'lady.'

'Ralph's my best pal from Flight Academy, Aurora. He likes to exaggerate and stretch the truth a little – remind me to tell you some very interesting stories some time when we have a chance – but he's a genius at analysing navigation software clusters.'

'And the mission has Ethan to thank. He did a Herculean job of wangling this posting for me. It was touch and go whether I was going on this mission or not. He had to do a shipload of grovelling to get that old warhorse admiral to give me the go-ahead.'

Ethan looked as if he just wanted to find a hole and hide, thinking, *Who needs enemies when you have got friends like this walking disaster?* He said aloud, 'Uh, Ralph, I guess you just forgot that the "old warhorse", as you put it, is Aurora's dad.'

''Course not! I – everyone knows that! I was just pulling your leg.' He said this with a bit of a tremble in his voice.

'Ooh, that's funny, Ralph!' Aurora smiled with obvious insincerity. 'I can't wait to tell my dad; he'll think it's hilarious!'

'Now look what you've done, Ralph,' Ethan whispered. 'You ruddy idiot.'

'Heavens! I didn't realise an angel could be so touchy. If I've offended you or your father, Aurora, then I'm really sorry.'

'You haven't, Ralph. Actually, I was only pulling your leg back. Good one, eh?'

'Well, you were very convincing. You should go into movies or something. Remind me, though, not to get on the wrong side of you in a sandstorm.' He turned to address Ethan. 'Anyway, Commander, the reason why I'm here in the first place is to tell you there's a crew drill at 21.00 hours. Looks like it might be the real deal.'

Looking at his wrist chronometer, Ethan exclaimed, 'Yoicks! That's only five minutes from now! Let's go. Did you walk or take the cart, Ralph?'

'We're rolling, sir. And, I may add, your carriage awaits, m'lady.'

'Thank you, kind sir. You are now forgiven. My tired legs forgive you also.'

As they arrived at the launch site, the Eden II had definitely come to life. Large, insulated hoses were feeding liquid oxygen and hydrogen into the launch vehicle's tanks. Space-Command Police, wearing white armbands, were escorting arriving crew members into the fit-out module to get into their take-off gear. It was all running according to drill, and even Ralph was following strict military protocol.

'Commander! Sir!' He saluted Ethan smartly. 'Should I escort Lady Aurora to safer confines?'

'Thank you, Lieutenant Baxter, but I'm sure the SCPs will show her to her designated station.'

A female SCP appeared as if on cue, saluted, and said, 'This way, Miss Gazers,' and led her to the control module, where her father was already seated. Biker was nowhere to be seen.

After getting rapidly fitted out in the special uniforms they wore for the high level of Gs that accompanied lift-off, the entire crew walked in a line down a ramp to the open-backed hover-transporter that would take them to the hydraulic lift to where the Eden II was perched atop the launch vehicle.

Ethan looked about and saw that all the ground crew seemed to be at their stations and all the rest of the base's personnel were settling into seats in a viewing station outside the range of the launch rockets' blast.

The crew came to attention just outside their transporter, facing the control module. Then Biker emerged from the fit-out module, kitted out in the blast-off uniform. Biker's inclusion as part of the crew was a complete surprise to everyone but the admiral, the rear-admiral and the fit-out support crew.

A panel in the front of the control module slid open and Admiral Gazers, wearing a tiny microphone attached to his uniform collar, stepped out onto a platform, looking intensely serious. 'We have finally come to the end of a long, hard road,' he told those assembled; 'one which has been fraught with all sorts of dangers along the way. We have encountered enormous obstacles and seemingly insurmountable barriers and we have met each of our challenges gallantly, head on. Unfortunately, this process has not been without some compromises, personal injury and even deaths.'

He paused and looked around at everyone. 'Due to the mounting pressure and threats from criminals and political villains, we have found ourselves in a position where we have to take some chances. Without exaggeration, never in human history have we been faced with such a crisis. So far, we have risen above all adversity, keeping one step ahead of destruction. The success or failure of this mission will determine our destiny. I, for one, will keep one eye open when I sleep from now on.'

He took a deep breath and composed himself. 'Would you now join me and welcome our illustrious leader, Supreme Ruler Ziekiel Landon, to the podium?'

Flanked by those members of the Special Operations Force who had recently demonstrated their loyalty to him, the Supreme Ruler of the Grand Assembly made his appearance.

Aurora now had no doubt that Ethan was going to leave her this evening, especially after her father's poignant address, and she was feeling very sad for her two men. She thought she could see Ethan looking straight into her eyes, as if he were reassuring her that everything would be all right and that she was to be brave. His mature tower of strength steadied her emotions a little and she glowed proudly, thinking, *He is so much like my wonderful father!*

Landon took over the podium. 'Thank you, Admiral Gazers, for your informative, honest, no-holds-barred address. I commend Rear Admiral Olansinju for successfully directing the preparations for this mission.'

He then turned to address everyone. 'Standing before us all is a group of professional, dedicated and brave individuals, both members of the Universal Defence Fleet and civilians, all sharing the same principles and aspirations. We are all normal beings, no matter from what place on Earth or in society we come. The difference is that these people have all undertaken to dedicate their lives for the next six months to ensuring the success of this mission. I am sure the word "failure" has no room in the conceptual universe of any of them. This evening, they will embark on a journey of discovery that will surpass any other expedition ever undertaken in our history.'

Everyone present looked at his or her neighbour to acknowledge this indirect announcement that they were not there just for a drill and a ceremony, that the rocket would carry the Eden II into space before the sun rose again.

Landon waited for the little murmur to die down before continuing. 'Such is the importance of the complete secrecy of this mission that some decisions, as Admiral Gazers mentioned earlier, had to be left to the last minute. Hence the inclusion on the mission of our famous flying hero, Biker Reed. He has volunteered to act as advisor and backup pilot under the direction of Commander Knight. To his credit, he only learned of this decision about an hour ago, having arrived here this afternoon thinking that he was here just to receive a routine briefing and to observe a drill. We are honoured, privileged and grateful that he has so unselfishly agreed to suspend his duties as a World Minister and to accept the invitation from Admiral Gazers and myself to take part in this mission without hesitation or regard for his own personal circumstances. Let us all wish Minister Reed, Commander Knight and his entire crew a successful mission and a safe return.'

The witnesses in the viewing station broke into spontaneous applause.

'Lift-off is now set for 23.30 hours. The countdown has already begun. Join me, if you will, in a cheer for our grand lady Eden II and her crew.'

Landon proceeded to lead the ground crew and those in the viewing station in a rousing 'Hip, hip, hooray.' He then turned to the flight crew and said, 'God speed and a safe return to you all.'

Chapter Thirty-Three

Aurora and her father embraced in a much-needed, emotional hug.

Ethan turned to Ralph. 'This is it, mate. We're going. How do you feel?'

'I don't know. I was looking forward to leaving; in fact, I thought the time would never come. Now that it's upon us, I truly don't know. I just feel numb.'

Ethan nodded. 'Biker's inclusion is a really pleasant surprise, though. He can be a real bundle of laughs – good for morale.'

'You'll need all the help you can get, pal, especially leaving that tasty number behind. Don't expect me to console you every night when you are sad and lonely and missing her badly.'

'Hey, that's my future wife you're talking about. Behave. Anyway, I have a mission to command, and that'll keep me occupied for a while – and please address me as "Commander", not "pal".'

The crew took their places on the open back of the transporter and started waving back in response to a standing ovation from all their work colleagues, the ground crew and the people in the viewing station.

Admiral Gazers stood with his arm around Aurora. Both were waving at the crew, although Aurora waved to Ethan in particular. The admiral glanced down at his daughter, who was both visibly swelling with pride and on the verge of tears, and murmured in her ear, 'We couldn't have picked a better set of safe hands to place Earth's future in.'

Leaning over the edge of the transporter's open back platform to wave at her friends, including Aurora, Dr Golly lost her balance and fell heavily onto the hard, blast-proof concrete surface of the launch pad three metres below. Several people witnessing this horrible mishap started screaming. Dr Golly herself screamed on the way down, but then she lay chillingly still and looked as if in serious distress.

Everyone reacted with disbelief and dismay, but Biker, being a man of action, immediately clambered down the side of the transporter to see what he could do, frantically calling out, 'Medic! Medic!' at the top of his voice. By this time, Dr Leah Longing, the crew's medical officer, had made her way back off the transporter in a much more careful manner and ran to render her assistance. By the time she got to Dr Golly, the injured scientist was already sitting up and having a coherent conversation with Biker.

'Talk about giving a bloke a heart attack just to get his interest,' joked Biker, trying to take the edge off the situation. 'You gave us all a fright! That's a sure way to leave an impact.'

'Oh, shut up, Biker, and let me get up,' she demanded. 'I need to see if I've broken anything.'

'It'd be better if you'd just stay put until I've examined you completely.' Dr Longing gave her instructions in a crisp, professional tone. 'How do you feel? Did you lose consciousness?'

'No, I'm fine; just a little shaken. That's all.'

Aurora and her father couldn't believe they had actually witnessed such a nasty fall. 'Ouch, I felt that!' Aurora exclaimed. 'I hope she's OK. That's a long way to drop. Dad, what'll happen if Dr Golly is injured and not in a fit state to discharge her duties on the mission?'

'"I don't know" is the answer to your question, kitten. We haven't allowed for this type of mishap. The mission requires a fully qualified geophysicist, so I don't know what we'll do. Unless we think of something, we'll just have to postpone the launch until either she recovers or we find a replacement, and that'd be catastrophic. The launch rocket's fuel is too volatile to remove and then reuse, and resources are so scarce it's taken us years to transport it here in secrecy. Replacing it now in any reasonable time would blow the base's cover for sure. It'll make us more vulnerable than ever.'

'Dad, it may not come to that,' Aurora said excitedly.

Further examination of Dr Golly's condition confirmed a probable small stress fracture of the tibia in her right leg, which had swollen like a balloon. Dr Longing, speaking to the control module over her hand communicator, also reported a possible concussion requiring scans and several days of tests and observation to ensure there had been no localised memory loss, temporary or not. She definitely could not possibly take her place amongst the crew.

Having received Dr Longing's report, Landon called an urgent meeting to try to come up with an alternative plan. Biker Reed and Ethan came at a run to join Admiral Gazers, Rear Admiral Olansinju and Landon in the control module for some decision-making.

The launch vehicle under Eden II, meanwhile, remained primed, with little more than an hour available before the fuel situation would force the mission to abort. Obeying orders Ethan issued before going to the control module, the rest of the crew took up their stations inside the Eden II so they could continue to prepare it for take-off and monitor the launch vehicle's readiness from the inside.

Minutes seemed like hours to Aurora as the five decision-makers discussed the situation in a conference cubicle inside the control module. Then they emerged from the meeting, her father glowing like a red beacon.

'It's all over, sweetheart,' he told her. 'It's off. We can't take the chance; it's too risky. There's no one else on base qualified enough to take Dr Golly's place on the crew.'

'Dad, there is one person,' Aurora reminded him.

'Oh, no. I know exactly what you're going to suggest, kitten, but it's not on! I cannot allow it; you are all I have. Don't put me in that position, please.'

'But, Dad! I've done all the training! I'm regarded as number one in the world in my field. It makes sense! Think about it!'

'No, you are not going! I need you here with me. It's far too dangerous!' Admiral Gazers pressed the palms of his hands to his forehead, thinking, *I can't cope with this dilemma.*

'Father, with all the crap that's been going on here on Earth – I mean, with two abduction attempts on me in a week, and gunfire in the streets, and Orlando Sung and his nasties still at large, surely it'll be safer for me to be out of harm's way for a while out in space. Just think logically and not emotionally for a moment. I can be your official representative. Wouldn't it be great to have your daughter's first-hand experience when we land on the planet? I've already been earmarked for the second mission, anyway, so it's only a matter of time.'

'I can see your point, Aurora.' The admiral took a deep breath. 'I'm not happy about it, but, if I suggest your proposal to Landon, the rear admiral and Ethan and they don't agree, will you promise to let the idea drop?'

'I promise I will never mention it again, providing that you leave the final decision up to them and consider what they decide as final.'

'OK, let's do it! But remember, you've promised.'

Admiral Gazers returned to the small conference cubicle, where Landon, Olansinju, Ethan and Biker were glumly looking out of a window at Eden II sitting on top of the launch vehicle. The admiral cleared his throat to get their attention.

'I have been reminded,' he said, 'that we do have one qualified scientist on site whose inclusion as a last-minute replacement would allow the mission to go ahead.'

All four turned to face him, the unspoken question of 'who?' in the eyes of each.

'My daughter. Aurora. She's volunteered. She's more than volunteered: she's put her case to me forcefully.'

Landon scowled and immediately snapped, 'No.' Ethan was stunned and said nothing.

'She says,' the admiral continued, 'that, with what's been going on lately, she'll be safer going through hyperspace than sitting, surrounded by troopers loyal to who-knows-whom, in Nevulae's Queen's North Side.'

Landon, now reflecting rather than reacting, stroked his chin, deep in thought. 'That's probably true.'

Advocating for his daughter, the admiral went on. 'Ziekiel, do you remember telling me once that you thought it would be a great idea if the planet were initially inhabited and developed by children? Are you still of the same opinion?'

'Well, yes, but not on the first mission. We don't know what dangers lie ahead of us. There's so much to consider here.'

'But we will never know if we abort now, will we?' The admiral asked this thoughtfully. 'If our intention is to send our children to the planet in the future, then why wait? Aurora has shown that she is extremely close to those children underground. Her gaining first-hand knowledge of the planet might help her recruit child settlers. And, after all, her credentials are exemplary and speak for themselves. Fleet Command has already all but decided to place Aurora on the crew of the second mission, anyway.'

'Yes,' Landon said, slowly. 'I recognise that our species is in deep trouble. It is our responsibility to do what is best for humankind.'

Admiral Gazers looked over at his old friend. 'Biker?'

'I guess – yes, I, too, would like the mission to go ahead. We do have all of humanity to consider here. I reluctantly vote the same way.'

'Obidinga?'

'My primary focus is the success of the mission. Whatever it takes.'

'Then, young Ethan, it is down to you,' said Landon.

Shaking his head, Ethan said, sadly, 'I don't have it in me to even think about trying to overrule such senior people, all of whom I respect totally. And I do desperately want the mission to go ahead as scheduled.'

Waiting out in the main room of the control module, Aurora could tell from the five faces emerging from the conference cubicle what the decision had been and, before any of them could say anything, brought her fist up in front of her breast and said, emphatically, 'Yes!'

She ran up and hugged first her father, then Biker, then Landon, then Rear Admiral Olansinju, and finally, and a bit more lingeringly, Ethan.

Admiral Gazers looked at her with eyes filled with emotion. 'I'll miss you, my princess.'

She kissed him on the chin, and then smiled cheekily. 'I'll bring you back a souvenir.'

'Listen, sweetheart, I understand now that this could be your destiny. I give you my blessing. Just bring yourself back safely to me; that's all I ask.'

'I promise, Papa!'

'Now, you had better go and get kitted up; you don't want them to leave without you after all your clever manipulation, do you?'

'I'm on my way! See you in six months!'

Chapter Thirty-Four

The countdown recommenced immediately, and within fifteen minutes Biker, Ethan and the newly fitted-out Aurora had joined the rest of the crew in the Eden II. Ethan and Digby Flack ran through the final checking and double-checking of all instruments, systems and programmes with the flight controllers in the control module.

Finally, the voice of the Chief Flight Controller came in over the headsets of everyone in the Eden II, saying, 'We now have one minute before ignition. Good luck; the world owes you all a great debt.'

The countdown proceeded smoothly; ignition and lift-off went without problems, and the giant launch vehicle, with its enormous booster rockets thundering and the Eden II on top, moved majestically up through the crater to the starry sky above. Immensely powerful pneumatic suction pumps built into the sides of the volcano's crater assisted the boosters by creating a powerful upward draught.

At the crater's mouth, 3,200 metres above the launch pad, the crater-boosters detached and were grabbed by steel booster hooks, and the atmospheric boosters ignited flawlessly. They rose into a clear, black night-time sky filled with billions of stars.

Ethan was in his element, monitoring every read-out, dial, gauge, oscilloscope image and screen with lightning eyes and reflexes, despite the 3.2 gravities bearing down on him, and keeping up a running report with the control module.

Within minutes, they had escaped Earth's gravity and, weightless, were soaring through space towards the Bifrost Three High-Orbit Spaceport. Ethan made a few small, 1.35 G adjustments to their trajectory and then cut the launch vehicle's engines, saving its remaining fuel for rendezvous, docking and spaceport-refuelling purposes.

Outside the Eden II's view-ports, the Earth slipped behind in all its tarnished beauty, growing smaller in perspective as they hurtled further from it.

Tech One Elliot Bingham, who had the responsibility for communications contacts, reported to Ethan that he had a mutually-decrypted channel open with Commander Leonie Parsch in the Bifrost Three.

Ethan keyed in his communication screen and the image of Commander Parsch, her white-blonde hair, streaked with grey, cut close to her head, her face lean, high-cheekboned and strong, came into focus. 'Greetings, Commander Knight!' Her voice came through the connection as clear, strong and full of authority.

'Greetings, Commander! I expect to be able to dock by 06.45 hours MLT.' MLT was Mount Love Time, used for space missions controlled from the Mount Love Space Centre.

'I hope they remembered to pack away some goodies for us.' Part of their mission was to resupply the Bifrost Three's stock of provisions.

Ethan smiled. 'Consider us Santa Claus, Commander Parsch.'

Exactly when expected, Bifrost Three became visible through Ethan's view-ports. Using his controls to divert the launch vehicle's fuel lines and to ignite its auxiliary engines, he deftly and expertly manoeuvred the Eden II into position for docking as if he had been doing it for years.

Commander Parsch's face came up on his viewscreen. 'Well done, Captain,' she announced heartily. She seemed to be the sort of person who tended to announce things, rather than just say them. 'Well done! I've never seen a docking manoeuvre done in less than twice that amount of time before in all my tours of duty here. I can start to see why you received this assignment.'

Once the Eden II had locked onto the Bifrost Three, Ethan immediately had all the launch vehicle's remaining fuel pumped into the spaceport's storage tank. Then Commander Parsch fired her axis-turn rockets, also called the pinwheel rockets, at 35% power for 3.2 seconds, bringing the gravity level in the combined Bifrost-Eden assemblage to .40 gravities.

All the able-bodied spacehands from both crews fell immedi-ately to the tasks at hand, with Ethan, Taylor Grimes, Agnes Gantts and Digby Flack on the Eden II, and Commander Parsch and her team on the Bifrost Three, operating the mechanised and robotic aspects of the processes from their command-and-control stations.

The first task was to detach the launch vehicle from the Eden II. In olden days, launch vehicles had been treated as expendable and allowed to fall into the sea after the boosters had done their job. Since the advent of hyperspace travel and the accompanying need to maintain the Bifrost spaceports, the launch vehicles, which created no drag when free from the atmosphere, came to be seen as vital resources for the spaceports to use. The UDF's engineers began designing them, first of all, with large cargo holds for transporting the provisions and supplies necessary to maintain the lives of the spaceports' crews. Secondly, the spent vehicles themselves became sources of metals, fibre-optic cables, plastics and other basics for the crews of the spaceports' workshops to use in the construction and maintenance of both the hyperspace velocitors and extensions to the spaceports themselves.

After detaching the launch vehicle and securing it to the Bifrost Three's workshop pod, the next job was to unload its provisions and to stow them securely away in the spaceport's storage pod. Once this had been accomplished, at about 20.20 hours on the day of initial docking, the Eden II's crew came into the spaceport through the dock-hatch and joined the Bifrost Three's crew in a traditional shared dinner, the officers in one mess and the ratings, techs and warrant officers in another.

As soon as Commander Parsch had finished her short, formal speech welcoming the Eden II's crew onto the Bifrost Three, Ralph and Seal hunted down the spaceport's chief science officer, Lieutenant First Class Ibrahim Subramanian, and asked about when they could start inspecting the cybernetic hardware and interfaces aboard the hyperspace velocitor.

Ibrahim, a short, dark, trimly-bearded fellow with a quick, brilliantly white smile, laughed. 'Right after dinner.'

'What's so funny?' Ralph wanted to know. 'We only have four days before our scheduled departure for our hyperspace spiral, and all these systems are new and have to be checked for consonance, especially since the hyperspace navigation software cluster on the Eden II has been reworked significantly from what you probably have on your specs because of an application-software glitch we found.'

'Well,' Seal added, 'it might very well be funny for the First Lieutenant here, but we're the ones who get to die horrible deaths if anything goes wrong.'

Recognising that these two were all business at that moment, Ibrahim apologised profusely and promised to show them what was what on the velocitor as soon as they had finished their ice cream. 'I don't want to get into the habit of apologising,' he said, 'so I'll just have to plead guilty to a weakness for ice cream.'

Raising her hand, Seal said, 'Me, too.'

Ralph's hand also went up. 'Me, too.'

'But now I suppose I really should apologise again,' Ibrahim said, with a sigh, 'but you're going to have to eat your ice cream and some other stuff over there, Seal,' – he gestured towards a hatch in a nearby bulkhead – 'while Ralph and I eat over there. We still observe the segregation of officers at meals here at the Bifrost's mutual dinners. We just don't have one mess large enough for everybody on both crews.'

Over the next three days, both crews, working in shifts almost around the clock, laboured to attach the Eden II to the hyperspace velocitor and the surface explorer. It was exacting work, with over 12,000 significant details to be checked off to tolerances that were, in any practical sense, nil.

After breakfast following their first sleep since arriving, the four pilots who would be at all likely to take the controls of the hopper made their way to the part of the velocitor where the hopper was berthed in order to inspect it and – as far as they were concerned, most importantly – to get their hands on its controls so they could get a subjective impression of how they felt.

'Yes, son,' the senior surface-explorer pilot, First Lieutenant Miles Mahoney, explained to the junior surface-explorer pilot, Second Lieutenant Skip Slider, 'it's the same with any flying machine as it is with a woman: until you know like your second nature how she feels all over, you can't really say that you know her.'

'I remember when you first came up with that line,' exclaimed the piloting advisor and reserve pilot, Commissioner Biker Reed.

'It was when we were stationed outside La Paz during the Corporation Wars.'

'A nasty campaign, but I suppose somebody had to fight it.'

'And you developed that relationship with that banker's widow who hung out with us in the Cantina Real, with its absolutely beautiful local lager – golden sunshine over the Andes with bubbles; it was – right by the base's front gates. What was her name – the one with the great, big, uh, eyes? She kept her pink llama tied up in front.'

'That's right – Graciela.' Miles reminded him.

'That's right, Graciela.' Biker remembered.

'What a woman! Not only could she toss back the local *cerveza*, matching me one-for-one all the way and all night long with that glorious, golden Andean brew, but it was through her that I learned how the Braille of piloting and love are one and the same.'

'You're such a funky poet; y'know it?'

Throughout all this, fleet command liaison and co-pilot, Commander Digby Flack, had remained impassive, as if he wasn't hearing a thing. Skip, however, couldn't resist the temptation to say, 'Y'know, any team selected to go out and bore for the UDF against the other services would have to have you two blokes at the top of the line-up. Now, let's stop skiting around and check this bird out!'

Meanwhile, Ethan, absolutely dedicated to every aspect of the mission proceeding with maximum smoothness and safety, kept a supervisory eye on everything and worked for sixteen hours out of every twenty-four. The concepts of 'day' and 'night' lost their relevance quickly for people working in deep space.

Aurora wondered why she had been so excited to be on a mission with Ethan when she only saw him when she reported on her review of the astrophysics of their position. She was putting in a good nine or ten hours out of each twenty-four herself, taking readings on the relative positions of Bifrost Three's transit along its Earth orbit, the Earth's orbit around the sun, the angle of attitude of the solar system to both the matching planet's solar system and the particular megayottaherz wave they needed to catch to get there, called the Zappa wave, and the current oscillation pattern of that wave. This last one required extremely delicate observations, as the indicators of the wave's position were extremely subtle and the wave's oscillations could change without warning as a result of factors beyond the ability of current science to detect and analyse. Furthermore, observations made from the Bifrost Three were more robust and finely accurate than those made through the Earth's atmosphere, requiring deft, sometimes almost imperceptible adjustments to the data already in place, which the hyperspace navigation software needed to process.

At the end of her first shift in high orbit, she stopped off at Ethan's work station before retiring to the crew's quarters. He was bent over a monitor, transferring figures from one spreadsheet onto another. She came up softly behind him and put her hands gently onto the sides of his head.

He sighed loudly. 'I do hope that's Aurora,' he said, 'and not somebody else.'

'It is indeed, my love. Do you have to work much longer?'

'I'm sorry, Aurora. I'd estimate I have about four or five more hours' work to do before I can turn in.'

'I know. The responsibilities of command come first. I should have known better than to expect anything else.' She leaned over and kissed him softly by the side of his right eye.

Ethan closed his eyes for a moment. 'Mmmm – that feels so good! It gives me the strength to go on.' He reached up and took one of her hands from the side of his head, brought it down to his lips and kissed it gently. 'You'd better go now. I've got to get my full attention back to preparing us for a safe and successful jump through hyperspace.'

'I know,' Aurora responded, sadly taking her hands away from him, turning and walking out into the cramped corridor without looking back.

She walked to the crew's mess, took a vacuum-packed egg salad sandwich and a packet of UHT milk from the galley, and sat down at one of the small, round tables with Dr Longing, who was reading a magazine. 'Do you mind if I join you, Leah?'

'Not at all. Please do.'

Aurora chewed her sandwich silently for a moment, swallowed, and then asked, 'Have you ever been in love, Leah?'

'What?' the doctor said, laughing. 'Is this a professional consultation, then?'

'Well, y'know, I may have all these qualifications in geophysics and the martial arts and all that, but the truth is that I'm only sixteen and know precious little about feelings.'

Leah smiled. 'Don't worry about it. What you're experiencing is the ordinary interaction between psychology, culture and hormones that everybody goes through. Just bear in mind that what society expects, what your mind tells you and what your biochemistry is doing can all work in harmony if you never lose sight of honesty and integrity.' She laughed. 'Now, didn't that sound pompous and entirely too mature. But I believe it's true.'

'Hello, ladies. Mind if I join you?' Skip Slider slid into a vacant chair next to Aurora without waiting for an answer.

'We were having a sort of private conversation, Skip,' Aurora told him.

'Oh, come off your high horse, Prin— I mean, Aurora. This is a spaceship. The quarters are too cramped to allow for that sort of thing, especially when there's a dashing and devoted and – dare I say? – handsome young officer offering his attentions.'

Leah looked at them both with an air of scientific curiosity, but said nothing.

'Please, Skip – I don't want to hurt your feelings, but I really don't welcome your attentions right now.'

'Oh, come on, Aurora! I'm really being vastly underutilised during this phase of the mission. All I'm asking is for you to consider allowing me to be of some assistance to you in any capacity. At any time.'

'Thank you. I'll give your offer all the consideration it deserves.'

He smiled broadly. 'That's great. And here; maybe this'll help you in your deliberations.' He put a small box of Swiss chocolates into one of her hands, closing her fingers around it in an intimate gesture.

Aurora said nothing, not even 'thank you'. She put the box down on the table, rose to her feet and, taking what was left of her sandwich and milk with her, left the mess and walked sadly to her quarters.

Over the next few days, Skip continued to take every opportunity he could grasp to chat her up, making her wary about spending off-duty time in the mess with the others, making friends. After Skip's first three charm offences, and after listening to Biker and Miles tell the same old war stories about as often, she took to eating and otherwise spending her off-duty time in her quarters, lying on her bunk and reading a book on applied ethnology and cultural anthropology. There was no telling what sort of society they might find where they would be exploring.

Aurora felt relief when Ethan, Ralph, Seal, Taylor and Agnes were satisfied that the Eden II was properly hooked up to the velocitor, Ethan called the crew to quarters and they cast off from the Bifrost Three.

Ethan skilfully manoeuvred the Eden II velocitor away from the spaceport and towards the point in space about 118,000 kilometres away where they would begin to accelerate into their parabolic spiral. Aurora felt an intense, multidimensional thrill as she fed adjustments in her readings to Ralph's and Seal's and Digby's and, most of all, Ethan's hard drives so that Ralph and Ethan could make continuous navigational adjustments under the watchful, backing-up eyes of Seal and Digby. She felt the basic animal thrill of heading into something fast and dangerous and full of consequences; she felt an oddly, indescribably and indefensibly spiritual thrill at this extremely close and intimate interaction with one of the grand waves, the big notes – the music of the universe.

Within a few hours, Ethan had the velocitor ready to head into the spiral. Over the Eden II's announcements communicator, he simply said, 'All hands at hyperspace stations. We hit the spiral in ten seconds from the tone.' A short, sharp electronic tone sounded over everyone's headsets, synchronised with a visual readout on their screens if their duty required them to have one. 'On the next tone, we're surfin' that wave; six, five, four, three, two and one…'

The tone sounded again and the whole crew reacted as one. The Eden II velocitor began its acceleration, subjecting everyone on board to surging, throbbingly changing increases in gravity pressures. The data were flying from Aurora to Ethan and Ralph to the navigational software and controls as fast as their agile young fingers could process it. The spiral got tighter, and, outside the view ports in the control cabin, the stars streaked by dizzyingly. Within a minute and a half, the velocitor was on its own, controllable only by the hyperspace navigation software cluster. Ethan threw back his hands and could only watch as the streaks of light that signified the universe going by started to throb in wave patterns, like the strings of some cosmically, incomprehensibly huge double-bass, and then, *wham*!

They popped through hyperspace. For those in the control cabin, there was no time to marvel at the radically different arrangement of the lights in the sky, at the sudden apparent stillness or at the proximity of the moderately-sized planet off at ten o'clock to the Eden II's attitude, or even at the wonder of still being alive. They immediately had to take the readings to show if they were indeed on target and, if so, how far from the target. Within three minutes Ralph was able to announce that what they saw over there was indeed the matching planet, and a cheer went up amongst the crew.

It was almost anticlimactic when Digby announced that they were 247,614 kilometres from the planet and should be in an approximately 350-kilometre orbit around it within thirty-nine hours. They still had plenty to do, but the sense of urgency relaxed.

Miles, Skip, Biker, Aurora, Leah and CWO Winston Garang, the chief of the technical personnel in the landing party, headed for the hopper in order to double and triple-check the systems for the descent to the surface and to do the same for the landing party's gear.

After their first meal on the other side of hyperspace, the crew watched from their viewports as the side of the planet facing them started to emerge from the darkness of the planet's night-time to the brightness of its day.

As more and more of the planet revealed itself to them, the crew became increasingly quiet. In one glaringly obvious way, this matching planet was clearly not like Earth. Many of the crew kept waiting for some sign of variation as the planet's sun's light crept across its surface, but, when it was still less than half-illuminated, Spacehand First Class Faridah Adnani finally said the obvious aloud into her headpiece's microphone for all aboard to face up to: 'It's brown. The whole bloody place is lifeless brown.'

Chapter Thirty-Five

Ethan took the Eden II into orbit around the brown, brown planet. Aurora and Ralph and their crew of techs were busily taking and analysing readings from the Eden II's various types of cameras and other sensors trained on the planet. Chief spectro-analysis technician Rodney Low, after a few moments considera-tion, softly said, 'Aurora, I think you'd want your attention called to this,' into his microphone headset.

'Then please call my attention to it, Rodney.'

'The configuration of the planet's atmosphere is both surpris-ing and troubling, ma'am.'

Aurora clicked her computer to bring up the atmospheric spectro-analytic screen; Rodney had just finished directing data to it from the gas-sensitive cameras and performing the initial analysis on it. 'Please do a redundancy check to establish that this is correct, will you, Rodney?'

'Aye-aye, ma'am.'

Aurora waited while Rodney went back over his work. The initial readings showed that the planet did have an oxygen-nitrogen-based atmosphere, but that it extended to little more than three kilometres above the surface, and most of it was exceedingly thin. The readings showed that the atmosphere was insufficient to support any life at all at more than one to two metres above the planet's median surface altitude.

'Review confirms all inputs and analysis accurate, ma'am.'

'Thank you, Rodney. I'll call this to Commander Knight's attention now.' Aurora entered several codes to obtain direct access to Ethan's headset and told him of the latest development.

The landing party, equipped with insulated uniforms and oxygen tanks and masks, assembled on the hopper. Ethan left the command of Eden II in Digby's hands and kitted up to join them. Additional data and analysis had revealed that atmospheric pressure at the surface varied with the altitude, but that a landing party could get by without pressure suits if the hopper were to land in one of the deep rift valleys on the planet's scarred and blistered surface.

The hopper, with Miles Mahoney at the controls, launched itself silently from the Eden II and slowly descended towards the brown planet. With considerable navigational assistance from his co-pilot, Skip, Miles brought the hopper down along a long, flat strip at the bottom of the deepest rift valley that the instruments had been able to locate. His landing was flawless, light as a feather.

Almost all of those in the landing party, however, took little joy in the technology and skill that had put them where they were, for where they were disappointed and dispirited them. Their mission had been to save their species by finding another place for humans to live, but outside the hopper's viewports they saw no signs of life or anything that would support it.

Still, each of them knew his or her duty and each did it. The landing party descended onto the surface, not using the auxiliary oxygen tanks and masks each was carrying. Under Ralph's and Winston Garang's supervision, the tech crews set up various seismic, sonargraphic, x-ray and other sensitive environment-monitoring devices.

Sitting in the hopper, Ethan and Aurora reviewed the data inputs from all the sensors on the surface, integrated with data accumulated from aboard the Eden II.

Ethan shook his head. 'I don't get it, Aurora,' he said. 'You being the scientist in the present party, I suppose you'll have to explain it to me: how come we have a perfectly breathable atmosphere and pressure environment down here in this gully, which requires the presence of CO_2 and water – well, at least water vapour – and yet we get no readings indicating the presence of any life at all?'

'What troubles me,' Aurora said, in an almost dreamy voice, 'are the absolutely negative seismographic readings. This is not a planet like any other about which we have data. The uneven surface strongly suggests the presence of at least instability in the planet's crust – y'know, latent volcanoes or earthquake faults – but the instruments show nothing of the sort, or even any sign of ancient weather patterns. This gully is certainly here, but we have no data showing us why it's here or how it got here.' She looked into his eyes and put one of her hands on one of his. 'This planet's either absolutely pure, featureless granite beneath the surface, uniform in composition – composed more like a rock potato than a planet – or something out there, or down there, is blocking us from getting complete data.' She shrugged with puzzlement.

'Well,' Ethan said, 'what do you suggest we do about it?'

Aurora thought about this for a few moments. Finally, she said, 'I'm going to leave the data-analysis with Rodney for now. Let's get out there and see what the place is about for ourselves!'

The able-bodied spacehands, having secured the various sensors and cameras to the surface, were returning to the hopper as Aurora and Ethan climbed down from it. Winston Garang, who had been supervising the spacehands, and Ralph, who had been testing the equipment and verifying that all the instruments were functioning properly, were standing at the bottom of the boarding ramp, looking dejected.

'Not a sign of anything,' Winston said softly, shaking his head in sadness.

'And you don't need to ask me,' Ralph blurted out, 'because Rodney's been badgering me about it over the headset, and there's nothing wrong with any of the instruments, so the data you've seen, which, I take it, is grim, is the real deal.'

Aurora spread her hands in front of her in a gesture of frustration. 'It's not just grim, Ralph. It's strange.'

'Strange?'

Ethan's natural impatience with non-action burst through and he started walking towards where the rift valley narrowed and descended into a barren canyon-like crevice, saying back over his shoulder, 'Tell him about it as we go explore, Aurora.'

Aurora and Ralph took off after him. Winston stayed behind, calling out, 'I have to supervise the spacehands!'

Ethan slowed down a bit to let Aurora and Ralph catch up. 'Maybe,' he speculated, as they strode, 'there's something about this planet that throws our Earth instruments off. Let's consider what our human senses tell us and look for clues.'

'Well,' said Aurora, 'if there is anything to find, I'd say the lower the altitude – the further we get from space – the more likely we'll be to find it.'

Forty-five minutes later, they reached the end of the crevice. They stood on a flat area only about three and a half metres wide, the planet's surface rising sharply towards the pale, grey-blue sky in all directions except along the path they had followed. They had found no sign of possible life along the way.

Aurora ran her hand gently along the rough, hard surface of the solid stone wall in front of her. 'I guess,' she said, softly, 'it was all too good to be true. I've so much wanted for you and me to save the human race together, Ethan, that it never occurred to me that we might not succeed.' She choked back a sob. 'And now, all those beautiful, innocent children are going to spend their lives hungry in dirty air, with bad water, in holes on sick old Earth.'

She sat down in the dust and started to cry. Ethan kneeled to comfort her.

Ralph's mind suddenly focused quickly on the single topic: dust. Some of Aurora's tears fell into the dust, watering a tiny seed hidden deep within it. The seed had been waiting for water for a long time and almost instantly sent a shoot up out of the ground.

Looking gloomily down at his sobbing girlfriend and science officer, Ethan spotted the rapidly-growing shoot of green plant life and almost shouted, 'Look!'

Aurora gasped as they watched the shoot continue to grow, branch out and sprout long, thin leaves.

'I can't believe I was being so thick,' Ralph announced, in a tone of wonder and awe. 'All along, our clue was dust. If there'd never been life here, the ground would have been solid, like these rock walls.'

More plants started to shoot out of the ground. Ethan cupped his hand around the stem of the first one and interlocked his fingers with Aurora's. The soil beneath them began to crumble, and Aurora and Ethan started falling into what had become in an instant a large sinkhole.

Ralph jumped back quickly enough to escape falling in. He looked on helplessly for a brief moment as Aurora and Ethan slid deeper into the crumbling soil, then called out, 'I'll go for help,' and started running back up the canyon.

Ethan and Aurora, meanwhile, spiralled downward, out of control, along what seemed to be something like a chute through the planet's crust. In the soil around them they could see many signs of life, from plant roots to mould to fungi to bugs, but the adrenaline stimulated by the speed with which they were crashing downward kept them from wondering why all their instruments had failed to detect any of it.

They could suddenly see a pinprick of light ahead that slowly glowed larger and brighter as they approached it. When they finally stopped falling, slowing to a halt in a small heap of rubble, they hardly had time to catch their breath before what they saw took it away again.

At length, Aurora was the first to find words; words which she knew, were inadequate, but she didn't care. 'Oh, Ethan,' she breathed. 'It's so beautiful.'

NAME THE
LOST PLANET!
Win £10,000

in equipment for your school, or, if over
the age of sixteen, an equivalent cash prize.★

BOOK **II**

What can you contribute to
building a new life on the planet?

You can have a say on the development of the lost planet in
the next book in the series. The name you choose could be
part of the story! All you have to do is cut out this page, fill in
your details on the back, and return it to:

DEPARTMENT 444
Wolsey House
46 High Street
Esher
Surrey KT10 9RB

Closing date for Competition:
19 May 2008

For more information go to:
www.23rdcenturychildren.com

If I were part of the construction team,
I would call the planet:

_____

Name: ....

Address: ....

....

....

Postcode: ....

Telephone Number: ....

Please tick the box that describes you:

☐ I am under the age of sixteen and therefore eligible for
the prize of £10,000 in equipment for my school.

☐ I am over the age of sixteen and therefore eligible for the
cash prize of £10,000.